To

Enjoy a trip to the lake

Joe Van Rhyn

BORN YESTERDAY

Finding love while searching for the past

A novel by

Joe Van Rhyn

ISBN: 978-0-9986798-0-8

The author may be contacted at:
joevanrhyn@cox.net

On Facebook @ Joe Van Rhyn, Author
Website: www.joevanrhyn.com

This novel is a work of fiction. All names, characters, objects, businesses, organizations, places and incidents are fictional. Any resemblance to actual events, locals, organizations, or persons living or dead are coincidental.

EL CID PUBLISHING
2722 Horseshoe Drive
Las Vegas, Nevada 89120

To my wife Elaine,
my rock and my friend,
thank you for a lifetime
of love and support.

With special thanks to
Kathy,
for your inspiration

Pine Lake Scrapbook

Pine Lake is located in central Wisconsin. It is known for giving up trophy-sized Lake Trout.

The Glen Nursing Home - Pine Lake

The Town was established shortly after the Civil War and has been a popular vacation spot ever since.

The Ice House was built in 1918 using logs from the large Norway pines taken from the area.

The Ice House - Pine Lake

In winter ice was harvested from the lake, stored in it, and later sold to people for their iceboxes.

White Wings - Pine Lake

The White Wings was an early steam-powered launch.

It was used to transport people and goods across the Lake.

Sailboat racing is a major sport on Pine Lake.

The Snipe is a two man sailboat. It provides speed and agility, making it one of the most popular boats to race.

Introduction

It was the spring of 1964, just five months after that tragic day in Dallas when an assassin's bullet silenced a sitting president. The news clips of Jackie Kennedy, in her pink Chanel suit cradling her husband's lifeless body, were still fresh in everyone's mind.

Civil rights divided the nation. Riots and protests brought unrest in most cities and towns in the South.

Sitting in your living room was like having a front row seat to the killings and horrors of war, as the Vietnam conflict played like a television series on the evening news. High school graduates were running off to Canada to avoid the draft and young people from all walks of life rebelled against authority.

Families lived on a little more than five thousand dollars a year. Gasoline was thirty cents a gallon, a loaf of bread cost twenty-one cents, and hamburger sold for thirty-five cents a pound.

A boy had to cough up a buck fifty to take his girl to the Friday night movie, while Dad and Mom could stay home, enjoy TV and a six pack of beer for less than a dollar. The Beatles had the top five songs on the pop charts and Beatlemania affected every girl in America, over the age of ten.

Ford shocked the automotive world by introducing a small, sporty family car. The Mustang sold in the same price range as a Chevrolet four door sedan. A new three bedroom home sold for less that fifteen thousand, with payments under a hundred dollars a month.

Hand held, wireless phones were popular in science-fiction comic books. The state of the art telephone was a black rotary dial contraption hanging on the wall or sitting on the living room table. In some rural areas, four to six neighboring farmers shared a "party line."

Computers were primitive with basic capabilities, most were bigger than a refrigerator, some the size of a Volkswagen. No one besides the government and Fortune 500 companies had one. The post office was the only option for sending mail to a friend. Stamps cost five cents each.

In spite of everything, America was on the cusp of rapid economic growth. People had more leisure time for traveling, planning vacations, and spending money. The demand for consumer products, such as TV's, stereos, and automobiles was so strong it pushed the stock market over the 1000-point threshold for the first time in history.

Pine Lake, a small resort town located in the central part of Wisconsin, was counting on the Farmers Almanac's prediction of a long hot summer, to bolster their tourist season. Local business people were crossing their fingers, hoping nothing would happen to spoil it.

BORN
YESTERDAY

Finding love while searching for the past

A Man is Found in the Park

"Julia, c'mere. Did you hear about the guy they found in County Park last night?"

The hoarse nasal voice of Pine Lake's postmistress and gossip queen made Julia cringe. She had put in a long night at work and wasn't in the mood to listen to a bunch of chinwag. All she wanted to do was drop her tax return in the mail and go home to bed.

Reluctantly, Julia stepped to the counter. "I wondered what the ruckus was about. Those police cars woke everyone at the nursing home."

Dolly continued sorting the handful of letters in her hand. "That no good Cory Bradley had the Harvey girl in the park at one in the morning when this guy stumbled out of the moonlight and fell against their car. They were probably doing the dastardly deed..."

Julia cleared her throat. "What about the guy?"

"Oh, right. He's got blood streaming down his face, his eyes were glazed and he cried, "help me," before crumbling to the ground."

"My God. What happened to him?"

"When the police got there, the guy was unconscious and a bloody mess. He had all these cuts and wounds to his head. One of the cops said he looked like he'd been hit by a freight train. The doctors at the hospital did

1

everything they could for him but he never came out of the anesthesia."

Julia clutched her throat. "He died?"

"Slipped into a coma."

Julia breathed a sigh. "Who is it? Someone from town?"

"That's the best part," Dolly said with a grin. "Nobody knows. His pockets were empty, no billfold, no identification, nothing." Dolly tossed the letters in a mailbag. "I heard too, the Harvey girl missed her period and her folks are sending her to a home in Green Bay."

Julia had heard the rumor but wanted no part of trashing the girl. "Sorry Dolly, I've got to run. I left my car running." Seeing Dolly's frown, Julia added, "Thanks for the information." On the way to her car an icy blast of air blew her jacket open exposing her cotton uniform. She shivered and pulled the jacket collar tight around her neck. Yesterday it was close to sixty degrees and today the cold cut clean to the bone.

"Jules, wait up." Her friend Doug trotted up to the car. "Haven't seen you in a while. What say we go to Teddy's for pizza tonight?"

Julia searched for her keys. "Pizza sounds great. I'm working at the hospital until four. Can we meet at five?"

"I suppose you've heard the news about the guy in the park."

Julia thumbed toward the post office. "Dolly gave me the whole scoop. I cringe every time I have to listen to her garbage. She never has anything good to say about anyone."

"That's Dolly's stock in trade. In this town gossip travels at the speed of light."

"I think every police car in the county drove past The Glen last night with their stupid sirens blaring. They woke everyone. It scared the living daylights out of some of our patients. They thought the place was on fire. I had a devil of a time calming them down." Julia held her collar closed. "Do they know what happened to the guy?"

"No, Sheriff Joe talked about it in the coffee shop this morning. He doesn't have much to go on."

"Is it a young guy? An old guy?"

"Joe said, he's Caucasian, twenty-five to thirty years old — no tattoos or physical markings, nothing in his pockets, or anything that could be used to identify him."

"That's what Dolly said." Julia nodded to the post office. "It's a little scary, don't you think?"

"Councilman Harris is afraid it could have a negative effect on summer business. You know how jumpy people get around here if they think something will prevent people from coming. He's planning to ask the Middletown paper not to make a big to-do of it."

"Do they think he was beaten up or something?" Julia asked, arching her brow.

"Harris said that until we know for sure what happened, we should say the guy got hurt in a fall or something like that."

"Are people that upset about this? Like it's some big crime thing?

"The sheriff isn't ruling that out. He's sending the guy's fingerprints to the FBI and checking arrest warrants and missing person reports in a four state area to see if he can find a connection. You know Joe, he's not the brightest star in the sky, but he figures solving a case like this could get him re-elected in the fall."

Most people were still scratching their heads at how Joe Christenson was elected sheriff in the first place. Everyone thought it was a joke when he declared his candidacy. His opponent in the race, the chief of police from Middletown, was a well-respected, highly trained officer with thirty years' experience. The chief should have won by a landslide. Fate handed Joe the job when a month

3

before the election the chief suffered a mild heart attack and withdrew from the race. Joe barely beat "none of the above" to win.

Julia gave Doug a wry smile. "Let's hope our illustrious sheriff can find out who this person is. It's scary having someone found that way and not knowing who he is or what happened to him." Julia got in her car. "I'll see you at five."

ℒeaving ℱlorida

Julia Parsons had moved to Pine Lake two years ago. She needed to leave Florida. Her personal life was in shambles and she wanted to get as far away from ex-fiancé Brad Holton, as humanly possible. She threw everything she owned into her '53 Chevy and headed north.

She had grown up in Milwaukee and as a twelve-year-old, spent a wonderful two weeks at a summer camp on Pine Lake. Having no better place in mind, she kept driving until she landed here.

Pine Lake offered her a place to regroup, to start over and begin building a new life. The people were friendly and the pace of living suited her. In Tampa everything was hustle. She worked full time in the campus bookstore while completing her Practical Nurse's training. Her boyfriend, a high school star quarterback, got a free ride football scholarship to the University but took to drinking and partying and flunked out after one semester. Wedding plans were put on hold as Brad tried to "find himself", and were scrapped when Julia found him in bed with her roommate. To make matters worse, he tried to blame her for never letting things between them get past kissing and petting. He called her a prude for wanting to bring her virginity into their marriage. She packed up and left the next day.

Julia felt fortunate to have landed the job at The Glen,

5

a locally owned nursing home. There weren't many year-round career opportunities available when she arrived, especially for young people. Her Practical Nurse Certificate was the door opener and she gladly accepted the graveyard shift. It also helped her land a part-time job at the hospital. Even having to work two jobs to make ends meet she loved small town life and quickly embraced her new home.

Her shift at the home went midnight to eight in the morning. She'd grab a few hours' sleep and, then be at the hospital helping out in the therapy room from one to four. This schedule raised havoc with her sleep regimen, but she loved both jobs.

Julia pulled up to her place and ran to the back door. Her fingers shook as she fumbled to put the key into the lock. She quickly closed the door behind her, threw her jacket over the kitchen chair and hung up her purse. "I've just about had it with this cold weather!"

In minutes she was out of her uniform and into her warm, toasty, flannel pajamas. She cheated, set the alarm for twelve-thirty instead of noon, pulled down the shade, and crawled under the covers. Her thoughts of the man found in the park lingered. Who was he? Where did he come from?

The alarm clock made its usual annoying buzz and Julia was quick to hit the button. She threw back the covers and ran her fingers through the tangled backlash of what was left of yesterday's hairdo. In the mirror she faced the obvious, strands and curls pointed in every direction. It was going to be a wash and ponytail day.

It took a while for the water in the shower to heat up. She let it run to warm the room before undressing. At twenty-four, five foot six and a hundred twenty pounds, she had a body most girls would die for, and most boys would lust after. Her soft features, creamy complexion, and high cheekbones turned heads wherever she went.

She sped up her routine and walked into the hospital with a few minutes to spare.

Julia opened the therapy room door and mimed an imaginary fork to her mouth and chewing, to show she intended to get a quick bite to eat. Phyllis acknowledged Julia's crude sign language with a laugh. Phyllis Morgan, an Osteopathic physician, believed muscle manipulation and exercise were essential in the healing process. She pressed for a physical therapy department at the hospital, a relatively new concept in the early sixties.

The cafeteria was packed. The hot station was lined with people waiting for steaming food. Julia opted for the cold station, which had one man looking over the sandwich display. She grabbed a tray, took an apple, an orange, and a small carton of milk. She side stepped the man and grabbed a ham and cheese sandwich before scanning the dining room. "Hi, Florence," she said to the woman at a corner table.

An elderly woman, nattily dressed with silvery hair wrapped in a bun, looked up from her plate. A smile brightened her face. "Julia, so nice to see you." Florence was the front desk supervisor and privy to everything that went on in the hospital.

"Have a busy morning?" Julia asked.

"Fridays are always busy. You know, you've worked the desk before."

"For a year-and-a-half." Julia tried not to appear overly interested. "How is the young man doing? The one they found in the park."

"He's in a coma." Florence gave Julia a puzzled look. "Why do you ask?"

"Just curious," Julia said, picking up her sandwich. "Was he beaten? Do they know who he is?"

"The doctors don't know what happened to him. If

7

somebody did beat him, they did a pretty good job of it. Besides all the nasty cuts and lacerations to his head, he's got a broken nose, a busted eye socket, and probably sustained a concussion. Doc Richardson did a marvelous job of patching him up. It was a shock to everyone when the fellow failed to come to. His vitals are good, and they continue to monitor him in ICU." Florence put her napkin on the tray. "How do you like working with Doctor Morgan?"

"I love it. Phyllis wants me to take some classes at community college this fall. I'm hoping to become a physical therapist someday." Julia took another hurried bite of her sandwich. "So...nobody knows who this man is?"

"He's listed as John Doe. It's funny no one has come forward to claim him." Florence stood and brushed off her dress. "Come sit with me at the front desk sometime. I miss our little chats."

"I will, I promise." Julia stood. "I've got to run too, I'll talk to you later." Grabbing the apple and orange off her tray, she hurried to the therapy room.

Phyllis wasted little time getting her protégé involved by having her help a recent surgical patient walk around the room. This was the part Julia enjoyed—seeing people making meaningful strides in their recovery. The afternoon went by quickly. When the clock signaled the end of her day, Julia jumped to her feet, grabbed Phyllis's hand and danced around. "It's Friday," she squealed with delight.

"Got a big date tonight?"

"Not really a date. Doug Foster and I are meeting at Teddy's for pizza."

"Well, have a good time, and I'll see you on Monday."

Julia gave Phyllis a quick hug, threw her jacket over her shoulders, and skipped out of the therapy room. In the hall she stopped and took a tentative half step towards the intensive care unit. Shaking her head she zipped her coat and made a dash to her car.

Doug, A Townie

Date? Julia mused over Phyllis' question. No, it wasn't a date. Doug was a great guy, but she viewed him more like a brother than a beau. She recalled the day they met. Having just arrived in town, she was getting gas at the Shell station when he drove up in his pickup truck. He jumped out and smiled her way. She pretended to be disinterested, but was intrigued with this slender, six foot, middle-twenties guy sporting a flattop haircut.

Doug was a townie, born and raised in Pine Lake, as was his father. His grandfather built the icehouse that stood next to the bait and liquor store. He sold ice for people's iceboxes, until shortly before World War II, when refrigerators put him out of business.

Nora, the manager and head nurse at The Glen had clued Julia in about Doug's family. His mom was from Chicago, sort of a wild hare. They met when his dad worked construction down there. The couple was only married a few months when the grandfather passed away, and had to come back to Pine Lake to take over the store.

One day, when Doug was still in grade school his mom just up and left. Gossip offered a number of scenarios and reasons for her departure, but Doug's dad never gave credence to any of it. John Foster took his wife's leaving hard and soon tried to find solace in the bottom of a bottle.

9

His son pretty much had to fend for himself. Doug could have used this as an excuse to cop out on life. Instead, he was determined to make the liquor store a success.

Doug pushed the idea of boyfriend and girlfriend when they first met, but Julia resisted. She wasn't ready for another close relationship. The sting of Florida was too raw. Brad's infidelity had crushed her, and sent her self-esteem through the floor. She fought depression, and struggled with anxiety if a man showed any signs of affection. Doug must have sensed her resistance, but she was still surprised when he backed off and agreed to just be friends. Their platonic relationship seemed to work fine. She slowly built a trust in him, and although she learned to enjoy doing things together she wasn't ready to take it beyond that. Date? No, in her mind this wasn't a date.

Julia parked in front of the bank and hurried inside. There were lines in front of every teller. A lady was telling anyone listening, "Sheriff Joe has had no luck identifying the man in the coma. He suspects foul play but doesn't have a crime, a motive, or any suspects. As far as Joe can tell the guy isn't a missing person, nobody's looking to arrest him, and the FBI said it would be a month before they would have any information on the guy's fingerprints."

A man in the next line laughed. "I heard Ol' Joe was so mad when he heard that he kicked the dog and stomped out of the office."

Julia chuckled as she peered ahead to see what was taking so long with the guy at the window.

People continued to discuss the man's plight. One lady wondered if this could be connected to the Kennedy assassination. "It's only been six months since that happened," she said. No one thought that, but one man was sure it had to be a drug deal gone bad.

"That's highly unlikely," said a nurse in uniform, who

claimed to have been in the operating room when the man was brought in. "He didn't have any drugs in his system." She praised Doc Richardson. "For a small town general practitioner he did a swell job of patching him up."

Julia finally made it to the window and withdrew twenty dollars. She frowned at the single digit account balance in her passbook. Somehow she'd have to make this stretch through the week.

*F*riday night was Julia's night to relax and enjoy herself. It was the same for most locals. They'd throw back a few beers, scarf down a plate of fish, and sleep in late Saturday morning.

A night out at Teddy's was easy to dress for, nothing fancy. Most people would be in their work clothes. Julia chose a white blouse, blue jeans, and white canvas shoes. She tied a blue handkerchief around her neck and moved the knot to the side. A well-scrubbed face, pink lipstick, and a matching blue ribbon to hold her ponytail achieved her intended look.

*C*ars lined both sides of the street in front of the tavern. Julia found a place to park around the corner. Loud music and voices drifted into the street long before she reached the front door.

"Jules! Over here!" Doug yelled as she walked in.

Cigarette smoke hung in a heavy gray cloud. The sweet smell of pizza covered the faint odor of stale beer. People laughed and talked loudly trying to be heard over the jukebox that was cranked up to the max. No one seemed interested in the TV, where helicopters were evacuating wounded from another bloody skirmish in Vietnam. The crowd, standing two and three deep at the bar, forced Julia to weave her way to the pool table where Doug was lining up a shot. The cue ball sent the nine ball to the corner

11

pocket.

"Dang! No way does that ball not go in." He leaned the cue against the wall and pulled out a chair for Julia at a nearby table. "What would you like to drink?"

"A draft will be fine." She hung her purse on the back of the chair and took a seat.

Lonnie stood from the table and nodded her way. "Hey, looking good." He picked up the cue and looked at Doug. "Is it my shot?"

"Yeah, you've got solids." Doug returned a few minutes later with a pitcher of beer and a frosted glass. "Fred called. He can't find his keys. I've got to run over and lock up the store."

"That's okay. I'll wait here with Lonnie." Julia poured herself a beer.

Doug cupped his hands around his mouth. "I'll be right back," he yelled.

Lonnie backed off his shot and raised the cue. "You trying to mess me up?" He repositioned and finished the stroke. "Dammit, I'd ah made it the first time if he hadn't yelled." He laid the cue on the table, and poured himself a beer. "When are you guys gonna get hitched?"

"What?" Julia choked on the beer. "Why would you ask that?" The question sucked the air from her lungs. "Has Doug said something?"

"Nah, but you guys spend so much time together, I just thought it's about time you tied the knot. I know he's crazy about you."

"Doug and I are really good friends. He..., I..., we've never talked about...it"

"It's none of my business. I just figured you'd make a good couple. Doug's a great guy, a hard worker, and he owns two businesses."

Just the word marriage sent Julia into panic mode. She had no answer. "Yes, but can he fly and leap over tall buildings in a single bound?" She bit her lip, angry that she had said something so silly.

Lonnie gave her a flat stare.

"I'm sorry, I didn't mean...I was just trying to be funny." She felt herself cascading down into the grips of anxiety. Her throat constricted, her breathing became short and shallow. She kneaded her numb fingers. "Shit," she murmured as the feeling of dread momentarily consumed her.

Lonnie got up, drifted over to the jukebox and dropped in a coin.

"Sorry about that," Doug said throwing a leg over the back of the chair. "By the time I got there, he'd found his keys. They had fallen behind the counter."

The jukebox came alive and Julia used the distraction of bass notes bouncing off the walls to alter her thought pattern and conquer her feelings.

Doug grabbed his glass and the pitcher. "It's the weekend. Let's go in back and order up a pizza!"

Lonnie returned and downed his beer. "You guys go ahead. I'm going to make it an early night. See ya, around."

"You don't have to go," Julia protested. "I'm sorry for what I said."

"I shouldn't have stuck my nose in your business. You guys enjoy yourselves."

Doug led the way to the back dining room. A couple were just getting up and Doug moved quickly to claim the table. He cleaned the remaining dishes and pulled out the chair. "Should we get another pitcher, or would you like something else?"

"This is plenty of beer for me. I'll have a root beer with the pizza."

Doug waved to the waitress and put in their order before settling back and taking a swallow of beer. "What was that about, between you and Lonnie?"

"He asked if we were getting married. What have you been telling him?"

Doug leaned forward. "I haven't said a thing, but it is an interesting question."

"I thought we agreed to be friends."

"Hell, that was two years ago. You said you needed time to get settled...that your schedule didn't allow time for a relationship. Are you any closer to being settled? Being friends is great, but will we never be more than that?"

"It's complicated. I mean ..." Her mouth dried and she had trouble forming the words.

"I guess I would like to know where I stand," he said, taking a drink of beer.

"It's not you, it's me. I probably should have told you long ago."

"Told me what?"

Julia straightened in her chair. "I left Florida to escape a bad relationship. I was crushed. When I got here I was a wreck. I hated all men. I just wanted to run away and hide."

"Why didn't you tell me?"

"Ashamed, I guess." Julia took a hanky from her purse. "Silly, right?" She dabbed the corner of her eyes. "I find the guy in bed with my roommate, and I'm the one feeling ashamed.

"You can't judge everyone by that one jerk."

"I know, but on top of that my dad cheated on my mother. He broke her heart, and mine, too. That's how I ended up in Florida. After the divorce mom and I went to live with my grandparents."

"It's a trust thing, right?" Doug took a swallow of his beer. "I don't know if you knew, but my mom up and left when I was in fifth grade. No good bye, no see you later, nothing. For the longest time I blamed myself for

14

her leaving. It's hard to put your trust in people because you never want to hurt like that again."

Julia nodded as she wiped the tears that had gathered on her cheeks.

Doug took her hand. "You know I think the world of you, but I won't force the situation. If it's meant to be, it will be. Don't worry about Lonnie, I'll have a talk with him. Did he say anything else?"

"He thinks you're some kind of Superman." She couldn't believe she was still using that silly analogy.

Doug fell back laughing. "More like Batman and Robin. We grew up together. He's been my best friend since first grade. As kids, every day was a new adventure for us. Some days we'd be at the swimming beach terrorizing the girls, or we'd be catching crabs under the bridge by the falls. For spending money we'd go night crawler hunting."

"Night crawler hunting?" Julia giggled. "Is that a joke?"

"Nah, night crawlers, big worms, you know, for fishing. My dad would pay us a penny a worm for all that we could bring him. Sometimes we would have three or four hundred in our pail. Those worms bought a lot of candy bars and cokes."

"How did you hunt them?"

"When it rains they crawl out of the ground and go slithering in the grass. We'd shine our flashlights and grab them before they had a chance to get back in their hole."

"You picked them up with your fingers? Yuck!"

Doug laughed. "That's enough about worms. Have I told you about the sailboat? You should see it." His voice rose a full octave.

Julia welcomed a change in conversation. "You mean the one you bought last year? You called it a bird or something."

"It's a Snipe. You won't recognize it. I've had it in the icehouse since right after the first of the year. I stripped it

15

down to bare wood, sanded the hell out of it and put on three coats of this new urethane paint. It's bright red and the hull is as smooth as glass. It should slide through the water like a greased eel."

"So you think you'll do better this year? I don't mean to burst your bubble, but I seem to recall you came in last place in every race last year."

"I know, but I had Lonnie crewing for me. He'd never sailed before, and I never skippered a boat. We were like Frick and Frack out there."

"I thought you told me you didn't do well because your boat was too heavy."

"That was part of it. A wood boat is heavier, but it was the boat to beat before everyone switched to fiberglass. We may still be a bit heavy, but we'll overcome that with superior skill."

Julia failed to hold back the laugh that exploded out of her mouth. "Superior skill! Those Lakeshore kids have been sailing all their lives. How do you think you're going to beat them at their own game?"

"Johnny Kinard."

"Kinard? The Lakeshore kid? Isn't he the one that's been in trouble with the law?"

"Yeah, petty larceny and stuff, but he's one hell of a sailor. Back a few years ago he won practically every race. With him on the tiller and me on the jib, I think we have a chance to win a race or two."

Julia smiled. "So when is the maiden voyage of this new and improved boat?"

"I'm hoping to have it ready by mid-June, but for sure I will be in the big trophy race on the fourth of July. It's going to be so neat."

Julia laughed. I don't know why you get so fired up about sailing. That's a Lakeshore thing."

"That's just it. They think they own it. None of us

16

town kids had parents with the financial wherewithal to buy us a sailboat. It was strictly by chance that I got to ride along on that E scow. That one time was so fantastic I was hooked. I'm still in high school, working in the store, when this guy comes in and buys a bunch of sodas and things. He looks out the window, sees the wind raising havoc with the trees, and asks if I'd like to go sailing. 'It's going to be a wild ride out there,' he said. 'We could use the extra ballast.' E's are those long, flat bottom sailboats. They normally carry a crew of four or five and will give you the ride of your life."

Doug leaned forward. "It was great. I loved everything about the competition. It was the craft accelerating through the water and the wind billowing against the canvas that excited me. Every Saturday thereafter I'd cruise along Chicago Avenue on my bicycle hoping for another chance to sail. Those Lakeshore guys weren't happy having a townie hanging around chasing after their sisters. They made their message loud and clear, but I could never shake my desire to sail."

The waitress set the pizza and drinks on the table.

"I never realized that you were this passionate about it." Julia put a slice of pizza on her plate. "You never talked that much about it."

"There's nothing to talk about unless I can win a race." The table went silent as they gave their undivided attention to the cheesy pastry.

The bar room cleared some when they came out of the dining room. "Would you like a little Crème de Menthe?"

Julia put her hands to her stomach. "I'm too full. I think I am ready to call it a night."

Doug took her hand and walked her to her car. "Don't pay attention to Lonnie, just friends is fine… but if you ever change your mind, just let me know."

Julia smiled. "Thanks, and thanks for the pizza." She

got in her car. "I'm looking forward to seeing your boat." She gave him a big smile and drove off. She had to admit, Doug would be a real catch for any girl. Maybe she was being foolish. Unless she wanted to be an old maid she would have to give dating and romance another try. She felt the knot in her stomach tighten. The mere thought of kissing a guy scared the pants off her. Consecrating a marriage would be near impossible.

Her Curiosity Continues

Julia came out of a sound sleep. Sunshine poked around the shade and sent a splash of light up the wall. She rolled over, stared at the ceiling and wondered what she would do today. She punched up her pillow and soaked up the warmth left in her blanket. The man in the coma stoked her curiosity, and although she cautioned herself about doing something foolish, she dressed, grabbed a piece of toast and went out the door. Jumping down the two steps off her back porch, the nip in the morning air halted her in mid-step as goose bumps bristled the hair on both arms. She retreated into the house and grabbed her sweatshirt off the clothes tree. Flipping up the hood, she made a mad dash to the car.

Julia pushed the hood off her head as she scurried down the empty corridor. The hospital hadn't come to life yet. The staff change was still an hour away, and it was much too early for visitors. Horace, the elderly gent with the kind face and full head of gray hair, sat at the front desk. He looked up from his newspaper and removed the glasses that hung on the end of his nose. "Julia, so nice to see you, are you working today?"

"Ah..." Julia searched for an answer. "No, I left my jacket here yesterday," she fanned the bottom of the garment, "I just came to pick it up." She came around the

19

desk. "I haven't talked to you in a long time, mind if I sit for a while?"

Horace folded his paper. "By all means, be my guest. Weekends are pretty quiet around here."

Julia sat. "So what's going on, anything new?"

"Not much, same old stuff. People get sick, they come in, they get well and they go home."

"What about...?"

"Who, our mystery guest? Still in a coma. He's doing well, breathing on his own, but showing no signs of waking up."

"Have they identified him, yet?"

"Nope! The sheriff was here a while ago. He's fit to be tied. He's checked every which way he can think of but can't find a thing on this guy. He's come up empty at every turn. Joe wondered why this guy's family hasn't come looking for him."

"Is he still in Intensive Care?"

"They moved him to two-oh-four. He's no trouble. He just lays there."

Julia stood. "I guess I will be on my way. You have a wonderful day."

Horace opened his paper. "Thanks, and you do the same."

At the end of the hall Julia stopped, looked back to make sure the old gent still had his nose in the newspaper, and scooted up to the second floor. There was no one at the nurse's station and two-oh-four was just across the hall. Taking one last glance up and down the hallway, she rushed through the door.

In the dimly lit room it was difficult to get a good look, but the man appeared to be resting peacefully. The machines and monitors hooked to him blinked and beeped in an odd cadence. Julia took a step closer. His head was heavily bandaged and the only features visible were the tip of his nose, his mouth and chin. She leaned over to get a closer look when the sound of voices froze her to the floor. The fear of being discovered sent blood racing through her veins like hot lava. As the voices moved closer, panic gripped her. There was no escape, and no feasible place to hide. Her eyes focused on the door. "Dear God, please don't let them come in here. "Her prayer went unanswered when a spear of light shot across the terrazzo floor as the door opened. A woman pushed a scrub bucket into the room and kicked down the doorstop. She plunged the mop up and down a couple of times, as another gal pushed in a cart of cleaning supplies. Julia held her breath. She had the presence of mind to duck behind the door and was somewhat concealed by it being propped open.

Pressing the handle to squeeze out the excess water the mop lady began swabbing the floor. The cart lady turned on the bathroom light and began wiping the back of the toilet. "No one seems to know what to do with this guy," she said, her voice echoing in the tiled room. "The administrator would like to free up this bed. He said the hospital has done everything it can for him."

"So, what are they going to do?" asked the mop lady.

"Nobody's got an answer for that," said the cart lady, her words partially drowned out by the toilet flushing. "The hospital would like to push the problem off on the county. The county treasurer is balking, says there ain't money in the budget to take care of him. The poor guy has become a political football, and everyone is trying to kick him to the other side."

The mop lady put the mop in the pail and pushed it out of the room. "You about done in there?"

"Just need to give the mirror a once over." The woman threw her towel on the cart and stripped off her rubber gloves.

21

The mop lady held the door and used her foot to bring up the stop.

Julia tried to hold her breath, but the door pressing against her caused her to let a puff of air escape through her nose. The woman leaned her head back and stared in Julia's face.

The woman screamed.

Julia flipped up her hood partially covering her face and pushed her way past the woman. She tore out of the room and descended the stairs two and three at a time, not stopping until she reached her car. She was long gone before anyone knew what had happened.

Arriving back at her place, she slumped in the seat. "I can't believe I was so stupid!" She pounded on the steering wheel. "What was I thinking? If those women recognized me, I'm dead. What do I say? Oh sorry...I was just curious. They will think I'm some kind of nut case." Curious or not, she was not about to try anymore stupid stunts like that.

Life Moves On

Gladys Iverson started The Glen Nursing Home. Raised in Pine Lake, she had been a big city nurse at Chicago General until her mother had a stroke. Her dad had passed a few years earlier, so it was left to Gladys to come home and take care of mom. In an effort to generate income Gladys converted the family farmhouse into a nursing home, catering to patients requiring around the clock care.

The big two-story colonial house had a covered porch on three sides and sat on five acres overlooking Pine Lake. The name, The Glen, came from the wooded ravine you drove through coming up to the house.

When Gladys' mom died she sold the home to a group of local businessmen and returned to her big city job. The group offered Nora Jensen, an ER nurse, the manager's job. The Glen became Nora's whole life, especially after Duke, her live-in boyfriend, passed away four years ago. Nora was working the emergency room at the hospital the night they brought Duke in. He had been bowling with the guys and suffered a massive heart attack. He flat lined on the way to the hospital and no amount of effort could bring him back.

Nora worked days. Carol, a recent graduate from nursing school, worked swing, and Julia covered midnight to eight in the morning. On the weekends, Nora brought in a couple of her retired nurse friends to take care of things. For Julia it was not only her place of employment, but also her extended family.

Julia hung her jacket on the rack behind the front desk. Carol busily wrote in a patient's folder. Without looking up she asked, "Did you have a nice weekend?"

Julia muffled a chuckle with a snort. "Yeah, fine, just went by too fast. How about you?"

"I heard you had all the excitement the other night."

"Those sirens scared the bajeebers out of everyone. I ran my butt off trying to keep everyone calm. Have you heard anything? Have they found out who the guy is?"

"Not that I've heard, but they did have something strange happen. The cleaning ladies said there was someone hiding in the guy's room."

"Do they know...?"

"The women said it all happened so fast they didn't get a good look, and couldn't say whether it was a guy or girl."

Julia picked up a folder and pretended to study it. *I hope they don't talk to Horace, he's the only one who knows I was there.*

"It's crazy, especially here in Pine Lake, Dullsville, USA," Carol said. "The mystery surrounding this guy get weirder by the day. Maybe they'll know something at Teddy's." Carol stood and gathered her things. "I hope you have a peaceful night."

"What is the attraction of sitting in a tavern at one in the morning?" Julia asked. "What kind of husband do you hope to find sitting on a barstool? Someone, who will beat you up, spend your money, and break your heart?"

"I'm not looking for a husband. I just need a couple of drinks to relax me. I'm too keyed up to go home and straight to bed."

"A warm glass of milk helps me," Julia offered.

"Eck, I'd puke." Carol put on her jacket. "See you tomorrow night."

Julia waved. *I should be the last person to give advice on picking out a husband.*

Her first order of business, see that everyone was bedded down. She especially enjoyed caring for the two gentlemen at the home. Robert was her charmer. When he got better, he promised to take her dancing and show her a night she would never forget. Robert was in his eighties, his dancing days were over, but she humored him and told him she would be ready when he was.

George had dementia. Julia never knew what to expect when she went into his room. Sometimes he'd be wandering around the room in his birthday suit. She'd have to corral him, get him into his pajamas and back into bed. Normally, he'd balk and put up a fight. Tonight he complied without a fuss. The rest of the shift went smoothly and it turned out to be just another routine night at The Glen.

The next three weeks flew by. The warm sunny weather was like money in the bank. People streamed into town. Stores and restaurants were crowded, and the lake gave up bag limits of lake trout, walleye and northern pike. A Green Bay TV station came down and did a segment for their sports report. Once it aired, Doug's phone rang off the wall with requests for his guide services.

Julia, too, found herself immersed in spring-type activities. Her yard had sprung to life. The soft yellow crocus in her front planter faded as the tulips burst forward in a carnival of color. The long cold winter was a distant memory.

Someone New For The Glen

The first shards of light came through the front door glass and reflected off the highly polished floor. It was time for the early risers to wash, brush their teeth, and be ready for their breakfast tray. Julia checked her watch as she finished with the last patient. She walked to the front and was surprised to see Nora sitting behind the desk. "What are you doing here this early?"

"Big things are happening. We're getting a new patient, the man in the coma."

"What!" Julia spun in her tracks. Did she hear Nora correctly? "They're bringing him here?"

"Yep! I was at a meeting yesterday afternoon with the doctors, the hospital administrator, and the county treasurer. The administrator needs the hospital room for regular patients. The treasurer, that chintzy bugger, wants to save money on the cost of his care."

"That's wonderful. Can we do it? I mean...are we capable of taking care of him?"

"The doctors believe we can. They'll bring all the equipment and monitors with him. One of their nurses will instruct us on his feeding, how to handle waste, and things like that. They want me totally involved with his care, so most of the stuff, like his feeding and hygiene, will be taken care of on day shift."

Julia could hardly contain herself. "Will there be things I will need to do?"

"Yes, they want us to monitor him around the clock, so you will be checking his vitals and logging them every hour."

"I can do that," Julia said. "When is he coming?"

"This afternoon," Nora said. "I'll have Carol fill you in. If you encounter any problems you are to call me immediately. Understood?"

A million thoughts bounced around Julia's brain as she tried to visualize things she would do once he arrived.

"Julia!" Nora cut into her thoughts. "Girl, you'd better get your head out of the clouds. Those people are counting on us and I promised them there wouldn't be any problems."

"Sorry, just tell me what to do. You don't have to worry about me."

"That's exactly what worries me." Nora settled in the desk chair. "He should be bedded down by the time you get here tonight."

Julia's alarm went off at eleven. Her pulse rate kicked up a notch, sending a shot of adrenalin through her body. She had trouble containing her excitement and was preened, dressed, and out the door much quicker than normal.

In The Glen parking lot she reminded herself to remain cool. The last thing she wanted was to look unprofessional. She rubbed her stomach and hoped the butterflies would go away.

Carol looked up at the clock. "You're early."

"I thought you could tell me everything I needed to do, you know, for the man. He's here isn't he?"

"Room Six. There isn't a whole lot you'll need to do for him. He sleeps like a baby."

27

"I thought we had to keep track of his vitals."

Carol handed Julia a clipboard. "We do, blood pressure, pulse, blood oxygen and temperature. It all registers on the one machine just above his head. Nora wants it done once an hour."

"Is that all?" Julia tried to hide her disappointment. "I guess I thought there would be more to do."

"Actually, it's a piece of cake, he's a lot less trouble than our other patients." Carol stood up. "Unless one of those machines starts whistling or banging he'll just sleep the night away."

"Whistling... Banging...?"

"In that case you call Nora." Carol stood and put on her sweater. "As long as you are here I'm going to take off, okay? Do you want me to show you the machine before I go?"

Julia sensed that Carol was in a hurry to get to Teddy's for her nightcap. "No, I'm sure I will know which one it is."

"You can't miss it. It's the one with all the red numbers. It's right above his head." Carol grabbed her purse and hustled to the door.

Julia stood for a moment, not sure what to do first. Carol's last entry was at eleven. Julia decided to do her first monitoring. Entering the room she took note of the equipment that surrounded the patient, and zeroed in on the one with the red numbers. She picked his hand off the bed and studied his breathing pattern. It was slow and easy, no sign of pain or stress. She lifted the covers and traced the feeding tube going into his stomach. The catheter and temporary colostomy were new to her. It was not a part of her practical nurse's training.

She squeezed his arm. The muscle seemed surprisingly firm. She expected more atrophy. She bent and looked closely at his face. There was a hint of bruising on his

28

forehead and around his eyes but very little swelling. She parted his hair and saw the sutures had healed nicely. "Once you get a regular haircut those scars will never show." She straightened the bed linens.

Julia judged him to be six-feet tall, between a hundred eighty and a hundred ninety pounds. His well-proportioned body reminded her of an athlete, or someone who got a fair amount of exercise. She stepped back and smiled. "You're quite the handsome fellow, aren't you?"

"I guess I better take care of business." She took the cap off her pen and read off the numbers: Blood pressure, one twenty seven over eighty two, pulse, sixty nine, blood oxygen, ninety eight, temperature, ninety eight point seven. She patted his arm. "Those are some pretty good numbers." She looked for a response, but none came.

Julia went about her normal routine of tending to the other patients, but at the top of each hour she was at his bedside. There were only minuscule changes in the readings. On her final visit she lingered for an extra few minutes. "Who are you?" she asked. "What happened to you? Why hasn't someone come forward? Don't you have family... friends... anyone who's missing you?" Julia straightened his covers. "So many unanswered questions and you just lie there, sleeping peacefully." Weeks went by with no change in the man's condition.

Her Special Patient

Julia's alarm went off at eleven. Instead of getting up, she turned it off and fell back to sleep. She woke thirty minutes later, jumped out of bed, and hustled to get ready.

"Damn," she said as she pulled on her sweater and skipped along trying to get her foot into her shoe. "What a dumb thing to do." She grabbed her purse and stumbled out the door.

She kept an eye on her rear-view mirror hoping the police hadn't decided to cruise the area. The last thing she needed was to have her name and age in the newspaper. The drive to The Glen normally took ten to twelve minutes. Tonight she made it in the near record time of eight.

"Sorry, I'm late," Julia shouted, as she flew through the door. "I'll make it up to you, I promise."

"Not a problem, but I will hold you to it." Carol shuffled a stack of folders. "I just finished the updates."

"How's our sleepyhead doing today?"

Carol glanced at his folder. "No change that I can see. It makes you wonder if he will ever wake up. I'd sure like to know what the hell happened to him."

"Me, too. Anything I should know about?" Julia asked, watching Carol gather her things.

"Nope, everything's copasetic. Have a great weekend, I'll see you on Monday." Carol waved and went out the door.

Julia picked up the clipboard. "Time to record some numbers."

Walking into the man's room, she gazed at each machine. Everything seemed to be working properly. She read off the red numbers and copied them down. "Your vitals look good," she told him. "If you were awake you'd be in the pink."

When they brought the man to The Glen, he seemed so helpless. Julia immediately assumed a self-imposed responsibility for his care. She'd tend to the other patients, making sure their needs were taken care of, and then hurry to his room for the last hour or two of her shift.

At first, she just sat and talked to him, keeping him abreast of what was going on in town and the world. She also used these nightly sessions to discuss the things that weighed heavily on her mind, notably the events that caused her to leave Florida. It was almost like going to confession. "It may not change your life," she caught herself saying, "but up until now I couldn't even think about Florida without the fear of plunging into a full blown panic attack."

During one of those evening sessions, he seemed restless. His arm twitched and Julia massaged it to quiet him down. Massages soon turned into nightly therapy sessions. No one told her to do it. It wasn't prescribed. She figured it would keep him in relatively good shape for when he woke up. It was all stuff she learned working with Dr. Morgan.

It was near five in the morning when Julia finished with the other patients. She hummed as she entered his room. "Okay, Buster, time for some therapy." She took his hand and lifted his arm straight in the air, moved it across his chest, and then straight up again before laying it by his side. Again and again, she moved his arm in this manner.

31

"How was your day? Mine was a disaster." She then proceeded to tell him how one crazy thing after another had befallen her. She continued to move his arm, folding, bending and stretching it in all directions, without missing a word of her story.

Julia enjoyed the nightly sessions. Even though their conversations were one-sided, she giggled, "You're the perfect man for me. You don't interrupt and you never disagree with a thing I say."

Making sure the arm was securely by his side, she walked to the other side of the bed and began the same ritual with the other arm. She was gentle, but made sure each movement flexed and toned his muscles. Finished with the arms, she moved to his legs, going through a regimen of exercises with each one.

She stepped back and looked for any sign of change, any movement, but saw none. Everything seemed normal. He appeared to rest peacefully. She covered him and turned out the light. On her way to the front desk, she peeked in each room to make sure everyone was okay. She picked up each folder and wrote a few comments about the patient. When she got to his, she simply wrote, NO CHANGE.

"Ready to start your weekend?" Nora asked, as she threw her purse on the desk.

"You bet," Julia shot back. "I have three hours at the hospital, but after that, I'm ready to live it up."

"Are you still helping Dr. Morgan?"

"Yes, I love it. It's so rewarding seeing the improvement people make as they get better and stronger."

"Speaking of improvement, any change in room six?"

"No. It's such a shame. He just lies there."

"He can't be alone in the world. Somebody has got to be missing him. Where is his family?"

Julia took her sweater from the hook. "Someday he is

going to wake up and tell us everything we're dying to know."

"I hope you're right." Nora headed for the kitchen. "Right now I'm dying for a cup of coffee."

"See ya Monday!" Julia said on her way out the door.

Was It All A Dream?

It was almost five weeks since the mystery patient arrived. Julia had marked the days off on the calendar. He was her special patient and made her eager to come to work.

Julia bid Carol good night. She took a moment to glance at each patient's chart before making her rounds. After restraining George in bed with an extra sheet, she stepped into her charmer's room. "Good night Robert, don't let the bedbugs bite." She turned out the light and closed his door. So far, the night held no surprises.

Glancing at her watch, she noted the time, four forty-five. She turned and entered the room where the young man lay in a deep sleep. She studied the monitor with the red numbers. His blood pressure numbers were somewhat elevated from what she had charted the previous hour. In the many nights she spent with him, she was in tune with his breathing pattern, tonight it was different, quicker, with deeper breaths. The average person wouldn't have noticed the difference, but Julia did.

"Are we a little restless tonight?" she asked, squeezing the saline bag and checking the port in his chest. "Having a bad dream?"

Not knowing what these changes meant, she decided to forgo the full therapy session and instead, just massage his arms. She lowered the bed rail and brought his arm toward her.

His forearm tightened against her grip, he'd never responded that way before. She was sure she heard a huff of air come from his nose. The monitor beeped and his red pulse number jumped two digits

She turned quickly and could have sworn his big toe moved. Not a big move, but she was convinced the toe moved. She'd never noticed that happening before.

"What's going on here?" Taking a step back, but still focused on his big toe, she asked, "Am I hallucinating or did that toe really move?" She waited, looked away and then back again, as if it were a game, still no movement.

"Okay Buster, what was that all about?" She gave him a slap on the shoulder and resumed massaging his arm, but kept an eye on his toe.

"There!" she yelled. "It moved again. I saw it this time. That toe moved."

She reached and gently took hold of his toe. "Can you feel this?" she asked, in a high squeaky voice. The lump in her throat choked off any further response, when the toe move forward and back in her hand.

She let go as if it was a hot potato. Her heart beat so that she felt her pulse in her neck. "If you can hear me, wiggle your toe."

This time the movement was stronger.

"Oh my God! You can hear me! That's fantastic. You can hear me!" Julia danced. "I've got to let somebody know. Nora! Call Nora." She ran from the room, down the hall, grabbed the phone, and dialed Nora's number.

She listened. One ring, two rings, three rings, "C'mon," Julia pleaded, "please answer."

Nora finally came on the line. "Who is this? What time is it?"

"Nora, Nora, he wiggled his big toe," Julia shouted

35

into the phone.

"Wiggled his what? Is this a joke?"

"Nora, it's me, Julia. Our sleepyhead moved his big toe. I asked him if he could hear me and he wiggled it again. What should I do?"

Nora must have realized what was happening and spoke firmly. "Just sit tight, I'm on my way."

Julia hung up the phone and hurried to his room. The man had turned on his side. "Lie still," she commanded. "We don't want you falling out of bed."

She yanked up the side rail. The sound seemed to startle him and he reached in her direction.

"Lie still," Julia repeated. "There are people on their way to help you." Flustered, she stroked the back of his hand. His arm relaxed and she took a deep breath. His head suddenly came off the pillow. With his eyes still closed, he turned from side to side as if searching for something.

"What are you doing? Don't try to move. Please, just lie still." She felt his finger slowly and gently squeeze her hand. "Oh, God. C'mon, Nora. Where are you?"

Without warning, he jerked her to his side and let out a blood curdling, "Watch out!"

"Oh Jesus! What are you doing?" She pulled from his grip and stumbled backwards, losing her footing.

Nora entered and caught her before she fell. "Whoa. Hang on there."

Julia burst into tears. "Oh my God, am I glad to see you. He's moving. He squeezed my hand. He yelled and scared the crap out of me."

"Go to the office, call the hospital and see if they can send over one of their emergency room doctors."

"But what if..." Julia protested, wiping the tears from her cheeks.

Nora pushed her out the door. "Just do as you're told."

The next few hours blurred in chaos. Julia tried a couple

of times to get back into his room, but Nora ushered her out each time. Doctors and nurses filed in and out, pausing to converse in the hallway. Julia eavesdropped whenever she could, but couldn't ascertain his condition.

Nora finally came out of his room and walked up the hallway.

Julia ran to her. "How's he doing? Is he going to be alright?"

"It appears he's going to be fine, but stay out of the way and let the doctors do their job." Nora stopped to look in the mirror. "Good Lord, look at this dress, it went out of style ten years ago. I was in such a hurry when you called, I grabbed the first thing I put my hands on. Didn't bother to comb my hair either." She grabbed her purse. "I'll be back in a bit. I'm going home to clean up."

Julia still had thirty minutes left to her shift. Sitting at the desk, and knowing he was going to be all right, released the tension in her body. She crossed her arms on the desk, laid her head and fell asleep. She woke to Nora's touch.

"Is he?" Julia asked, unsure if this was a dream or the man had really come to.

Nora looked her normal self, crisp white uniform, hair combed, and just enough makeup to hide the lines and creases she claimed were truly deserved. "I just checked on him. He's sitting up, talking and responding to questions. He doesn't remember anything, but the doctors think that could change at any time."

Julia looked down the hall. "Can I go see him?"

"Why not leave that for tomorrow? The doctors are still with him. Besides, it's eight o'clock and you need to get your buns out of here." Nora pointed to the front door. "We don't pay overtime you know."

Julia felt torn. She really wanted to see him, but the prospect of him being awake frightened her. Their relationship was the world she created for the two of them. But what would it be like now? She decided to heed Nora's advice and face the unknown tomorrow.

Would Life Change

Julia woke shortly before eleven and immediately bombarded herself with questions. Would he like her? Would she like him? It finally dawned on her-he was a complete stranger. She knew the face and the body, but not the person. Nor did she know the color of his eyes or the sound of his voice. For all she knew, he could be a foreigner, or from outer space. She was comfortable with him being her silent friend, but his waking, seemed to have ended that.

"Oh, God, what if he's married?" Julia had checked for a ring the very first night, even tried to determine if there was a ring groove. It didn't matter until now. "Julia," she called herself out. "The man just came out of a coma, he hasn't said a single word to you and you're worried if he's married." It was no use, the questions continued to pound at her senses.

Her stint at the hospital went by in a blur. Arriving home, she barely remembered anything she did. She opened the refrigerator, leaned against the door, and tried to decide if there was anything there she wanted. She fought the urge to drop everything and go running to The Glen.

The compressor started with its usual clickety-click, jarring her back into the moment. She was neither hungry nor thirsty. Closing the door and kicking off her shoes, she walked to the bedroom. She took off her blouse, threw it on the bed, and pulled the ribbon out of her ponytail on the way to the bathroom. One glance in the medicine cabinet mirror convinced her going to The Glen was a bad idea. "Look at you," she moaned. "You're a wreck. You don't want him seeing you like this."

She studied her reflection. "What would I say to him?" She washed her face and toweled dry. Holding the towel under her chin she again addressed the image in the mirror. "You have to stop thinking about him or you're going to drive yourself crazy." She dropped her slacks and put on her robe. With little forethought, she began tidying up the room. She wiped the counter, put her toothbrush and paste in the drawer, and neatly positioned her shampoo, conditioner and other beauty products on the sterling silver tray she won as top debater in high school.

Satisfied with the way the bathroom looked, she found herself on a mission as she went through the house on a cleaning rampage. By six o'clock, she was completely worn out.

It felt like she had just closed her eyes when her alarm woke her with a start. She wasted little time getting ready. The thought of their first meeting still frightened her, but him waking excited her and was what everyone had hoped for. The adrenaline rush had her ready and out the door earlier than normal. Her anxiety level continued to rise as she approached The Glen.

There were extra cars in the parking lot including one in her normal spot. She parked at the far end and hurried inside.

"What's going on, why all the cars?" Julia asked.

Carol looked at her and then at the clock. "Fifteen minutes early? Wow, I think I'll write that in the logbook.

We wouldn't want this historic event to pass unnoticed."

"Is everything all right? Is he all right?

"They've brought in a specialist from Milwaukee."

"He's okay, isn't he?"

"Fine, I guess. They haven't let me in the room, so I'm not sure. I think they've run every test known to man. They are talking about moving him to the hospital. They've removed the feeding tube; no solid foods yet, but he did eat some Jell-o."

"Is he talking? Does he remember anything?" Julia picked up his chart.

"From what I'm told, he's talking but still pretty confused. The doctors think it could take a while for his memory to come back."

A man, with a stethoscope slung over his shoulder, leaned across the desk. "I need to use the phone. I want that ambulance over here."

"He's going to be alright, isn't he?" Julia interrupted.

The doctor laughed. "He's doing fine. The lucky devil gets to have the catheter taken out and surgery to reverse the colostomy."

"Tonight?" Julia asked.

"The OR is open first thing in the morning and we can get all that taken care of. If everything goes okay, he could be back right after lunch. He will probably be a little groggy so you might want to keep an extra eye on him, just in case."

"He's coming back?" Julia tried to mask her excitement at hearing the news.

"The hospital's full. They don't have a bed for him. Besides, he's doing fine. We're all shocked at what really good shape he's in, considering all he's been through."

Julia hid a smile with her hand. She didn't dare tell them about all the therapy she had given him.

When the ambulance pulled up to the door, the

alternating red and yellow flashes of light danced off the walls like the reflected light of a ballroom mirrored-ball. The doctor met the driver at the door and turned him around. "This isn't an emergency, douse those lights. We don't need to wake up the whole damned town."

Julia stood by his door and watched as they lifted the man onto the gurney. He looked at Julia as they wheeled him by and she saw the bewildered look of a confused man. Her heart sank. All the nights she spent with him, she had only seen his sleep induced peaceful expression.

The evening went by slowly. Julia went through the motions caring for the other patients, but her heart and mind were focused on him. All the questions she struggled with, whether he was nice, or whether he was married, seemed unimportant. Her only concern now was for him to get better.

By the time Nora arrived to relieve her, Julia's energy was spent. She quickly filled Nora in about the young man being taken to the hospital. "He's probably out of surgery by now," Julia said. "The doctor thought he'd be back sometime after lunch."

"I'll call over there and find out what's going on. You get your tush out of here. You look like you could fall asleep standing there." Nora took Julia's sweater from the rack and threw it to her.

Julia one-handed it out of the air. "You're right. I'm beat."

She left a trail of clothes from the kitchen to the bedroom, was barely awake putting on her pajamas and was asleep the moment her head hit the pillow.

Julia poked her head into the therapy room to let Phyllis know she would be back in a few minutes before rushing off to check on the young man.

"He left here about ten minutes ago," Florence said.

42

"They took him back to The Glen."

"Were there any problems?"

"Everything went like clockwork. They put his plumbing back in order and he should be just fine. The only thing that's not working well is his memory. The poor lad doesn't remember a thing before waking, not even his name. Hopefully it will all come back to him in a couple of days."

"Is that the doctor's prognosis?" Julia asked.

"No, mine, the doctors aren't saying anything. They really don't know what's going to happen. Right now, they are just happy he's doing well physically."

"Thanks, Florence." Julia turned and rushed back to the therapy room.

The afternoon went by quickly. Getting in her car, she thought about going to The Glen. She was anxious to see him, to talk to him, but still apprehensive about that first meeting. The decision of seeing him now or waiting until she arrived at midnight was no surprise. She decided to wait.

"Girl, you're such a *Fraidy Cat*," she said. "You'll have to face him sooner or later." She put the car in gear and let out the clutch.

Carol was at the desk busily shuffling papers when Julia arrived to start her shift.

"How is he doing?" Julia asked.

"You mean Wonder Boy?"

Julia gave her a cross look. "Why did you call him that?"

"It's a wonder he woke up and now he's wondering what the hell happened to him." Carol seemed amused by her attempt at humor.

"I don't think that's funny at all." Julia then softened her tone. "Have you talked to him? What's he like? Is he

43

nice?"

"Well, he hasn't bitten anyone...yet."

"Carol," Julia scolded. "You've had a chance to talk to him, I haven't seen or talked to him since he wiggled his toe for me." Julia realized how silly that sounded and let out a giggle.

"He hasn't said much to any of us."

It was now or never, Julia walked to his room and opened the door slowly. The man was lying on his side facing the window. She greeted him the same way she had on numerous other nights. "Hello, sleepyhead. I'm glad you finally decided to wake up?"

He rolled and quickly sat up. He appeared to study her from head to toe. "It's you," he said, his voice rising. "I didn't know if you were real. I remember your voice, but wasn't sure if you were real or part of a dream."

"I'm real." She walked to the side of his bed. "I was with you when you woke up. I'm the one that grabbed your big toe and you wiggled it for me."

"Everything's so confusing, it's like I was trapped inside my own body sitting through a never ending movie. All these images flashing through my mind, but nothing made any sense. Your voice was the one thing that gave me peace. I longed to hear it. I waited for it."

"You could hear me?" Panic gripped her. She had told him everything about herself but he wasn't supposed to hear it. "Do you remember everything I said to you?"

"I don't remember what you said. I just remember the sound of your voice. That's silly isn't it? Why would I remember something like that, when I can't remember anything else."

Julia breathed a sigh of relief. She was touched that he remembered her voice and wiped the moisture that collected in the corner of her eye. "Every night since you got here I came into your room and talk to you. I'd give

44

you back rubs, massage your arms and legs and even give you whole sessions of physical therapy. I hoped it would help when you woke up."

"What made you do that?"

"I don't know, it just sort of happened. The first couple of nights, I just sat and talked, keeping you up on all the local news, most of it was just gossip."

"You gave me physical therapy?"

"I help out in the physical therapy room at the hospital. I was practicing the things I learned."

"You're telling me I was your guinea pig?" His smile negated any attempt to sound indignant.

"I asked a couple of times if you wanted me to stop, but you didn't answer so I just continued." Julia had all she could do to keep from laughing out loud.

"I think you took advantage of the situation."

"What can I say," Julia shot back. "You snooze you lose?"

He laughed. "You are too much. Does the voice have a name?"

"Julia, Julia Parsons."

He gave her hand a squeeze. "Very pleased to meet you, Julia Parsons."

"I don't suppose you have a name for me?" Julia asked, but wished she hadn't.

His tone went sober. "Sorry, I wish I could, but I come up with nothing."

Julia quickly backed to the door. "Listen, I've got to tend to my duties. We do have other patients. You get some rest and I will be back in a couple of hours."

"Promise?"

"Promise," she said walking out of his room. She felt her heart beat all the way up into her throat.

"Well, did he bite you?" Carol asked as Julia came bounding up to the desk.

"No, he's really nice." Julia tried to control her excitement. "He's a very nice guy."

"I got that, he's a nice guy," Carol said. "But was he able to tell you anything about himself, like maybe a name?"

"He remembered my voice, and thought I might not be real," Julia said, in a bit of a swoon.

"Oh, you're real alright, but maybe you need to get your real butt in gear and tend to our other patients."

Julia realized the chitchat session was over. "I'm going," she said, and hurried down the hall.

It was close to the end of her shift before she found herself at his door. "Knock, knock, anybody home?" she said in a soft voice. She peeked in and was surprised to see him sitting on the edge of the bed moving his leg up and down.

He switched to the other leg. "Hi, come in."

"What are you doing?" Julia asked with mocked dismay. "You just had surgery. You don't want to pull apart your stitches. Besides, you know you shouldn't try doing that on your own, are you trying to take my job away?" she scolded playfully.

"The stitches are fine," he said. "I'm just trying to get some strength back in my legs, so I don't feel so wobbly." I'm a little stiff, but the doctors are surprised how quickly I'm regaining my strength."

"You didn't tell them about therapy, did you?"

"No, should I have?"

Julia straightened the blankets on his bed. "Oh Geez no, I probably would have gotten into a lot of trouble for doing that. How did things go at the hospital?"

"Piece of cake. They shot this stuff in my arm and the next thing I knew I'm back here in my bed. It feels great to be rid of the catheter and that other thing." He pulled his gown around enough to show her the patch on his side.

"Looks like you are doing great." Julia took a step

backwards to avoid a breach of privacy. "I'm about to go off shift, but I will be back again tonight at midnight. Will you still be here?" She said with a giggle.

He made a magnanimous gesture with his hand. "I can only assume my whereabouts will be somewhere close to this bed and shall await your return."

Julia laughed and waved as she left the room.

Nora tossed her purse on the desk and began straightening folders and loose papers. "Did you do this, or did Carol leave this mess?" She gathered pens and paper clips and placed them in the drawer. "How can anyone work with such a mess?"

"I never got a chance to sit down. I've been on the go the whole shift," Julia said in her own defense. "Nothing crucial. Just everyone needing extra attention."

"So, no time for updates?" Nora asked.

"There's nothing new, everyone is fine. Please don't make me stay and do them."

"Go, get out of here. Other than our man in six, things don't change much around here on a day to day basis. You could probably copy yesterday's notes and not be too far off."

"Thanks," Julia said. "You're the greatest."

"Yeah, yeah, yeah, I know. Just get out of here before I change my mind." Nora picked up a chart and waved it in the air. "By the way, how is our celebrity guest doing?"

"He's sweet," Julia said walking to the door.

Nora just shook her head. "Medically speaking, how is he doing?"

"Doing just fine," Julia said as she pranced out the door. She skipped to her car, pleased their first meeting went so well.

Very Pleased to Meet You

*I*t was a bright beautiful morning and Julia couldn't stop smiling. She rolled the car window down and let the wind blow through her hair. "Very pleased to meet you, Julia Parsons," she mimicked. No one had ever said her name so sweetly. She wanted dearly to return to The Glen, to spend more time with him. The thing that held her back was that she didn't want to come off like some girl on the make.

She sang the Beatles', "I love you, yeah, yeah," as she walked into the house and continued singing while putting on her pajamas. She pulled down the shade, took a running leap onto her bed, and rolled on her back. Looking at the ceiling, she repeated, "Very pleased to meet you Julia Parsons." She closed her eyes with a vision of him in her mind.

*J*ulia thought about calling in sick and going to see the man instead of going to the hospital. She straightened the collar of her blouse, picked up her comb and made a final pass through her hair. She brought her face closer to the mirror. "For Pete's sake woman," she said, pointing the comb at the mirror, "You don't want to go running over there like some moon struck school girl." She convinced herself to stay away from The Glen until the start of her shift." She threw her comb on the vanity. Her reflection returned her disappointed look. "I don't believe it," she said, laughing out loud. "He's got me talking to myself." She grabbed her purse and skipped out the door whistling a cheerful tune.

Phyllis was quick to notice Julia's happy demeanor. "What are you so happy about?"

"That fellow woke up from the coma and I was there. He's a really nice guy."

"He's nice? What does that mean?" Phyllis raised an eyebrow to the woman she was working on.

"I've talked to him, he's really...nice."

Both women saw Julia's face flush and smiled.

Julia turned away quickly and helped a new arrival straddle the stationary bike. She also refrained from talking about the man for the rest of the day.

Walking out of the hospital, she had a few hours to kill. Pulling into the Shell station, she rolled down her window. "Can you do an oil change?" she asked, as Charlie approached.

"It would be my pleasure. Leave it running. I'll do it right now."

Julia got out and took a seat in the small waiting area next to the front counter.

Charlie's wife, Stella, came out of the restroom wiping her hands on a paper towel. She looked out into the garage. "Car problems?" she asked, tossing the wad of paper in the basket.

"Just an oil change."

"I heard that fellow came out of the coma, but doesn't remember a thing. Someone was saying that he may have brain damage."

"That's not true." Julia tried to remain calm. "He is having trouble remembering things, but he's doing very

49

well. The doctors think it's just a matter of time before he gets his memory back."

"One of the girls at the beauty shop said a doctor told her, he thought the memory thing was just a put on. That he was using it to conceal some wrongdoing."

Julia jumped to her feet. "I don't believe that for a minute. I've talked to him. He's polite and very sincere. Why is it when something happens to someone, everyone wants to make a bad thing out of it."

"I'm just repeating what I heard," Stella said putting her hands in the air.

"I'm sure the gossip mill is cranking out stuff big time." Julia stomped her foot and made a large swinging gesture with her arm. "Why can't everyone just be happy he's awake and give him time to recover?"

Charlie entered the office and had to duck as Julia's arm came around over his head. "Whoa girl. What's got you all riled up?"

"I think Julia's got the sweets for that fellow at The Glen," Stella said.

"Don't be silly. I would just like everyone to give the poor guy a chance to heal before judging him." Julia opened her purse. "How much do I owe you?"

"Two-dollars for the oil change and seventy-five cent for the grease job." Charlie gave Stella a cross look while handing the keys to Julia.

Julia paid and turned on her heels. Yanking open the car door, she felt her face flush. "Nobody has to tell me who I have the sweets on," she mumbled. Starting the car, she squealed the tires driving off.

Julia drove onto the grass in front of her place. She needed something to do to work off the aggression that churned in her stomach. Grabbing a pail and a couple of old towels, she unwrapped the hose, filled the bucket and sprayed the car. Rinsing off the last of the soap bubbles, she toweled it dry. Granted, her car was eleven years old, but she always liked the way the green metal flake sparkled when it was freshly washed. She emptied the pail, coiled the hose, and hung the towels on the clothesline. A sense of pride brought out a big smile as she went into the house.

Julia turned on the shower. She stood, with her eyes closed as the hot water ran down over her body. Recalling her blowup at the Shell station, she grit her teeth. "Maybe I am sweet on him," she whimpered. "But I don't need Stella telling me I am.

Carol was hunched over at the desk. Julia hung up her sweater and peered over Carol's shoulder. "How's he doing?"

"By him, I'm assuming you're referring to our guest in Room Six?" She said, without looking up.

"You know who I mean." Julia tickled Carol's ribs.

Carol rolled away in the chair to escape Julia's attack. "He's doing great and stop tickling me. I have to go to the john and you're going to make me wet my pants."

"Then give me all the information you have on this guy or these fingers will attack again," Julia said, wiggling her fingers.

"Don't come near me," Carol said, rolling back to the desk and picking up his chart. "He's been walking in the hallways every two hours, sat in his chair from seven to nine this evening, went number one and number two, which means his plumbing is working fine. He had chicken and mashed potatoes for supper plus two helpings of ice cream. Anything else you'd like to know?"

"Is he awake?"

I checked on him twenty minutes ago and he was sound asleep. I think we pooped him out."

"Has he remembered anything more about himself?"

"Nope, still drawing zeros," Carol said. "He remembers

everything that has happened since he woke up but nothing before that."

"Do you think he has brain damage?"

"The specialist from Milwaukee said as far as he can tell his brain is functioning properly. He's not mentally incapacitated. The doctor thinks this memory thing should clear up in time. Why would you ask a question like that?"

"The gossip mill is spewing out stuff in high gear. That's one of the things they're saying."

Carol threw his chart on the desk. "You know better than to listen to that crap. He's doing fine. It might just take some time for him to get his memory back."

"I'm going to peek in on him." Julia started down the hall. Carol was right. He was asleep, even snored a little. She backed out and returned to the front desk. "He's asleep." Julia said, trying to hide her disappointment. "Anything else I should know about?"

"Just normal stuff, George has been unusually restless, you might want to keep an extra eye on him. It's been fun having Six awake and being able to care for him." Carol threw her sweater over her shoulders. "We need to come up with a name for him, we can't keep calling him 'the man, Six, or Hey you.'"

Julia laughed. "I guess you're right. See yah," Julia yelled to Carol's wave.

Three times during her shift she peeked in on the man, each time he was asleep. Finally, a little before six she found him sitting up in bed. "Good morning," she said. "How are you feeling today?"

His smile stretched the width of his face. "Fine, a lot stronger, especially my legs. The walking helps. I'm not quite as shaky."

"I can work on those legs if you want, or how about a back rub?"

"A back rub sounds wonderful."

Julia cranked the bed flat. He rolled over and brought the sheet around to cover his buttocks. She untied the strings on his gown and let it slide off his shoulders. As she put her hands on his back, he stiffened.

"Ooooh, your hands are cold."

Julia slapped his back. "Don't be such a pansy." She scolded him and pushed her hands toward his neck. It was more of a massage than a rub. She worked on the muscles up and down his spine. He groaned as she increased the pressure on each tight spot. He moaned especially loud when she hit the pressure points in his neck and shoulders.

"You need to relax," she said. "You're like in one big knot." She retied the strings of his gown and helped him roll over. His gown got tangled in the sheet and in trying to straighten it out, he pulled on the gown, exposing his lower body. "Whoops," she said, as she quickly pulled the sheet over him.

"I don't know who designed these gowns, but they're absolutely worthless. Do you have time, or do you have to go?"

Julia looked at her watch. "I've got some time."

"Could we talk?"

"Sure, what do you want to talk about?"

"Where are we?"

"You are at The Glen. It's a nursing home."

"I guessed that," he said. "But where are we, what city, what state?"

"Oh," Julia chuckled. "You're in Pine Lake, Wisconsin." She waited and watched him ponder the words. Not seeing a reaction, she continued. "Small town, big lake, a hundred-twenty miles north of Milwaukee, lake trout fishing. Does anything ring a bell?"

He shook his head. "I have to believe I was in some kind of accident, but how did I end up here."

"You want the long story or the short one?"

53

He shrugged his shoulders. "The long one I guess. I've got a bunch of things floating around in my head and a lot of blank spaces I'm trying to fill."

Julia started with the young people smooching in the park, the ones who called the authorities. She described his injuries, how Doctor Erickson patched him up, and being moved to The Glen when the hospital needed the bed. "Do you remember anything about what I've just told you?"

He shook his head. "The name Mary keeps popping up in my head but I have no idea why." He gazed into space. "Is there a Mary here?"

"No, none here and I don't know of any Marys' at the hospital. Sorry, I guess I can't help you."

"That's strange," he said. "It's like I'm calling her name."

An awkward moment of silence hung between them. The young man was about to say something when Julia turned her head, at the sound of the front door bell. "It's too early for Nora. I'll have to see who it is. I'll be right back."

"Promise?"

"I promise," she said.

An Unexpected Visitor

Julia opened the door. Sheriff Joe Christenson stormed in carrying a brown paper sack. A stump of a man, his belly not only hung over his belt, but swayed side to side as he walked. People joked about him never passing up a doughnut or a meal. He was a dull, unattractive character, who barely made it through school. His appearance was further degraded by a mouthful of crooked teeth stained from years of chewing tobacco.

As sheriff, he could chose to wear street clothes but preferred the two-tone blue policeman's uniform, that included the pointy blue cap with gold braid, shiny visor, and badge on the front. The popular take on Joe, "the lights are on but nobody's home."

Charging up to the desk, he slapped his hand on the varnished surface. "I'm so dang mad, I could spit. I take a couple days off and no one bothers to tell me the main character in my ongoing investigation has come to." Joe looked around. "Well," he said distastefully. "Are you going to show me where I might find this person?"

"Yes sir, this way." Julia walked swiftly down the hall. The sheriff, his short legs moving a click or two faster than his normal gait, struggled to keep up.

The young man came forward in his chair when Julia and the Sheriff burst through the door. The sheriff stuck his thumbs in his gun belt and sucked in a big gulp of air. "Well, young fella, I'm glad you finally decided to wake up. We need to get to the bottom of what the hell this is all about."

Julia stepped between them. "He's having a little trouble remembering things."

The sheriff shot her an angry look and continued to question the man. "I'm here to question the young man. If you would kindly step out of the way and let him answer my questions." He motioned her aside. "What can you tell us about yourself?"

"Not much, I get these images in my head but nothing makes any sense."

"Some people in town think you might be faking this amnesia business. Have you got something to hide?"

"That's silly. Why would he do that?" Julia interrupted.

Joe ignored her intrusion. "Does the name Josh mean anything to you?"

"Should it?" The man asked without making eye contact.

"Well," the sheriff removed a pair of boxers from the paper bag, "you were wearing these shorts when they brought you to the hospital. See here, someone wrote the name Josh on the label. What do you make of that?"

Julia turned away and pursed her lips trying to stop the giggle that shot from her mouth.

"Ma'am!" The sheriff held up his hand to her and pressed the boxers to the man's face. "Is that your name?"

"I don't know, I guess it could be."

The sheriff leaned again. "Do you remember being in a car accident? We found tire marks on the highway above County Park, the day after those kids found you. They lead right into a high bank on the side of the road." Joe waited before proceeding. "Now, if someone driving a vehicle fast enough to make those marks on the pavement,

56

hit that bank, it could have caused that person, or persons riding in that vehicle to be thrown into the windshield with enough force to cause all sorts of injuries to that person's head. Do you remember anything like that?"

The young man sat motionless.

"The problem is, we don't have a vehicle. Are you following me on this? If you was in an accident up there, what the hell happened to the vehicle?"

The young man shrugged. "I wish I could tell you. I'm just as confused as you are."

The sheriff straightened. "What we have here is a real mystery." The sheriff walked to the window. "We've sent your fingerprints to the FBI, your picture, as beat up as you were, to every missing person request in four states, and got nothing. You don't match any arrest warrants and the FBI said you have no criminal history. There is just no information on you. It's like you was born yesterday and fell out of the damned sky... and landed in my damned county." He tipped his hat to Julia. "Sorry ma'am, for my colorful language."

The sheriff took off his cap and scratched his head. "There's also the mystery of who and why a person would be hiding in the room while you was in the coma."

Julia choked and turned away.

The sheriff gave her a cross look before pressing the man. "Any thoughts on that?"

The man looked blankly at the officer.

"I guess until you start remembering something, we ain't got much to go on, just the name Josh, that you, your wife, or your mama wrote in your underwear."

Julia completely lost it and burst out laughing.

"Ma'am, this is an official police interrogation. If you continue to cause an interruption, I'll have to ask you to step out of the room."

"I'm sorry. It won't happen again, I promise," she said.

57

Joe folded the bag. "The rest of your clothes: pants, shirt, shoes, were full of blood. We sent it all to the crime lab in Madison. It was common department store stuff, nothing out of the ordinary."

The sheriff started for the door. "I'm going to ask you not to leave Pine Lake without contacting my office. We still don't know if any crimes have been committed. So until we get to the bottom of all this, I'm going to need you to stick around."

"Sure." The man rose from his chair. "No problem."

The sheriff tipped his cap to Julia and nodded in the direction of the man. Julia escorted the sheriff to the front door.

"Go!" the man shouted when she returned. "Where am I going to go?"

Julia was startled and stepped back.

"How can I go? I don't have any money." He threw his hands in the air. "Hell, I don't have any clothes except for this hospital gown and a pair of boxer shorts."

"The gown stays," Julia said.

"What?" He looked puzzled.

"The gown stays. It's belongs to The Glen." Julia fought to keep from laughing.

"Oh, that's cruel." They both laughed.

"So, do you think your name is Josh?" Julia asked.

"My underwear thinks it is.

"So, is it okay if we call you Josh?"

"Sure, just call me 'good old Josh,' the guy with no money, no place to go and no clothes to go in. I can't believe people would think I would fake being in a situation like this. And what did he say, someone was hiding in my room?"

Julia swallowed. "I did hear something about that." A chill sent a shiver down her back; she knew she'd dodged a bullet. Thank goodness, Horace never connected the

58

dots of her being at the hospital that day and she was not ready to fess up to being the one at this time. The sound of the front door closing provided a break. "Oh my Gosh, it's Nora. I've got to go."

Nora set a large plastic bag on the desk when Julia came scurrying up.

"His name is Josh," Julia blurted. "The sheriff was here. It was written in his boxer shorts."

"Girl, will you slow down and make sense. Let's start with 'the sheriff was here.'"

Julia composed herself and gave Nora a blow-by-blow description of the sheriff's visit.

"At least that's something. So, other than the name Josh, the sheriff still has no clue of who he is or what happened, huh?"

"I guess not." Julia walked to the desk. "What's in the bag?"

"Keep your nose out of there." Nora grabbed the bag and placed it on the floor. "Anything special I should know about our other patients?"

"No, everything is good. The sheriff said some people think he's faking the memory thing."

"That's stupid, but, if he is, it's an Oscar winning performance," Nora said. "Let's hope he remembers something soon and stops all this bullshit gossip."

"I agree." Julia ran down the hall and stuck her head in Josh's room. "Would you like some company this afternoon? I could skip going to the hospital and come back."

"That would be great." He held the key in the air. "This could unlock the mystery of my past, but for the life of me, I haven't a clue of what it's to."

A Pleasant Afternoon

Julia made a detour to the kitchen. The cooks were loading breakfast trays with French toast, bacon, syrup, and cartons of vanilla yogurt, chocolate milk and orange juice.

"Mmmmm." Julia reached for a cardboard container. "Do you mind if I take some on the run?"

The cook shook the spoon in her hand. "Okay, but you better eat every bit of it or I'll give you a good spanking."

"I will! I'm starving, but I need to be on my way."

Arriving home, she put the food on the table, took a swallow of juice and searched her purse for a mirror. It had been weeks since she had her hair trimmed. She picked up the phone. "In an hour, perfect. Thanks Myra, I'll see you then." Julia soaked the French toast in syrup, put a large piece in her mouth and added a chunk of bacon. She grabbed the juice and headed to the bedroom.

Stepping out of her uniform, she stood in front of her closet. She moved hangers trying to decide on a blouse to wear for their afternoon visit. She held a green one to herself and looked in the mirror. Throwing it on the bed, she gave a white one a quick look. One-by-one she pulled tops from the closet giving each a long look before either putting it back, or tossing it on the bed.

He'd only seen her in uniform. Maybe she needed to

60

go to the Bargain Barn and pick out something new. She shook her head. "That would be foolish. Besides, I don't have any extra money for that."

Throwing on a pair of jeans and a purple t-shirt she returned to the kitchen, popped the rest of the French toast in her mouth and washed it down with the last of the juice. She put the yogurt and chocolate milk in the refrigerator, picked up the last strip of bacon and bounced out the door.

The ladies at the Cut & Curl hung on Julia's every word. They wanted to know everything about the mystery man and especially enjoyed the part of the name Josh being written in his boxer shorts. Julia wished that she hadn't told that part. He'd probably want to kill her if he ever found out. Julia jumped out of the chair and checked the cut in the mirror. "Looks great." She made a few passes with a brush, pushing and patting her hair to get it just the way she liked it. She paid and waved goodbye to the girls.

The bed was a rainbow of colors with all the tops she had laid there. She chose the pink scoop neck and a pair of white Bermuda shorts and hung the rest back in the closet.

She woke a little after one refreshed and anxious to see him. Once dressed it only took her a few casual strokes with the comb and a few squirts of spray to get her hair to lay just right. White button earrings, a light coating of Sensual Pink lipstick and a dab of My Sin perfume by each ear were the finishing touches. She stepped back from the mirror for one final look. Her first thought was to start over, but decided this was it. She grabbed her purse and hurried out the door.

She hummed along with Elvis on the radio, on the short drive to The Glen. She took one final look in the rear-view mirror before going in.

Nora sat at the desk, her head down, looking over some

61

papers. She looked up as Julia approached. Throwing her hands in the air in a silly gesture of surprise, she exclaimed, "Well, look at you, darling, did you get all dolled up just for me?"

Julia waved off Nora's obvious attempt at humor. "I was just...he said... he'd like some company this afternoon."

"Now that's what I call going above and beyond the call of duty," Nora said with a big grin. "Coming back on your own time to sit with a patient?" Nora put her elbows on the desk and put her chin in her hands. "Did you come to see Robert? He'll probably want to take you out dancing."

"Oh please." Julia said, as she walked down the hall. She heard Nora's laughter as she approached his room. The door was partially closed so she tapped before poking her head into the room.

Josh stood looking out the window, not in his normal stylish hospital gown, but in a plaid western shirt and blue jeans. "Wow!" Julia exclaimed. "You look great."

He spun on his heels. "I should say the same about you."

"Where did you get the clothes?" Julia straightened his collar.

"My Sin?"

"What?"

"Your perfume, My Sin isn't it?"

Julia blinked. "It is, how did you know?"

Josh shrugged his shoulders. "I don't, it just came out." There was a long moment when neither spoke.

Finally, Julia broke the silence. "Where did you get the fancy clothes?"

"Nora." Josh extended his arms in a casual pose. "She brought them in this morning. I guess they were her husband's."

"Probably Duke's, her boyfriend. They never got married." Julia looked at the other clothes on the bed.

"It feels great to be dressed in something other than that stupid gown. I guess we were pretty much the same size. Same shoe size, too." Josh picked up his foot to show her the white canvas shoes he had on.

"Will you excuse me for a minute? I'll be right back." Julia went straight to Nora and gave her a hug. "That was really nice of you to give Josh those clothes."

"Silly me," Nora said. "I would buy all these clothes for Duke and a lot of it he wouldn't wear. I gave away a bunch of his things when he passed, but there were some things I just couldn't part with. I thought Duke looked so smart in that western shirt and jeans."

"That's what was in the bag you brought in this morning wasn't it?"

"Yeah," Nora confessed. "Some shirts are still in the package. He never got to wear the two pair of nice slacks." Nora fussed with some papers on the desk before pulling a hanky from her sleeve and wiping both eyes. "Did you see those tennis shoes? Fifteen dollars. He never wore them either. The only shoes that man ever wore as long as I knew him were cowboy boots. I felt a little foolish for hanging on to that stuff, but now I'm glad I did. I'm sure Josh will put them to good use."

Julia gave Nora another hug with an extra squeeze and headed back to his room. That's so typical of Nora, she thought. She would literally give the shirt off her back. Julia chuckled. Of course, in this case, it was Duke's shirt she gave.

"What's so funny?" He asked as she entered the room.

"Oh nothing, I just had a nice thought about someone." Walking straight to him, she poked her finger in his chest. "Now, I think you need to explain how you knew the name of my perfume."

"I wonder that myself. It just came out."

"Maybe you know someone who wears it, maybe a

63

girlfriend, or this girl, Mary?" Julia bit her lip and wished she hadn't said that.

Josh appeared to ignore the question. Looking out the window he pointed to a large building in the distance. "What is that?"

Julia looked to see where he was pointing. "That's the county courthouse. The town is Pine Lake, but we are also the Marshall County seat so the courthouse is here, too."

"How big of a town is Pine Lake?"

"It's small, less than a thousand people in the winter. From May to September, counting all the tourist and Lakeshore people, the town swells to probably fifteen times that many. We get a turnover of tourists every week or two. The Lakeshore people stay the entire summer. By Lakeshore, I mean the families that have second homes on the lake. Some of these properties are huge, sitting on two to three hundred feet of Lakeshore frontage. Many have been in the family for two and three generations. A lot of fellows from town work as caretakers on these estates. They also provide summer jobs for the high school kids mowing grass and doing yard work," Julia paused. "If I'm boring you with this, just tell me to stop."

"No, no, it's very interesting," Josh said. "I'm anxious to see the lake."

"Sorry, you got one of the cheap rooms. The rooms with the lake view are across the hall." Josh acknowledged the obvious humor.

"Lakeshore mothers and kids come up and spend the summer," Julia said, picking up her travelogue, "the dads commute and spend weekends. Lakeshore people tend to stick together. Their families are entwined, Lakeshore boys grow up and marry Lakeshore girls."

Josh smiled. "Is that a rule?"

"Not chiseled in stone. We're townies and they're... Lakeshore. It's like I'm German and you're..."

64

"Something else."

Julia blushed. "I'm sorry...you know what I mean."

"There's a difference."

"Right. In summer they pretty much take over the country club for their parties and social events. Their big thing is sailboat racing on the weekends. It's a battle royal between the local fishing guides, who are out there trolling for lake trout and having to navigate through a slew of sailboats. The Lakeshore guys will sail right in front of the fishermen or pass so close behind they cut the fisherman's lines."

"I sense there might be a little animosity between the locals and the Lakeshore people."

"There probably is, but Lakeshore people provide employment. They also pay a huge portion of our taxes. They spend money on groceries, buy gas and eat in our restaurants. We need them, but other than that there isn't much mingling between Lakeshore and the local inhabitants."

"How big is the lake?"

"Three miles wide and six miles long. It's over one-hundred-ninety feet deep in some places. Pine Lake got its name from the tall pines that line the shore." Julia extended her hand in the air to indicate the height of the trees.

Josh continued looking out the window.

"How would you like to take a ride?" Julia asked.

"A ride?" Josh turned. "Could we?"

"I could take you around and give you the grand tour. We could drive along the lake, down by the marina and out to the country club. That's where the big Fourth of July yacht club dance will be next week. I can also take you to a place that makes the biggest, juiciest, and best hamburger in town."

"Sounds delicious." His face lit up. "Do you think it would be all right?"

"Let me check with Nora. I'll be right back." Julia opened the door just as Nora was about to step in. "Oh Nora, I was just coming to see you."

"I was coming to make sure this wasn't a conjugal visit."

"Nora!" Julia blushed.

Josh smiled.

"Calm down. I was only kidding," Nora said. "The cooks want to know if they can fix you guys a little snack or something?"

"We were thinking of going for ride," Julia said. "I was going to show Josh around town and then maybe catch a burger later."

Nora looked at Josh. "Let's not rush this. He's doing good, but let's give it one more day. Tomorrow is Saturday. Why don't you two plan something for tomorrow?"

The two agreed.

"Okay," Nora said. "Now, that we have that settled. How about a snack? Maybe you'd like to have it out on the porch?"

"That would be wonderful," Julia said.

"I'll tell the cooks to fix you up."

The afternoon went by quickly as the two sat on the porch, munched snacks, and watched the activity on the lake. Julia kept the conversation light with stories of some of the things she encountered since moving to Pine Lake.

A cool afternoon breeze rustled through the leaves of the tall oak close to the house. Julia rubbed the goose pimples off her arm and checked her watch. "I should be going, if we both get a good night's sleep, we will be ready for our big ride tomorrow."

"Sounds great," Josh said. "I enjoyed the afternoon and I'm looking forward to the grand tour tomorrow."

Julia felt an extra bounce in her step as she went to her car.

Going For a Ride

Julia woke, embracing her pillow. She drew her pajama top up to her nose. The scent of her warm moist body mixed with the fading fragrance of My Sin filled her senses. The thought of spending another day with Josh sent a tingle through her body. Her legs wiggled with excitement and she tightened the hold on her pillow. She felt alive and cursed Brad for causing her to suppress the feelings of want and desire for so long. Her heart ached and she yearned to be with Josh. No matter how hard she tried to take her time, she was ready and fully dressed by seven thirty.

Josh was standing at the desk talking to Nora when Julia walked in. He had on a white short-sleeve shirt and plaid Bermuda shorts.

"I like the shorts," Julia said.

"More of the outstanding wardrobe this kind lady has provided me." He smiled at Nora.

"Okay!" Nora tapped her finger on the desk. "Here are the ground rules. Josh, I want you to take it easy, not too much walking and for heaven's sake if you get tired or start to feel out of sorts, get back here on the double. You've only been up and about for a few days." She turned to Julia. "And you young lady, I want you to have him back here no later than four o'clock, sharp!" Then added, "or your butt is toast."

Nora walked them to the front door. Holding onto Josh's arm, she felt him hesitate. "Are you sure you are up for this?"

"I'm fine, just a little nervous. It's a big world out there, but I'll have to face it sooner or later."

"Just take it easy, okay?"

Josh stood by the car and slowly panned the countryside. He turned abruptly and watched a speedboat cruise past on the lake below. Closing his eyes, he took a deep breath, and exhaled slowly. "Do you hear that?" He pointed to some birds chirping in the trees. Before she could answer, his head turned at the sound of a dog barking down the road. "The sounds, the pine scent, the sweet smell of fresh air, it's all so wonderful."

Julia laughed, then leaned across the seat. "Are you getting in or are we going to spend the whole day in the parking lot?"

"Sorry, I just want to soak it all in."

Julia did her best to point out the points of interest along the way, the elementary school, the high school and churches of each denomination. "The town is old. People settled here right after the Civil War. Some houses date back to before the turn of the century, but most were built in the 20's and 30's."

"That's the courthouse, right?" Josh said, pointing to the large building ahead.

"You remembered." Julia pulled into a parking stall and turned off the engine. "This is the main intersection of town, so dictated by the four way stop. We don't have any traffic lights, so that's as big city as we get. Do you want to walk around a little bit?"

"Sure." Josh got out and walked to the corner.

Julia led the way down the street. Josh stopped and looked in every store window. He spent extra time at the gift shops looking at the knick-knacks and souvenirs. She gave a little background information on each business. Pointing to the coffee shop across from the courthouse, "they make a really good breakfast."

Walking past the post office, "All news and gossip flows across its counter," Julia said, not giving him a chance to question her meaning. "That's Charlie's Shell," she said, pointing to the opposite corner. "That's where I get my gas."

"I love the quaintness, but I'm surprised to see the empty stores."

"Highway thirty-seven used to come right through Pine Lake," Julia said. "About six years ago, the state built a bypass on the outskirts of town. Before they moved the highway we had two grocery stores. That one closed." Julia pointed to the empty building next to the gas station. "The other was in the last building down the street. The owners closed and built a new store out on the frontage road next to the highway. In the other empty buildings we had a hardware store that moved out by the highway and a variety store that went out of business."

"That's a shame," Josh said. "Moving the highway must have hurt the other businesses, too."

"Most businesses here struggle to survive. Thank goodness we have the lake and all the people it attracts."

"The courthouse is quite impressive," he said. I love the red brick facade and those white columns by the front steps."

"The original structure was built in 1910 and underwent a complete renovation in the early 50's."

"You really know a lot about the town," he said.

"Thanks to Nora. She's lived here for twenty years and knows everything about the town. We've got to keep moving. We have a lot more to see." Julia walked across the street and pointed to a building at the end of the block.

69

"Down there, by the Budweiser sign, is the famous Teddy's Bar. It's where all the locals hang out. It's sort of run down but they make the best burgers. We'll stop there later."

"Where to now?" Josh asked, getting in the car.

The White Wings

"Our next stop is the Marina. It's the hub of summer activity. You can rent a boat, buy a boat, or go for a boat ride. You can also take a guided fishing trip on one of their pontoon boats. They sell snacks, souvenirs, and t-shirts with a Pine Lake print."

Josh laughed. "They should hire you to do their advertising."

"Look. It's the White Wings," Julia said as they pulled into the marina parking lot. A long white boat, with a full-length canopy top, glided across the water. The posts supporting the top were ornately carved and the edge of the roof was trimmed with white wood filigree. It moved effortlessly as it maneuvered to the dock.

"It's beautiful." Josh said.

"That boat is like fifty years old. It was built to ferry the men who worked at the Carnation plant at the west end of the lake. During the war, when gasoline was rationed, it was cheaper for people to go by boat than by car." The two watched as people began stepping off the boat.

"C'mon, let's take a closer look." Julia ran to the pier and threaded her way through the crowd. Standing by the boat, she waved for Josh to follow.

Acknowledging her wave, he stood to the side and waited for the crowd to filter past. Julia had already stepped down into the boat and sat on the bench seat along the far side. "C'mon slowpoke, sit over here by me." She patted the seat next to her.

He took his time looking at the boat from bow to stern. The beautifully varnished wood floors and trim glistened in the sunlight. An ornate captain's chair and steering wheel were located about halfway back along one side. The engine, under a padded cover, sat in the center of the boat beside the captain's chair.

Josh was still admiring the beautiful woodwork when the boat teetered. Turning, he was confronted by a young man wearing a white boating cap with shiny black visor.

"Next ride is four o'clock," the young man said. "It's our Happy Hour Cocktail Cruise. If you don't have a reservation I'm afraid we're sold out."

"That's okay, we're just looking at the boat," Josh said. "It sure is a beauty, all this wonderful woodwork. Are you the captain?"

The young man nodded. "The correct terminology would be to call her a launch. She was built to haul people and cargo."

"That's what she said," Josh pointed to Julia.

The captain looked at Julia. "You work up at The Glen, don't you? During the winter, I drive laundry truck. I remember seeing you there." Then turning to Josh, "Haven't seen you before. Where are you from?"

Julia spoke quickly. "He's here for a visit. I'm showing him the town."

"Well, folks," the captain said. "I've got to get the old girl over to the boat house and get her set up for the cocktail cruise." Josh made a move to leave. "Wait," the captain said, grabbing Josh's arm. "I'll give you guys a ride to the boathouse. It's just a hundred yards or so down the shore."

The captain sat in his chair, adjusted the shifting

72

lever to neutral and turned over the engine. It responded immediately and purred so smoothly neither could feel a noticeable vibration. Jumping on the pier the captain untied the stern and threw the line in the boat. Untying the bow, he used his foot to push the front of the launch away from the pier and jumped onboard.

He gave the horn a couple of toots and pushed the shifting lever forward. The launch moved ahead quickly. Instead of turning and going to the boathouse, he steered the vessel towards the channel. "I've got a few extra minutes. I'll give you the ten cent tour out to the buoy and back."

Josh smiled and acknowledged the offer. "That's fine with us."

The afternoon sun was warm, but gliding across the water made it feel cooler. "She's deceptively fast," the captain said. "She'll do eighteen miles an hour and could pull a couple of water skiers doing it. We cruise at about twelve miles per hour." He slowly turned the launch and steered towards the boathouse, where he expertly maneuvered it into the sleeve, reversing the engine at the final moment before hitting the front of the dock. The boat came to a stop, without touching either side, or the front.

"Well done," Josh said. "You made the landing look easy."

"You have a boat?" the captain asked.

"I don't know, but I feel comfortable on the water."

The captain looked bewildered.

Julia, sensing the conversation would end up requiring a lot of explaining, quickly moved on. "What do you have to do to get it ready for cocktail cruise?"

"Everyone brings their own snacks and what they want to drink—wine, beer, martinis, you name it. The bench seating that line the outside of the boat works fine for sightseeing, but with food and drinks we use these narrow

73

tables and lock them down in front of the benches." He mounted the first one. "It creates a row of cocktail tables up and down each side. The tops have bottle holders and a place for an ice bucket built into them. It saves a lot of bottles from rolling around the deck in choppy weather." The captain added a chuckle.

Josh stood up and took Julia's hand to help her up. He turned to the captain. "Julia said the boat, I mean launch, is over fifty years old, but she looks practically new."

"True. This is her second year on the lake since being restored. She first went in the water in April 1911. She not only hauled people to the milk plant on the west end, she also delivered food and laundry to the boys and girls camps around the lake." He locked in another table and continued his story. "The milk plant closed in forty-eight and some of the camps during the fifties. Speedboats and Chris Crafts became the rage. There wasn't much work for the old gal so she pretty much sat idle."

The captain continued working. "Cliff Nelson couldn't bear the thought of scuttling her or tearing her apart. He had her wrapped in canvas and stored in a steel shed on some farm. She sat in there for some fifteen years. When Cliff died, his grandson, Joe, thought it would be a tribute to his grandfather to restore the old girl. He did all the refinishing himself, put in the new bench seating and as a safety feature had the seat cushions made to pass as flotation devices. Just in case we have to abandon ship. She was originally powered by a wood burning steam engine. Joe added the more dependable thirty horse gasoline engine"

"How did she get the name White Wings?" Josh asked.

"She actually has two names. Cliff named her White Wings after seeing her glide across the water, said she looked like a beautiful white gull soaring in the sky. The name we use to advertise our boat rides is, The Queen of

74

the Lake."

Julia tugged on Josh's sleeve. "We really should be going."

Josh shook hands with the captain. "So, who owns the boat, I mean, launch?"

"It belongs to Joe Nelson. The marina leases her for the summer."

Josh stepped out on the pier. "Thanks for the ride and the background story. This boat is a real treasure." Josh looked around. "How do we get back to the car?"

"Just go between those buildings and you will be back at the main pier."

First Kiss

A rriving at the car, Josh stopped and looked across the lagoon. "What is the big brown building over there?"

"That's the icehouse," Julia said. "Years ago, they cut ice from the lake. Before refrigerators people used the ice in their iceboxes to keep things cold."

"What's in there now? Anything?"

"It belongs to a friend of mine. He just uses it to store a bunch of junk. C'mon let's go see some of the Lakeshore homes. We can swing by the country club and see that, too."

Josh opened the car door then looked back at the icehouse. "That building is neat. It has rustic charm and it's right on the lake. I'm surprised no one has done anything with it."

"My friend said it would take a ton of money to put in the utilities. C'mon, we've got lots to see."

"This is Illinois Lane," Julia said as they drove along the lake. "The homes here are mostly owned by wealthy people from Chicago."

Large oaks and towering pines lined both sides of the street. The homes, each one more impressive than the next, were set back from the road, many with long driveways that circled around to the front door.

Josh noted the appeal of the large screened-in porches

that faced the lake. "Imagine how wonderful it would be to sit on one of those porches on a cool summer evening... sipping lemonade and watching the moonlight dance across the water."

"The taxes on some of these properties are more than a lot of people in town make in a year. It's like we have two separate worlds living side by side. Lakeshore people often spend more on a single party than someone from town would spend feeding their family for three months."

"Is the lake completely surrounded by homes or is there some place where we can get down by the water?"

"I'll take you to inlet road. We can drive right to the water's edge."

The ride took them away from the shore and along a county road. They passed homes and farms, drove through groves of towering pines, and fields of corn before coming to a clearing. The road stretched like a mile long ribbon with water on both sides.

"This is inlet road. The lake is on the right and Silver Creek pond is on the left." Julia pulled into the narrow patch of land on the lake side of the road. "Do you want to get out and put your feet in the water?"

"Yes, let's," Josh said opening his door. He went to the water's edge and stepped onto a large rock. "My God, what a beautiful sight."

Julia removed her shoes and socks. Stepping off a flat rock she lifted the hem of her shorts as the water came to her knees. "Are you coming?"

Josh quickly removed his footwear and gingerly stepped into the water. "O-o-oh, it's cold."

"You're such a sissy." Julia laughed. "Once you're in it's really nice."

He shuffled his feet on the sandy bottom to move close to her. Wrapping his arms around her, he drew her close. "Would it be alright if I kissed you?"

77

Julia was stunned.

Without waiting for an answer he leaned down and pressed his lips to hers. Julia felt his chest heave against her breast. His breath was warm and sweet. He parted his lips as his tongue searched for an opening between hers. Impulsively, she squeezed her lips tight, then slowly let his tongue probe deep into her mouth. She felt awkward, her hands hung at her side. Slowly, she brought her arms up and wrapped them around his neck. She felt the tingle of the kiss all the way down to her toes. Her stomach churned with emotion.

"I'm sorry," Josh whispered as they separated. "It just felt like the thing to do. I wanted to thank you for bringing me out on this marvelous excursion. I guess it turned into a little more than that."

"You don't have to apologize. It felt good to me, too." If that's his thank you kiss, she thought, what would an 'I love you kiss' be like? She climbed out of the water and walked to the car. Opening the trunk she brought out a blanket, spread it on a small patch of grass, and began putting on her shoes and socks. Josh joined her and did the same. She lay on the blanket and watched him finish tying his shoe.

Josh laid beside her, entwining his fingers in hers. "I could spend the whole afternoon watching these clouds drift by." He rolled on his side and faced her. "I'm thankful for whatever it was that brought me to this paradise. The lake, the town, they are so beautiful, and the people have been wonderful. I won't be disappointed in the least if circumstances allow me to stay." He moved toward her slowly.

Julia wanted another kiss, but she pushed him away. "Not here. Not with all the cars driving by." She sat up and looked at her watch. "It's after two. Aren't you getting hungry?" Julia stood and pulled the blanket from

78

underneath him.

"I guess we're leaving, huh?" Josh said, rolling to the side.

Julia folded the blanket and put it in the trunk. "I promised you one of Teddy's delicious hamburgers. You don't want to miss that, do you?"

"No, and now that you mention it, I am hungry."

On the drive back to town, Julia continued her travelogue about the lake, the people who settled here and the history of the area dating back to when the Winnebago Indians roamed the area.

Julia pointed to a sprawling building at the end of a grass lined driveway. "That's the Country Club. The yacht club dance will be there on the Fourth of July." The parking lot was full. "They must be having a big wedding. It's not local. It's either Lakeshore or out of town. Local weddings are usually down at the Legion Hall. Let's skip this part of the tour and head to Teddy's."

Sixty Years in Business

Julia parked in front of the bar. Josh got out and studied the building. It didn't look much like a tavern, more like a big old house, but the overhead Plexiglas sign and the blinking neon beer signs in the windows left little doubt of its real purpose.

Josh opened the tavern door for Julia and followed her in. The room was large with an array of mounted deer heads hanging on the walls. Josh stopped and appeared to be fixated on the stag with the large set of antlers, hanging on the back wall.

Julia saw the distant look on his face. "What is it Josh?"

"I just had a vision. A deer was running beside me. He was so close I could have reached out and touched him."

"You saw a deer, were you hunting?"

"I don't think so." Josh took the time to study each mounted head.

"Are you okay?" she asked.

"Yeah, I'm not sure what to make of it, seeing that deer seemed so real."

Josh continued taking in the bar's decor. The walls were covered with a variety of antique tools and old fashioned kitchen utensils. Above the bar, two mounted fish appeared to be jumping off the wall and a stuffed raccoon with white feathers in his mouth peered down

80

from a log pedestal. Interspersed among everything hung a variety of lighted beer signs that made the place come alive with color.

The twang of a country guitar streamed from the jukebox and appeared to be serenading the two guys shooting pool. One of them kept time to the music by nodding and tapping his cue on the floor. Two fellows threw darts on the right, while on the left, a half dozen people sat at the bar that stretched the length of the room. The ceiling tiles were smoke-stained, and a closer look revealed that everything in the place needed a good dusting.

Julia walked to the rear with Josh following close behind. Down the hallway, past the kitchen, was a small dining room. "Let's sit back here," she said.

Josh pulled out a chair for her. "This is quite a place."

"It's a local's hangout. Everyone's a fisherman, a hunter, a farmer or just plain red neck."

The waitress, dressed in jeans and a Teddy's t-shirt, brought them menus. "No one puts on airs around here," Julia added as she greeted the server. "Lo, Gretchen, who's cooking today?"

"Robby."

"Super, give us two hamburgers, grilled onions and fries on the side."

"Drinks?" the server asked.

Julia ordered herself a Coke.

"I'll have the same," Josh said.

Gretchen picked up the menus, then, looking at Josh, "Are you that man? We heard you came out of the coma."

"Gretch, please don't say anything. We don't need a bunch of people back here gawking at him."

"No problem," Gretchen said and walked toward the kitchen.

Julia realized, when the cook peered over the swinging

kitchen doors to look at Josh, that Gretchen meant she had no problem telling the first person she saw who was sitting in the dining room. Soon, a parade of people pretending to be going to the restroom, came to get a look at the celebrity guest. Then as quickly as the line started, it stopped.

A burly man of about forty came up to the table. "Those dodo heads have no manners. I closed off the dining room so you guys won't be bothered anymore."

"Thanks, Teddy," Julia said. "This is Josh's first time out and things are a little overwhelming."

Josh stood. "You've got quite a place. Did you shoot all the deer you have hanging on the walls?"

"Dad shot the two biggest ones. I got the spike when I was fourteen. I was probably twenty-five when I shot the six pointer. Some guys from town shot the others.

"I noticed the raccoon," Josh said. "Do you hunt those too?"

I raise chickens as a hobby and that bugger would raid my coop on a regular basis. I would sit in the dark with my twenty-two caliber pistol, at all hours of the night, waiting for him. When he didn't show I'd go to bed, and in the morning there would be a pile of feathers and I'd be out another good laying hen."

Josh laughed. "So, how did you get him?"

"This went on for a couple of months. I even went out to the sandpit and did some target shooting, thinking if I had a shot at him I sure as hell didn't want to miss.

"Did you miss him?" Josh asked.

Teddy settled in his chair. "Nah, never got a shot. I was coming home from the bar one night and ran him over with the truck."

Josh laughed as hard as Teddy.

"I had him stuffed so everyone could see who got the best of who." Teddy sat up in his chair with a big grin on his face.

"How long have you owned the bar?" Josh asked.

"The bar has been in the family for sixty years. My grandpa opened it in 1904 and ran it until 1935. Dad and mom ran it until dad passed away in forty-six. I bought it from mom in '48 and have been running it ever since.

"Sixty years," Josh said. "That's quite an accomplishment."

"During prohibition, Grandpa turned it into an ice cream parlor. Grandma sold ice cream in the front while grandpa was selling moonshine out the back door. He spent six months in the county jail for possession, but those revenuers never found his still."

"True story?" Josh asked.

"The gospel," Teddy said, pointing to the hallway. "There's a newspaper clipping telling all about it on the wall next to the men's toilet. Gramps was sort of a celebrity back then. Those federal guys tried catching him for three years and never came close. The only reason they got him, they raided the place when grandpa was out at his still cooking up a new batch. They found his stash hidden in the wall behind the icebox in the kitchen. When grandpa got back they gave him a choice, plead guilty to possession or they would charge grandma as an accessory. He did the time to protect grandma."

Gretchen brought their sandwiches and sheepishly apologized for telling people about Josh. Teddy got up, went around the table and gave Julia a hug. "I'll let you guys enjoy your burgers."

Josh lifted the bun. "It smells even better than it looks."

"I told you they had great burgers."

There Could Be A Problem

*I*t was exactly four when Julia pulled into The Glen parking lot. "I hope you had a nice day."

"Most enjoyable day...I can ever remember." They both laughed. "Seriously, I had a great time and learned so much about Pine Lake. It's a wonderful place."

Nora got up from her desk as the two came through the door. "I was just about ready to call the cops and send out a searching party." Turning to Josh, "How did you do out there? Any problems?"

"I did fine," Josh said. "Julia gave me the grand tour of Pine Lake. We took a boat ride, drove along the Lakeshore, and put our feet in the water by the inlet. We capped it off with a wonderful hamburger at Teddy's."

"Well, you are still under my care, and I say that is enough for one day. I want you to go to your room and take it easy." Turning to Julia, "and you, young lady, need to let the poor fellow come up for air. I know you and you probably ran the legs right off of him."

Josh took hold of Julia's hand and shook it gently. "Thank you, again. I had a really great time."

"I did too." They stood and looked at each other.

"Oh, for heaven's sake," Nora exclaimed. "Shake hands, hug, kiss, let's get a move on."

Josh gave Julia's hand an extra squeeze. "Will I see you

tomorrow?"

Nora took Julia by the arm and led her towards the front door.

"I'll come by in the afternoon," Julia shouted, as Nora ushered her out the front door.

Standing on the front step, Nora faced Julia. "Word of you two went flying through town like a white tornado. I got a call from one of the trustees wanting to know if I was aware that our patient was out on the town. I'm not sure I did the right thing letting you guys go off like that."

"I hope I didn't get you in trouble."

"We both may be in a little hot water over this, hopefully not too bad."

"What do you think they will do?" Julia asked. "They wouldn't fire us, would they?"

"No, I'm sure it wouldn't come to that. Just stay calm. We'll talk about it tomorrow."

Julia's ride home was anything but pleasant. It wasn't the greatest job in the world but what would she do if she got fired?

She threw her purse on the table and opened the refrigerator. There was no soda, no juice, no fruit, but in the back corner she spied a near full bottle of wine leftover from Doug's Christmas party. She poured a good amount in a glass and took a big swallow. Her face flushed as the wine made a mad dash to her brain. She took another swallow, kicked of her shoes and sat at the table. "What's wrong with taking him out for some fresh air? Fresh air is good for him. He wasn't in any danger. I was there and I'm a nurse." In between entreaties and going to bed, she finished the rest of the wine.

Morning came abruptly. Her head throbbed as if someone beat it like a bass drum. She immediately questioned the wisdom of drinking the wine. Just opening

85

and closing her eyes set off an explosion of pain in her head. Through blurred eyes she had to convince herself that eight fifteen was the correct time.

"Oh my God." She got out of bed, struggled getting into her robe, and skipped from the bedroom to the kitchen to get her slippers to stay on her feet.

She put water in the teakettle and set it on the stove. Grabbing a cup and the box of tea bags from the shelf, she searched for something to eat. Her stomach was floating. It needed something solid to anchor it down. Options were few, she decided on oatmeal.

Julia heard the ring. Confused, she glanced at the teapot before gently putting the phone receiver to her ear. "Hello," she said in a raspy voice.

"How would you like to go to Sunday brunch at the Country Club?" The sound of Doug's voice sent another round of pain coursing through her brain. Holding the receiver away from her ear she rolled her tongue around in her mouth and tried to gather enough saliva to talk. "Oh Doug, you can't believe how crappy I feel. I drank some wine and it feels like my head is ready to explode."

"Wine? You? What made you do that? Is it that guy?"

Julia was slow to process the question. "In a way, I guess."

"Okay, how about I pick up a couple of egg sandwiches and coffee from the Drive Inn. I'll be there in fifteen minutes." He hung up before she could protest.

"But," is all she got out before hearing the dial tone. She hung up the phone and was about to lay her head on the table when the shrill whistle of the teakettle brought her upright, sending a sharp spear of pain to both temples. She turn off the stove and stumbled back to the chair.

She woke to find Doug standing at her side, taking things out of a paper bag. He set a cup of coffee and sandwich in front of her.

"You want cream or sugar?" he asked. Seeing no response, he put some of each in her cup. He did the same for himself.

Julia used both hands to steady the cup to her lips. Taking small sips, she took a deep breath in between each one. "God, I must look frightful." She straightened the collar on her robe.

"You do look a little ragged. What made you dive into the wine that way? I've never known you to drink that much?"

"I ran into a little problem at The Glen. I may have ticked off some people and I could lose my job."

"Because of that guy, right?" Doug unwrapped a sandwich for himself.

"You heard about it?" Julia asked, her eyes opening wide.

"It's a small town. News travels fast."

"What did you hear?" Julia asked. "Tell me. What did you hear?"

Doug pointed to her sandwich. "I got one with bacon and one with sausage, which would you rather have?"

"Doug!" Julia shouted. "Tell me. What did you hear?"

"That you and he were seen down at the marina, out by the country club, and in the back room at Teddy's."

"I was just showing him around the town. He's been stuck in that room. He needed to get out... get some fresh air." She put her head in her hands. "What was so bad about that?"

"Nothing from what I can see," Doug said, "and from what I've heard, nobody's upset with you. It's the fellow that's got the problem."

"What do you mean?"

"Well, since it appears he can be up and about, the county doesn't want to keep footing the bill for him to stay at The Glen. The problem is no one knows what to

87

do with him. He has no money, so that puts everyone in a quandary." Doug took a bite of his sandwich. "The county treasurer would love to give him a couple hundred bucks and a bus ticket out of town, but doesn't know where to send him." Doug cut her sandwich in two and handed her a section. "Here, eat this, it will make you feel better."

Julia took the sandwich and put it back on her plate without taking a bite. "Well, they just can't throw him out on the street. Where would he go? How would he live? That is absolutely stupid."

"Hey, I'm just telling you what I heard. Why are you getting so upset?"

"I'm upset because I watched this man as he lay in that bed for close to a month. I was the one who was there when he woke up. Sure, he's awake now, but he still hasn't regained his memory. He could slip back into a coma at any time." Julia jumped up and marched around the table. "These people only think about what it costs. They've got to realize that they are dealing with a human being, a very fragile human being who can't possibly take care of himself." Adrenalin erased most of the effects of the hangover as she continued to rant about the situation.

Doug sipped his coffee. He wrapped her sandwich and put it in the refrigerator. "Jules, I don't know what they are going to do about this guy. It's a tough situation for everyone. I didn't come over here to get you upset."

"I'm sorry. You bring me breakfast, you've been there whenever I needed help, and I go storming around here like a raving lunatic. Please forgive me."

Doug cleaned off the table. "Nothing to forgive."

Julia tightened her robe. "I need to get dressed and get my head on straight. Can I call you later? Maybe we could go for pizza? How about six or so?"

"Sure, that would be great." His response was less than enthusiastic.

She came around the table and kissed him on the cheek. "You're the best friend a person could ever have."

Doug gave her a wry smile. "I just wish you would be as passionate about me as you seem to be about him."

Julia waved to him as his truck fishtailed on the gravel leaving the house. She knew he was upset, but her only thought was to get dressed and go see what was happening at The Glen.

Things Were in the Works

*A*rriving at The Glen Julia saw two strange cars in the parking lot. Inside, two men stood at the desk talking to Nora. Something was up. Sunday was Nora's day off, and she being in street clothes was not a good sign. Julia made a right turn and headed for the kitchen. She found a cup and filled it with coffee. "What's the big meeting about?"

"The young man. I think they're doctors," said the cook.

Doctors? Hardly, she thought, these guys, in their rumpled suits, were no more doctors than the man in the moon. She opened the door just enough to watch them.

The fat one seemed to be doing all the talking. Nora stood with her arms folded. The walrus of a man continued to wave his arms in swooping gestures until it appeared Nora had enough. She raised her hand and shook her head. With that, the men backed up and started for the door. Walrus man turned and shook his finger one last time before walking out the door.

Julia slipped out of the kitchen door and took a sip of coffee as she walked to the front desk. "What was that all about?"

"Just a couple of fathead politicians trying to throw their weight around." Nora gave Julia a puzzled look. "What are you doing here?"

"Doug Foster came over this morning and said the talk in town was that they were going to ask Josh to leave. Is that true?"

"That's part of what those two nincompoops were talking about. I told them no one was going anywhere until the doctors and I sign off on it. How some of these people get elected to office is beyond me. If brains were dynamite, they wouldn't have enough powder to blow their noses."

Julia threw her arms around Nora. "That's why I love you. You don't take crap from anyone." Then stepping back. "Are we in trouble?"

"No, we're fine, but the fact remains, he is not going to be able to stay at The Glen forever."

"Does Josh know about any of this?"

"Oh, yes. Those fellows were in there with him before I got here," Nora said angrily. "Otherwise, I would have thrown the bums out the minute they set foot in the door. Maybe you should go talk to him. I think he could use the support."

Julia had already moved in that direction. She knocked and opened his door. "Good morning. How are you doing?"

Josh stood in his usual place looking out the window. "Ok, I guess. There were some men here earlier wanting to know what my plans are."

"I know. I saw them leave."

"Plans?" Josh questioned. "I don't have a clue of who I am or how I got here and these guys want to know what my plans are? I wake up in a strange town. I've got no car, no money and I'm wearing hand-me-down clothes. It's hard to come up with a plan when you have so little to work with."

Julia went to his side. "Have you been able to remember
91

anything more? Anything at all?"

Josh shook his head. "I have things flashing through my mind. I see faces, buildings, places, but nothing makes sense.

"Have you remembered anything more about Mary?" Julia held her breath.

"I think she and I were in a car. She's driving and talking, but there's no sound. I don't know what she's saying."

"That's a good start...You're in a car...Coming from where? Do you know where you were going?"

Taking a moment, "We were heading north."

"North? How do you know that?"

Josh closed his eyes. "Because I saw the sun setting through the driver's side window."

"Can you remember anything else, landmarks, signs, anything like that?"

"I saw a 'Welcome to Wisconsin' sign."

"That's great," Julia said. "You're from Illinois."

Josh opened his eyes. "Or just passing through."

"Right. What about where you were going? Were you going home? Were you going on vacation?"

Josh stared out the window. "Couldn't tell you."

"What about Mary. Is she a girl friend? Is she your wife?" Julia crossed her fingers behind her back.

"I don't think so. I don't have a sense she's someone close to me, more like someone I might work with."

Julia was relieved. At least for now.

"Speaking of a wife," Josh said. "If I have one, wouldn't she be questioning where I am? Don't I have family, friends, co-workers, or anyone that's missing me? Am I that alone in the world to have no one who cares enough to look for me?" Josh blinked and wiped back a tear.

Julia grabbed his hand. "Listen, there has to be a reason people aren't out looking for you and we will find out why."

"May I come in?" Nora stepped into the room. Julia sensed this was not just a friendly visit.

"I just got off the phone with the board president. The county is sending a couple of doctors to check on Josh. Seems, since he's come out of the coma everyone is trying to figure out what to do with him."

"But Nora," Julia pleaded. "They can't just throw him out on the street."

"Don't get your underwear in a bundle, they're just talking. The county treasurer thinks if Josh is well enough to be out carousing around—his words not mine—that Josh could be released from The Glen and get help through social services."

Julia jumped up and stomped across the room. "Welfare? They want to put him on welfare? What kind of people are these? Don't they know he still needs help to get his memory back?"

Nora grabbed Julia's arm. "Calm down, nothing has been decided. The doctors have to check him over and approve his release and I'm sure I will be able to be a part of that decision."

"You can't let that happen," Julia pleaded. "What will he do, where would he go?"

"Let's cross one bridge at a time," Nora said. "The mind heals differently than the body. There is no timetable for something like this. It's also possible that he may never get his memory back."

Josh grabbed the back of the chair. "Do you think that could happen?"

"Don't even think like that," Julia said, then turning to Nora. "He has remembered some things. He just needs more time."

Nora came around the bed and put a hand on Josh's shoulder. "I know this is upsetting, but we will do

93

everything in our power to help you.

Josh forced a smiled. I guess it is what it is. When a baby comes into the world he has no plans. He has to rely on others to nurture him. I'll have to rely on you folks to help me through this mess."

Julia moved closer. "When are those doctors supposed to be here?"

"First thing in the morning," Nora said, moving towards the door. "I'll be there to help in any way I can."

Julia closed the door. "We'll get you through this, I promise."

"You've both been terrific. I just hope whatever happens--I don't hurt either of you. That would be devastating to me."

"That's silly. How would that happen?"

"What if I turn out to be some kind of bad guy, or worse, an axe-murderer or serial killer?"

"There is no way you could be either one of those," Julia said. Married would be the worst thing, she thought. "Listen, I know we were going to hang out today, but I've got stuff to do. I'll see you when I come on shift, okay?" She purposely left out the part of having pizza with Doug. She'd explain about Doug at another time.

"That's fine. I need time to digest today's revelations."

Julia gave a small wave and walked out the door.

Pizza With Doug

It wasn't a total lie, the house was a mess. She had left in a hurry and didn't put things away. The bathroom was the worst. Her comb, brush, and toothpaste added to the clutter of her shampoo and lotions on the vanity. When picking her pajamas up from the floor, she caught a glimpse of herself in the mirror. Her hair looked as if she'd combed it with an egg beater and she had a lipstick smudge in the corner of her mouth. Minor stuff compared to finding, in her haste to get dressed, she put on a striped blouse and checkered shorts. A choked-back laugh came with a burst of air. "Dear God, he must think I'm some sort of hayseed. Oh, well, I can't do anything about it now."

Grabbing a towel she went to the kitchen sink, washed her hair and toweled it dry. After combing it out she put in a line of sponge rollers. Dropping her shorts she turned back the spread and crawled into bed.

She woke refreshed. The nap had pretty much alleviated any residual effects of the wine, and unlike this morning, she no longer wished to die. She was still concerned Doug would be upset. It was not her intention to hurt his feelings. She had been so obsessed with defending Josh's situation she may have struck a jealous cord with him. She'd have to somehow soothe his bruised ego.

She picked out matching shorts and top, fussed with

her hair until she had just the right amount of curl, and guided the lipstick to stay within the boundaries of her lips. A dab of rouge high on her cheeks, a splash of My Sin perfume, and she was on her way.

Julia remembered when Teddy first started serving pizza. Some college kid from the Lakeshore suggested it. The kid said it was a popular snack on campus. People chuckled at first, a Pollock who grew up on sausage and sauerkraut making pizza. They didn't laugh long, as Teddy's pies began bringing in people from miles around. Some of the locals even experimented with putting kraut on their pizza. She and Doug always ordered a large with everything except anchovies and sauerkraut. Kraut on pizza just seemed all wrong to Julia, and neither of them could stomach the taste of anchovies.

Doug sat at the far end of the bar talking to Teddy. Men occupied nearly every stool and their heads turned in unison as she walked by. Julia was used to those lecherous stares and paid no attention. Doug slid off his stool and gave her a friendly hug. "Feeling better?"

"Much," Julia replied. "A nap really helped. I'm sorry about this morning."

"I understand. You were just trying to defend your patient."

Julia tried to read his face. Did he really believe that or was he wanting to defuse the situation? It didn't matter, she was happy to let things end on that note. "I've been thinking about pizza since I woke."

"I told Gretchen to save us a table in the back," Doug said. "Should I order?"

"Not yet, I'd like a beer first."

"Sure thing," Doug said, waving to Ted. "I'll have one with you."

Teddy tossed a cardboard coaster in front of Julia before setting down her beer. "There was a guy in here earlier asking about you."

"For me?" Julia looked up and down the bar. "Is he still here?"

"I think he left," Ted scanned the bar. "He said he knew you from Florida — medium build, bleached blond hair, sort of an arrogant cuss."

Julia stiffened. She only knew one person who bleached his hair. "What did he want? Did he say?"

"Just wanted to know if I knew you. I told him you might be in later."

Doug took a swallow of beer. "You seem to have admirers coming out of the woodwork."

Julia bowed her head and mumbled. "I can't believe he's found me here."

Doug and Ted saw Julia was visibly shaken by the news. "What is it? Who is the guy?" Doug asked.

"A nightmare from the past." She took a sip of her beer, trying to camouflage the emotional eruption that churned in her stomach. She felt nauseous. Sliding off her stool she ran to the ladies room. She burst into the stall, leaned over, and dry-heaved two or three times. Tears welled in her eyes and she couldn't stop panting. Sitting on the toilet she lowered her head and tried to rub feeling back into her fingertips.

"Are you okay?" Gretchen asked. "Doug sent me to see if you're alright."

Julia reached around and flushed. "I'm okay. I'll be out in a few minutes." Julia waited until she heard the door close before coming out of the stall. Looking in the mirror, she blotted around her eyes trying to salvage her mascara. She filled her cupped hands with water and rinsed her mouth. The sweat on her neck had taken most of the curl out of her pageboy. She looked and felt drained. "What is he doing here, what does he want?" she asked the image in the mirror.

97

Doug had retreated to the back dining room and held a chair as she approached. "Geez, are you okay? Do you know who this guy is?"

"I think so, but I have no idea why he's here. His name is Brad Holton. I haven't spoken to him in two years."

"He's not here to hurt you is he? If he is...I'll..."

"I don't think so. I don't have anything of his. I gave him back the ring."

"You had a ring? Were you married?"

"Didn't get that far." Julia took a drink of beer and watched Doug's eyebrows curl.

"If there's a problem, I can get a couple of guys. We can scout around and find this guy."

"It might not even be him. Maybe it's someone else altogether." Julia knew she was deceiving herself. After hearing the guy was arrogant, with bleached hair, she was sure it was Brad.

"You just say the word and we'll..."

"Let's not blow this out of proportion. I'm starved and I was looking forward to pizza." Having Doug get excited and threaten violence was not the answer.

"Do you want me to order?" he asked.

"Please. Remember, no kraut." She took a large swallow of beer hoping to calm her nerves.

Doug corralled Gretchen and put in their order. Returning to the table, he finished his drink. "Do you want another beer?"

Julia pushed her mug to him.

He grabbed the glasses and headed to the bar.

No one paid attention to the man that had slipped in the back door and stood in the far corner. As soon as Doug left, the figure approached the table. "Hello, Julia."

She swung around in her chair. "How did you find me? What do you want?"

"You," he said, drawing the word out. "I've missed

you terribly. Your mom told me where you were. She's hoping you will come back to Florida with me."

"My mother doesn't know what you did."

"It was a dumb thing to have sex with Rachel. It didn't mean a thing. I was just so mixed up and you didn't want to satisfy my needs."

"Your needs?" Julia exclaimed. "That's what it has always been, what you wanted, what you needed. I was stupid, infatuated with this big football star. Well, I'm not anymore. It's over."

"You can't mean that." His demeanor suddenly changed. He took hold of her arm and angrily spat. "I'm not leaving without you."

Julia yanked free. "I'm not going anywhere."

"I can't believe you would want to be stuck in this podunk town. You banging some country boy up here?"

"That's none of your business."

Brad reversed himself and tried to add charm. "Aw c'mon, Julia, I didn't come here to fight with you."

"You could have surprised me. Why are you here anyway? Is Rachel no longer jumping in bed with you?"

Brad continued to soften his tone. "She doesn't mean anything to me. I want you. I need you. I promised your mother I would bring you back with me."

"Another promise you won't be able to keep."

"Why are you making this so difficult?" he asked. "We had a good thing between us."

"Maybe we did, but you threw that in the toilet with Rachel." Julia tried to turn away, only to have Brad reach and grab her arm.

Doug walked up carrying two mugs of beer. "Hold it fella! I think you'd better back off and leave the lady alone."

Brad turned. "You keep out of this. It's between me and her."

"Wrong," Doug said, setting the beers on the table. "It's between you, me, and the ten guys at the bar, including Teddy, who keeps a baseball bat handy."

"This is my fiancée and I'm taking her back to Florida." the man said.

Doug grabbed Brad's arm and pulled him around.

Brad swung wildly at Doug, who parried with his forearm. Doug grab Brad's shirt collar with both hands and drove him backwards. They tumbled over a nearby table scattering chairs in all directions. Doug drew back, ready to plant a knuckle sandwich on the guy's chin.

Julia grabbed Doug's arm. "Stop this," she yelled. "Duking it up is not the way to handle this."

Doug kept his hand squarely on the man's chest, holding him to the floor. "Are you sure? We can settle this right here and now." A half dozen locals gathered around.

"It's alright." Julia pleaded with him. "Let me talk to him. Give us a few minutes."

Doug slowly got up. "I'll be in the bar. Yell, if you need me." Reaching down and extending his hand to the guy, he said, "You so much as breathe in her direction and I will be back here to finish the job."

Julia waited for Doug to leave before poking a finger in Brad's chest. "You listen. I am not your fiancée anymore. I don't know what you were expecting by coming here, but it's over. I've moved on with my life and you should do the same."

"I've lost everything," he said. "I blew the football scholarship. I messed things up with us, and I'm stuck working for the ol' man in the dealership. I've got nothing, I need something to hold onto. I need you."

Julia turned away. For the past two years Julia would have liked nothing better than to pound on him herself. Hit him until all the hurt she felt from his betrayal was appeased. Seeing him now, almost to the point of tears, made retribution seem meaningless. Life had dealt him more punishment than she ever could.

Brad came behind her and took hold of her shoulders. "Are you sure you wouldn't like to get back together? I've got two tickets for a flight out of Milwaukee in the morning."

Julia pulled free. "I'm happy right where I am." Julia saw Doug peek from behind the wall and waved for him to come. "Tell the boys in the bar they can relax, everything's fine. Nothing here for the gossip ladies, but I'm sure they would have loved a big rumble to talk about."

No one saw Brad's hand tighten into a fist. "Sorry if I acted out of line," he said, and then without warning took a wild swing at Doug. The blow missed badly as Doug drew back his head. Brad was not so lucky. Doug's blow caught him squarely on the nose, splattering blood over his face and shirt. Brad stumbled backward, falling over a table and getting tangled in the tablecloth. He finally shook free and spit a mouthful of blood in Doug's direction. "Are you the one she's putting out for?"

Doug was ready to finish the job, but Julia pushed him aside.

"Brad Holton, you're nothing but a pathetic jerk," she screamed. "Get out of here. I never want to see you again."

Brad stood and used the tablecloth to wipe his nose. He righted the table and slapped an envelope on its top. "The flight leaves at ten," he said. "Be there if you know what's good for you."

"I'll tell you what's good for me," Julia screamed. "It's for you to get out of town and stay out of my life." She raised her hand in an attempt to claw at Brad.

Doug grabbed and held her in check. "Don't waste your breath." He picked up the envelope and stuffed it into Brad's chest. "I suggest you take Julia's advice and stay out of Pine Lake."

Grabbing Brad by the back of his collar Doug pushed him towards the front door. "Let's make sure you find your car. We haven't had a tar and feathering in fifty years, but one more peep out of you and I think these good ol' boys could find the necessary stuff to do one on you." The room exploded in laughter, as Doug escorted the rejected ex-boyfriend out of the building.

Doug returned and escorted Julia to their table. "I believe that's the last we'll see of the 'Florida Flash.' He'd be a damned fool to ever come back here."

Julia tried to calm her breathing and wrung her hands to keep them from shaking. If there was ever a person she never wanted to see again it was Bradley Holton.

Gretchen set the pizza on the table. "What was that all about?"

Julia saw the look on Doug's face. "Don't even go there," she said, as she dragged a piece of pizza onto her plate. Doug made a comment about how good the pizza was. They were the only words spoken during the meal.

"I'm sorry," Julia said, as they got up from the table. "I didn't expect him to ever show up here."

"I thought it was entertaining. Your ex-fiancé comes all the way from Florida and wants to drag you back to Tampa. He takes a swing at me and thinks you... are my girlfriend. Hell, he doesn't even know about the guy, Josh, up at The Glen."

"You're upset, aren't you?"

"No, if I were upset I would sit you down and tell you to be careful. You have a rejected lover on one hand — him not me — and a guy you have no idea of who he is or where he came from. Either one could end up hurting you real bad."

"Thank you. Once again you've come to my rescue," Julia said, playing up to his bluster.

Just be careful, okay? I might not be around next time."

"Would you like a little Crème de Menthe to settle your stomach?" Doug asked, as they walked to the bar. "Or how about a little wine?"

"Very funny, my stomach doesn't need any more alcohol. I just need to go home, put on my relaxers, and take it easy." She saw the disappointment in his eyes but knew she needed time alone to sort out her emotions.

Leaving The Glen

Julia came out of a deep sleep. She had lain awake for hours before finally nodding off. If she had any doubts about her feelings for Brad, things were crystal clear now. She had left Florida in a huff, never faced Brad, or told him they were through. Just saying the words to his face put finality to their split. His betrayal had shaken her to the core, left her hurt, and fractured her self-esteem. She felt different. Free. She vowed to no longer punish herself for the breakup nor allow it to dictate her life in the future.

Rolling on her side, her thoughts quickly shifted to Josh. A broad smile broke across her face as she recalled them standing in the water at the inlet. She tried to convince herself the kiss had come so fast she didn't have time to react. Who was she fooling? She knew she could have stopped him, but deep inside she wanted that kiss as much, if not more, than he did. A warm sensation surged through her body and she cuddled with her pillow.

The feeling drained quickly as she remembered the doctors were coming to examine Josh in the morning. She exited the bed and got ready with military precision—clean uniform, hair combed, purse in hand, and she was out the door. "Those doctors better not think they can just throw him out on the street. If they do, they'll get a good piece of my mind," she said, jumping in her car.

Carol was at her usual spot behind the desk.

Julia hung her purse on the rack and peeked over Carol's shoulder. "Anything interesting?"

Carol tossed her pen on the desk. "Does anything interesting ever happen around here?"

"How is Josh?"

"Doing great. Nora brought him more clothes, even went out and bought him underwear. She can be one tough old cookie, but for this, Josh, she's nothing but a big softy."

Julia was pleased for Josh, but couldn't help feeling a little jealous. "Have you checked on him lately? Is he still up?"

"Asleep, the last time I checked. Did Nora tell you about the fourth?"

"No, what about it?"

"She's giving us the day off. She's bringing in some of her nurse friends to cover for us. What do you think about that?"

"Hallelujah!" Julia squealed. "Do we still get paid?"

"Yes, it's a paid holiday."

"That makes it even better." Julia twirled around with delight and waved goodbye as Carol walked to the door.

Skipping down the hall, Julia opened Josh's door and poked her head inside. The room was dark and his long even breaths confirmed he was enjoying a deep and restful sleep. Closing the door quietly, she proceeded with her nightly routine. She managed to keep herself busy but found herself watching the clock in anticipation of the doctors' arrival. She hoped they would choose to give him more time to heal.

The first rays of the morning sun reflected off the polished floor. Julia hadn't seen or talked to Josh in almost twenty hours. She knocked softly, went in, and was surprised to see him fully dressed.

105

"Good morning," he said. "I've been waiting for you."

Julia admired the light blue polo shirt and navy Bermuda shorts he wore. "I heard Nora brought you more clothes."

"She even bought me underwear. I'm beginning to feel like a real human being."

"How long have you been up?"

"Since six, I've got a lot on my mind. It's pretty certain they're going to ask me to leave The Glen."

Julia was ready to interrupt, but he raised his hand. "I know you're concerned, and I appreciate everything you've done for me, but I've got to start taking control of the situation. This is my problem."

"Maybe you need to wait to hear what the doctors have to say. You don't know — they may let you stay."

Josh shook his head. "I think the wheels are already in motion for me to leave."

"Have you been able to remember anything more?" Julia asked. "Anything more about Mary or being in a car? How about where you were going or maybe the reason you were going to where ever it was you were going?"

Josh smiled. "No, but I'm pretty sure the deer I keep seeing in my head is involved somehow. I would like to go where the sheriff believes I might have been in an accident just to see if it would jar my memory."

"We can do that."

"Nora and I talked a little bit yesterday."

"Oh," Julia said. "About what?"

"Nora said the board is putting a lot of pressure on her for me to leave."

"Is it because this cheapskate county wants to stop paying?" Julia shot back angrily.

"I have no complaints. They took great care of me at the hospital and I've had nothing but the best here at The Glen. I'm grateful, but can't ask or expect them to continue taking care of me this way."

"All they think about is how much money they can save."

"The county is not the bad guy here," Josh said. They've covered all the cost. It represents a great deal of money and I don't know how I'm ever going to repay it."

There was a long silence.

"So, what are you going to do? Where are you going to go?"

"Nora has graciously offered to let me stay with her until I can get set up with social services to see what help I will get from them."

Julia's facial expression showed her disappointment.

"We know they won't just turn me loose," Josh said. "They have to protect themselves from a lawsuit. Nora figures by me staying with her it will satisfy any qualms they may have. What do you think?"

Julia hesitated. She was angry but didn't want to say anything close to what she was thinking. "I guess it could work," she offered, "but, maybe the doctors will say you should stay here for a while longer."

"I know this is hard on you, it's hard on me too, but we have to face reality. It could take a long time for me to get my memory back." His voice lowered. "It's possible, like Nora said, it may never come back. I can't expect the county or anyone else for that matter to take care of me for the rest of my life, certainly not here at The Glen."

The door opened. "Good morning," Nora said brightly. "How are we all doing today?"

"I was just telling Julia about our talk yesterday," Josh said.

Julia held back her tears. "I don't think it's fair."

"Life is not always fair." Nora put a hand on Julia's shoulder. "But give this man credit. It's his life, his dilemma, and he's going to see it through. I've got that big

107

old house. The whole upstairs is empty. He can come and go as he pleases, and I'm sure the county people will go along with the arrangement."

"We can still do stuff on my days off." Julia contributed with a forced smile.

"You bet," Josh said. "I'm counting on your help."

Nora patted Julia on the back. "Listen, there isn't anything you can do and it's probably going to take the doctors some time to do, their thing. Why don't you go home, get some sleep, and come back this afternoon to see what the doctors decide." Nora stopped before going out the door. Turning back to Josh, "I'll let you know when they get here."

"I'm ready, he said.

Things were turning out differently than Julia had expected and it took the wind out of her sails. "I guess Nora is right I might as well go home, she said. "Is that alright with you?"

"Sure, I'm fine. I'm going to gather up my stuff and be ready for whatever happens."

"I'll come back this afternoon. They'll have to get along without me at the hospital." Julia left the room only to come back in. "For heaven's sake, don't just roll over and play dead for these guys," she blurted. "Speak up for yourself. You may be out of the coma and you might be able to get around, but you are not totally healed. I just think the whole thing stinks."

Josh smiled. "I'm sure everything will work out fine. Come, I'll walk you to your car."

He opened her car door. "Everything will work out, trust me."

Julia got behind the wheel and rolled down the window. "I'm sorry. I didn't mean to be so bossy."

"I appreciate your concern, and I promise I won't play dead if you will go home and get some sleep. The world will seem a lot brighter when you wake."

Julia waved and forced a smile as she drove out of the parking lot.

The Doctors Were Right On Schedule

Josh didn't have to wait long. The doctors arrived minutes later. They poked and prodded and asked a lot of questions, most of which he couldn't answer. In the end, as if anyone didn't already know, they declared him physically fit and capable of being released from The Glen.

The doctors' report had to have gone straight to the county treasurer. He showed up an hour later. "The county will give you two hundred dollars spending money and pay for a motel room until you get set up with social services," the treasurer said, but then admitted his plan had a flaw. "With the Fourth of July next week, there's not a motel room available in the whole town. To compensate, we can give you extra money for a round trip bus ticket and hotel room in Middletown. You can stay there and come back to Pine Lake after the fourth."

Josh let the man speak his peace before stepping in. "All of that won't be necessary. If I may, let me propose an alternative plan. Nora has offered to let me stay with her. I'll accept the two hundred dollars spending money with the stipulation that it is a loan I will be paying back. I'll make regular visits to the hospital so they will be able to monitor my condition, and hopefully social services will be able to help me get on my feet. I also intend to find

110

work of some kind so I can begin repaying the cost of my care."

The treasurer was almost giddy as he hastily agreed to Josh's proposal. He produced an envelope from his inside coat pocket. "There's two hundred and fifty dollars in here, consider it a loan for that much. Is that okay with you?" The two men shook hands.

The treasurer turned to Nora. "Thanks for letting him stay with you. That takes a lot of pressure off everyone."

"Oh, yeah, and it saves the county the cost of a bus ticket to Middletown," Nora said. "This is not the end of it. I will be going with him to social services to make sure he receives the help he needs."

"Yes, yes, of course," the treasurer said. "I'll put in a call to them and let them know you are coming."

"You keep your nose out of this," Nora said as she ushered him out of the room. "We'll handle it from here."

Nora stepped back into the room. "Sometimes I get so fed up with those penny ante politicians I'd like to give them all a Tabasco enema."

Josh chuckled at the thought.

"Why don't you gather your things?" she said. "I'll see if I can find something to put your stuff in."

Josh opened the envelope the treasurer gave him and thumbed through the bills. He folded it and put it in his pocket. "Well, Josh, if that's your name," he said. "You've got a place to stay, a basic wardrobe, two hundred fifty dollars cash, and more importantly, outside of a few scars and a faulty memory, you have your health."

"I found a couple shopping bags to put your stuff in," Nora said, tossing them on the bed. "I get off at four and we can head to my place after that."

"I've been thinking," he said. "If Pine Lake is where

111

I end up, it's not the worst place to start a new life. The people are friendly, the living is laid back, and you have that big beautiful lake."

"I came here twenty years ago and I wouldn't want to be anywhere else."

Josh finished putting his things in the paper sacks. "There, I have all my worldly possessions in these two bags." He drew an imaginary sword from his side and pointed it to the window. "It's time brave knight, to go out and seek thy fortune."

Nora laughed as she headed for the door.

Josh slumped into the chair. "Right now I'd give a fortune to know who I am." He laid his head back and closed his eyes as visions flashed through his mind in blinding speed. Clips of people, some happy, some angry, came at him from all sides. Buildings, trees and roads passed at various angles. Seeing himself being hurled into the side of an earthen mound caused Josh to sit up straight. His heart pounded as he tried to recall each thing and make sense of it. Was any of this connected to how he got here or was his mind just shooting him random images.

The door opened and Josh rose.

"How are you doing, son? I'm Doctor Erickson. I'm the one who patched you up."

"Doing fine." Josh extended his hand.

The doctor pointed to Josh's head. "Mind if I take a look?"

"No, not at all."

The doctor parted Josh's hair. "Everything looks great. You've got a healthy crop of hair, it's covering things nicely."

"Thanks, for a great job."

"Nora said you are being discharged but you still don't remember anything of your past."

Josh nodded.

"I'm not a psychiatrist, but I've discussed your case with a few of my friends who are. The way it has been explained to me is that sometimes when the brain suffers a traumatic injury it will put your memory in a vault for safekeeping. When you came out of the coma your brain began functioning normally. You remember things that are happening now. You also have the ability to reason. You can draw on a lifetime of knowledge of common things, like this is a bed, and that is a chair," he said pointing to each. "It's just that your brain isn't quite ready to let you access the part that is locked in the vault. That being the past and all the pertinent things about you."

"Will I ever remember?" Josh asked.

"In some cases people wake up one morning and their memory is completely restored, like walking into a dark room and turning on the light. Your memory could return that way. In other cases memory is regained a little bit at a time, but it can take days, weeks, months, or even years. There just aren't any easy answers as to how the brain operates. Unfortunately that vault may be locked forever."

"What do I do in the meantime?"

"Live," the doctor said. "This is your life. None of us are guaranteed a tomorrow and by the same token, you might be deprived of a past. If this is your new life, a life that is starting today, then live it. Do all the things people do, dream, plan, and strive to make your life better. Make friends. Hopefully you will be able to find family or friends that will help piece things together. Sometimes you don't remember the past but you form a new memory of your past life from the recollections of others. You are somewhat blessed, you know."

"Why is that?"

"Because you have both a future and a past to look forward to," the doctor said as he started for the door.

"Thank you for coming. You're right, it's time for me to focus on what I am going to do from now on. I'll still search for the past, but will concentrate on my life going forward."

"I think you are going to be fine." The doctor walked to the door. "Good luck, son."

Josh walked to the window. The sight of the outside world didn't seem quite so daunting.

Spending Time Together

Julia grabbed her purse and flew out the door before the noon siren went off. When she got to The Glen, she made a side trip to the kitchen, jumped behind the counter and poured herself a cup of coffee. Throwing a spoonful of sugar and a splash of milk in her cup, she grabbed a donut from the platter and exited before the cook had a chance to yell at her. Julia ran to the front desk. "How did it go with the doctors?"

"Slow down, girl," Nora scolded, "and don't choke on that food in your mouth. Everything is settled. He's coming to my place when I get off shift. I'm sure he will tell you all about it."

Julia didn't wait for Nora to finish her sentence before jogging down the hall. She gave Josh's door a quick knock before entering.

"Hello, anybody in here?" She peeked into the shopping bags. "Matching set of luggage, how cool is that?"

Josh laughed.

"So tell me, what did the doctors say?"

"That I am fit as a fiddle," Josh said.

"Did you plead your case? That you needed more time to regain your memory?" Julia recognized the guilty expression. "I knew it, you just let them roll over you, didn't you? I should have stayed. I would have given

115

those doctors a piece of my mind."

"Things will be just fine. I have my health and look," he pointed out the window, "there is a whole world out there and life to be lived."

Julia wanted to continue her protest, but he put his finger to her lips. "Dr. Erickson stopped by earlier and left me with some good advice. He said the past may be important, but we don't live in the past. We live today, tomorrow and all the tomorrows ahead of us. I'd love to know who I am or was, where I came from and all that stuff, but you, Nora, and even this town are a part of me now. So whatever we find out, it will have to blend into my life going forward."

"What if you have a wife?" Julia asked. "Or children? What if you have children?"

"What if I don't?" Josh countered. "You see, we can drive ourselves crazy with what ifs. I don't have all the answers. Some things will have to be dealt with as they occur. We can't solve a problem or situation until it presents itself. I may have a past, and maybe my past only goes back to the moment I woke up."

Julia knew life was full of uncertainty, but the thought of him being married and having children was almost more than she could bear. Tears welled up in her eyes.

"Are you okay?" He used his finger to wipe the tears off her cheek.

"I'm just being silly. I don't know why I'm getting so emotional."

"You're a very special person," he said. "I need you, no, I want you to be with me on this journey."

She mustered what bravado she could. "I will and we will deal with whatever comes our way."

"Promise?" he said, drawing her to him.

"Promise." She waited for his kiss. Their lips were about to meet when the door opened.

"Whoops," Nora said unapologetically. "Am I interrupting something here?"

Julia quickly turned away and grabbed a tissue from the nightstand to dry her eyes. Josh smiled and raised his eyebrows.

"Carol called, her car battery died and she's going to be late. I'll have to stay until she gets here. There's no sense for Josh to be stuck here. Why don't the two of you go somewhere? You can drop him off at my place whenever you get there."

Julia looked at Josh who quickly nodded. He grabbed the shopping bags, took one last look around and followed Julia out of the room.

"Have a nice afternoon. I'll see you when I see you," Nora said, yanking at the bed sheets.

"Where would you like to go?" Julia asked when they got to the car.

"I don't know. Maybe we could go where the sheriff thought there might have been an accident."

"Yes, let's do that. It might jog your memory about what happened."

As they approached the site, Julia took her foot off the accelerator. "You said you were going north because of where the sun was setting, so you would have been traveling in this direction. The trouble is we don't know exactly where the sheriff was referring to."

Josh turned his head, looking intently on each side of the road.

"We must be getting close. Look, over there is County Park." Julia pointed to the left.

Josh looked in that direction and then looked at the road ahead. "That big pine up ahead, I think...I would swear I saw that tree in one of the images in my mind."

"Are you sure?"

117

"I'm not positive, slow down when you get next to it."

Julia checked the rear-view mirror and slowly accelerated.

"Stop!" Josh shouted.

Julia stomped on the brake. "What! What is it? What do you see?" Her heart raced.

Josh pointed to the woods on his right. "It's here! This is it."

"What's here?" Julia asked, her voice raising an octave as she looked in the direction Josh was looking.

"That big deer. That's where that deer came out of the woods. It had a huge set of antlers. Mary swerved to the left and I watched this huge head running alongside the car. I looked into his eye and saw the fear. It all happened in a flash."

"Did you hit the deer?"

"I don't think so. Maybe we hit something else. In one of the images I'm running into a wall of dirt."

"Look!" Julia pointed to a huge mound of dirt on the opposite side of the road. "It looks like when they cut the road through here they left that big bank. They probably didn't want to cut down that big pine that sits on top of it. Do you think that is what you ran into?" Julia pulled over, got out, and ran across the road. "Is this a skid mark?"

Josh hurried over. It was just one mark near the edge of the asphalt, about three feet long. Time and weather made it hard to tell if it was or wasn't. "If we did come across the road and it was here that Mary hit the brakes, we would have still been going really fast when we hit that dirt embankment."

Julia went in the ditch. "Maybe we can find some car parts or something." The wall of dirt towered over her. Tree roots from that big pine and other vegetation were exposed. Erosion from the summer rains had also cut deep grooves in the dirt so it was hard to see if there was any

118

sign of an impact.

Josh used the angle of the skid and walked back towards the car. He returned in a straight line towards the bank, stopping at the edge of the pavement. "My guess, we would have hit right about there." He pointed to the dirt. "What's that?"

"What? Where?" Julia walked closer to the bank. "I don't see anything."

"Just ahead of you, reach out your hand. Higher. Higher. Right there."

Julia felt it before she saw it. She pulled the small shiny metal object from the dirt and handed it to Josh.

"What is it?" Julia asked, and watched Josh clean off the dirt.

Josh ran it up and down on his sleeve bringing it to a bright shine. "It's a chrome letter, like the ones they put on cars to spell out the brand."

Julia came out of the ditch and grabbed Josh's hand to get a closer look.

"It's an "O," or a zero." Josh said, handing it to Julia.

"Do you think it came off the car you were in?"

"It's possible."

"Maybe it's "O" for Oldsmobile," Julia offered. "What else could it be?"

"Well, there's an "O" in Ford, Dodge and Lincoln," Josh countered. "This could have come off any number of cars. And don't forget Desoto. It has two "O's." He turned and walked toward the car. "This may not help us that much, but I'm pretty sure that this is where we crashed."

Julia walked a short way down the road where the bank was lower. She climbed the mound and peered towards the lake. "Look down there, that grassy area is County Park. That's where you were found."

Josh surveyed the area.

"Oh, look," Julia said. "You can see The Glen from

119

here. We've got that big light in the middle of the parking lot. It was night. Maybe you got here and saw the light. You could have been going for help."

"For me, or for her?" Josh asked. "What happened to her? Where did she go? Why would she leave me?"

"Maybe you were trying to get away from her?" Julia said. "It was pretty strange that you had nothing in your pockets, no billfold, nothing. Maybe you were being kidnapped."

"That's an awful lot of maybes. I guess there is a lot we still don't know about what happened."

It was quiet on the ride back to town. Josh kept looking at the "O."

"It's good we found something," Julia said. "Maybe if we can find out what kind of car it came off of, it will help you remember the rest of what happened."

"Another big maybe."

"Sorry. Are you getting hungry?" Julia asked.

"I could go for another of those hamburgers from Teddy's and this time I'm buying. I've got this money burning a hole in my pocket." Josh pulled the envelope from his pocket.

Julia nodded. "All I've had to eat so far today is the donut I swiped at The Glen."

The lunch crowd at Teddy's had thinned out, but most tables still had dirty dishes on them. Julia cleared a table by the window. Gretchen came with menus and took their drink order.

"How're you guys doing?" Teddy said, walking to the table. "I heard they released you from The Glen."

"Kicked out, if you want to know the truth," Julia said. "Our illustrious County Treasurer doesn't give a hoot that he still hasn't fully regained his memory. All he cares about is how much money he can save."

Josh put his hand on Julia's arm. "I'm fine. I have to

start putting a life together and the county has agreed to give me a hand. I'm not complaining. It is what it is."

"Good for you," Teddy said. "Have a great lunch, I just wanted to say hello."

Julia pulled her arm away. "Aren't you just a little miffed about being asked to leave?"

"It would have happened sooner or later. I'm grateful for all the care I've received, especially the physical therapy." Josh flexed his arm. "Look at this body. I'm in tip top shape."

"You better believe it, if it wasn't for me, you would have withered up like an old prune."

"I'm forever in your debt," Josh said. "But I still think you took advantage of me while I was in the coma."

"You will never know, will you?"

Their eyes made contact and Julia felt a warmth circulate through her body. Josh made a move towards her, as Gretchen set their drinks on the table sending Josh back into his chair. He picked up his glass and Julia fumbled with the paper covering her straw.

Gretchen stood for a moment. "Do you guys know what you want, or do you want me to come back?"

"We can order now." Julia gave their order.

Josh waited for Gretchen to leave. "We are always talking about me and my situation. Let's talk about you for a change. Have you lived in Pine Lake all your life?"

"I moved here from Florida two years ago." Julia wondered how far she should take the conversation. Sooner or later, he would hear about the blow up last night, but she wasn't ready to defend that part of her life.

"Pine Lake is a long way from Florida," he said, taking a drink of coke. "What brought you all the way up here?"

"I lived in Milwaukee until I was thirteen. I spent a summer at one of the camps on the lake. Had a great time. So, when I decided to leave Florida it seemed like a nice

121

place to come."

"Did you have a job offer?"

"I had my Practical Nursing Certificate and I figured I would find a job when I got here. I just threw everything I owned in my Chevy and headed north. The Glen was the first place I applied. Nora hired me on the spot. She said I reminded her of her younger sister."

"You drove the car we're riding in, all the way from Florida? Wow, I'm impressed."

Julia laughed. "With me or the car?"

"Both! That's a big trip. Where did you stay along the way?"

"I pitched a tent in the KOA campgrounds. I never had a problem, made it in five days." The conversation paused as Gretchen set their burgers on the table.

"What made you leave Florida?" Josh asked, taking a bite of his sandwich.

Uh-o, how would she answer this? "I felt I needed to spread my wings, to get out on my own. I never really liked Florida. My dad got a job offer down there. I was a freshman in high school when we moved there. I never quite fit in, they called me a dang Yankee."

"Well, speaking selfishly, I'm happy that you ended up here. I'd be pretty lost without you."

Julia laughed and was happy he didn't press her for more details. "I never get tired of Teddy's burgers."

"They are becoming a favorite of mine, too."

The waitress came by, gathered up the dishes and laid the guest check on the table.

Josh reached in his pocket and brought out the envelope with his money. "The bill is three seventy, how much should I leave for a tip?"

"Seventy five cents should be plenty."

Josh handed Gretchen the check and a five-dollar bill. "It's good, keep the change."

"She is going to think you're the last of the big time spenders," Julia said as they walked out of the dining room. "Nora won't be home for a while. What do you want to do?"

"I don't want to go there until she's home, not this first time. I wouldn't feel right."

"We could go to my place and just hang out until Nora gets home."

"That would be great." Josh hurried to open her car door.

"Don't expect anything great, it's small, but what I can afford."

"I'm sure it will be just fine."

Spending Time at Julia's Place

"This is it." Julia tossed her purse on the table.
"It's a nice place, I especially like the vintage cabinetry, they looks freshly painted." Josh ran his hand along the light green Formica countertop.

"Come, I'll give you the fifty cent tour." Julia walked through the archway opposite the back door. "This is the living room."

The room was just a bit larger than the kitchen. A couch and easy chair faced a small TV that sat on a table in the far corner. A lamp with a long neck arched over the chair and an oval coffee table sat in front of the couch.

"The TV is an old black and white, but it still works. Besides, I don't watch much TV."

Julia continued down a short hallway giving Josh time for just a quick glance at the living room. She opened the first door on the left. "This is the bathroom. I don't have a tub but the shower is great." Again, Josh had just a quick peek before Julia opened the door on the right. "And, this is the bedroom."

Josh followed her into the room. "The bedroom?"

"Yep, one and only, but it's just me so it works fine."

"You have a wonderful place," Josh offered.

"It didn't look like this when I rented it." Julia led the way back to the kitchen. "We had to do a lot of cleaning, painting and fixing. The bed and the table and chairs in the kitchen were my first purchases. For a while that's all I had, a place to sleep and a place to sit and eat. I basically furnished the whole house with stuff I bought at yard sales."

"You mentioned we," Josh said. "Did you have help?"

"Doug," Julia blurted. "Doug Foster, he owns the bait and liquor store. He helped. He did all the painting."

Josh smiled. "He did a fantastic job on the cupboards."

"We met when I first came to town. We're really good... we're friends." Julia slipped past him and headed to the kitchen. "Want something to drink? I think I've got some lemonade in the refrigerator."

"That would be great." Josh continued looking around.

Julia poured them each a glass. "Come, let's sit in here." She carried the drinks to the living room.

Josh sat on the couch. Julia handed him a glass and plopped in the easy chair.

"Can I put my feet up here?" Josh asked, pointing to the coffee table.

"Sure, I do it all the time."

"You say he has a liquor store, this friend of yours."

"Yes, it's next to the icehouse. Remember, it's the big building across from the marina. He also has a pontoon boat and takes people fishing. He's been a really good... friend." Julia's face reddened. "It's not what you think. We're not like boyfriend and girlfriend."

Josh took a drink of his lemonade. "I wouldn't want to come between the two of you."

"No, no, it's not like that, we're just..."

"Friends?"

"Okay, no more cat and mouse." Julia sat upright in the chair. "Doug and I are good friends. We go to the movies and we have lunch together. In summer, we go to band concerts and boating on the lake. It's what friends do."

125

"I'm sorry, I didn't mean to upset you. I don't want to be a problem."

"We sometimes go weeks without seeing one another." Julia stood and turned on the TV. The tube crackled and finally delivered a fuzzy black and white image.

Julia adjusted the rabbit ears antenna. "I get three channels from Green Bay, and sometimes if the wind is right, I can pick one up from Madison." It didn't make much difference which way she turned the antenna, the picture remained fuzzy.

"If I had an antenna on the roof with a rotor box I would get a better picture," she explained as she continued to move the antenna. "Oh wait, here's old crooked nose with the weather. Let's see what it'll be like on the 4th." Julia jumped back into her chair. "Nora gave Carol and me the day off for the fourth."

"That's nice."

"With pay."

"That's even better," Josh said. "When is the 4th?"

"Friday! It'll be a three day weekend!"

"I've sort of lost track. What is today?" Josh asked.

"It's Monday, the twenty-ninth." Julia turned back to the TV. "Listen, here comes the weather."

The weatherman predicted lots of sunshine and light winds for the weekend. He said winds would be moderate and there was little chance of rain.

"That's great!" Julia jumped out of the chair. "Good weather, plus a three day weekend means the town will be loaded with people."

"Good for business, right?" Josh said.

"You bet, this town lives or dies with the weather," she said. "At best, people here have a hundred and twenty day window to make enough to survive the winter. Last winter seemed like it was never going to end. I was either shoveling my car out of six to eight inches of snow, or

126

adding more layers of clothes trying to keep warm during the spell of subzero temperatures we had in January. Would you believe, there was still a little bit of snow on the ground on April fool's Day? Some Joke."

"It's a lot better now," Josh said.

Doug says, good weather on the Fourth of July means the kids will have milk and honey on their Cheerios. If it rains, the kids have to settle for Kool-Aid and soda crackers."

"This Doug sounds like quite a guy. I'd like to meet him."

"I'll introduce you to him, we're..."

"Good friends?" Josh laughed.

Julia laughed too.

"Why do you call the weatherman crooked nose?"

"When he first came to channel three, he had this crooked nose, like someone punched him and broke it. When you watched the weather, your eyes would get fixated on his nose. No matter what he said or did, all you saw was his bent nose."

"I don't think it looks that bad."

"Not anymore," Julia continued. "One day he announced he was going on vacation and three weeks later he came back with a brand new nose. I can never remember his name so I call him crooked nose. That's pretty bad of me, right?"

"I think he said his name was Jim Jamerson."

"Yes, that's it." Julia went in the kitchen. "Do you need more lemonade?"

"I'm good. Are you coming back or should I come in there?"

"Just sit and relax. I'm just taking care of a few things." Julia dug in her purse and counted her cash. With a three-day weekend, money could be an issue. She looked in her checkbook and compared the balance to her passbook.

127

She tossed both on the table. "Why do I have such a hard time balancing this stupid checkbook?"

Josh came into the kitchen. "Are we talking high finance, here?"

"I wish just once I could find a few extra bucks the bank doesn't know anything about."

"Mind if I take a look?"

"Be my guest. Did you say you wanted more lemonade?"

"Sure." Josh lifted his glass.

Julia poured the rest of the pitcher into his glass. She set the pitcher in the sink, went into the living room and fell onto the couch. After a few minutes, Josh strolled in and sat in the chair.

"Did you find where I went wrong?"

"You made a couple subtraction errors and you missed entering a three dollar check to the Cut & Curl."

"Darn it, how much am I off?"

"Thirteen-dollars."

Julia counted the days in her head. "That's going to make things real tight."

"One thing is for sure, you don't need me causing you any extra expense." He took the envelope from his pocket and removed two tens. "Here, I want you to have this. It will cover your shortfall."

"Don't be silly," Julia protested. "That's your money. You're going to need it."

"It's for gas. You've been chauffeuring me around and I will probably need more rides. Please take it." Ignoring her protest, he put the money in her checkbook. "What I need to figure out is, where I can find a job."

"Balancing checkbooks?" Julia giggled.

"I should be able to find something. I'm not a cripple."

"That's because of the fine work your physical therapist did to sculpt that beautiful body of yours," she mocked.

Josh jumped from his chair.

Julia took off for the kitchen, around the table and back to the living room with Josh in pursuit. She squealed as they both tumbled onto the couch. He slowly lowered his head. Ever so softly, their lips touched. He pressed forward into a long, passionate kiss.

Their lips parted. Julia opened her eyes. "Was that another thank you kiss?"

Before he could answer, she giggled and pulled him down for another kiss, causing them to lose their balance and fall off the couch.

Julia rolled on her back. "It's too bad there isn't a job being a kisser," she teased. "You'd be perfect for that."

"I'm serious. I need to find a job of some kind."

"I don't mean to burst your bubble, but what would you put on a job application?" Julia held back a grin. "Picture this, first question, what was your last job? Answer, I don't know. Question two, what can you do? Answer, I don't know. You'd have a whole application of I don't knows."

"Dammit, I'm sorry if I can't remember what I did or what I can do. For all you know, I could be a criminal, an axe-murderer or bank robber."

"I'm sorry," Julia said soberly. "I didn't mean to upset you. I shouldn't have made fun of the situation."

Julia pushed up and leaned against the front of the couch. "I have an idea, maybe Doug can use some help in the liquor store? Let's go ask him."

"Now?"

"Yes, now." She stood and wiped the lipstick smudge from his cheek. "That wouldn't look so good for your first job interview. Let's walk, it's not that far."

Josh Meets Doug

The breeze coming off the lake made the walk comfortable. Julia pulled him close. "If you were a bank robber that would solve the money problem." She held back a grin, then burst out laughing.

Josh shook his head, drawing his lips into a wide smile.

"I know Doug's Uncle Fred works at the store, but maybe he can use some extra help. It won't hurt to ask."

"I don't know anything about a liquor store."

"Now, don't be an old poop," Julia said. "What's there to know? The customer takes a bottle off the shelf, hands you the money and walks out the door. What can be so hard about that?"

Approaching the store, Josh was surprised that the business was in a house. It was two steps up to the porch. The large bay window was nearly covered with colorful posters and in the oval front door window hung a blinking "open" sign. Julia opened the door and went in with Josh close behind.

Doug was behind the counter; his face lit up. "Jules!" he shouted. "What brings you down here?" His eyes were so fixated on her he didn't notice the man standing in her shadow.

"I want you to meet someone." Julia said, pulling Josh to the counter.

Doug's expression sagged.

"This is Josh. The guy in the coma. Josh, this is Doug." The men made eye contact and nodded.

Josh looked around the room as Julia tried to explain the whole situation. Coming to the part of him having to leave The Glen, Doug gave Josh an up and down look. "You don't remember anything? I think that's pretty strange."

"Doug, he just needs time for his memory to come back," she said. "It could come back any time, but right now he needs a job to start getting his life in order. I thought you might need some help in the store."

Doug grabbed Julia's hand and led her to the far end of the store. "What in hell are you thinking? You want me to put this guy in the store? Are you nuts? I don't know him from Adam, and you want me to let him run wild through my store, through my cash register? Are you serious?" Doug huffed and threw his arms in the air.

Julia pulled his arm down. "Don't be so dramatic. He's a good person. Please, he needs help right now."

Doug sighed before shaking his head. "Why can't I ever say no to you? I don't believe I'm doing this, but Fred has been bugging me to get someone to cover for him. He wants a couple of weeks to jump in his truck and go wherever it takes him." He pointed to Josh. "Tell him he can have two weeks work covering for Fred."

"Oh, thank you," Julia squealed. "Thank you so much. I know he'll do a good job for you and you won't regret it." Julia dragged Doug to where Josh stood. "Doug said he's got some work for you." Josh smiled and the two men shook hands.

"Come in tomorrow at nine," Doug said. "Fred will be here to show you the ropes." Turning to Julia, he said, "Have you fallen for this guy? Remember what I said last night, just be careful, okay?"

Julia gave Doug a kiss on the cheek. "I will."

"See, you have a job," she said, ushering him out the door. "Isn't that great?"

Josh shook his head. "Once again, you have saved the day. You are incredible, you know that?"

"Just another of my better qualities." Julia danced ahead of him.

"Is it true?" he asked.

"Is what true?"

"Have you fallen for me?"

Julia gave him a push backwards. "I'm not one to kiss and tell. You will have to figure that out on your own. It's after five, should we call to see if Nora's home?"

"I guess we could. I'll have to go there sooner or later."

Nora answered on the second ring. Julia held her hand over the receiver. "Do you want to go now?" she waited for him to acknowledge. "We'll be over in a little bit."

Going to Nora's

Josh was quiet on the ride to Nora's place.

"I work tonight, but I'm done at eight. I can give you a ride to the liquor store. You don't want to be late for your first day on the job." Julia parked the car in front of a large two-story house.

"That would be great." Josh gathered his belongings from the back seat.

The porch stretched the full front of the house. The architectural style was reminiscent of the 1930's with dormers and shutters. The yard was well kept and the house appeared to be freshly painted.

"Wait a minute!" Julia fumbled through her purse. She brought out a pen, scribbled something on a scrap of paper, and handed it to him.

"What's this?"

"It's my phone number. Just in case you want to call me."

"Thanks." He folded the paper and put it in his shirt pocket. Then, leaning back against the car he took a long look at the house.

Julia leaned over the seat. "Do you want me to go in with you?"

"No, I will be fine. I'll see you in the morning." He started up the walk, turned, and waved as she put the car in gear and drove off.

She didn't want him to see the tears that filled her eyes. She had to remind herself it wasn't a final goodbye, she would see him in the morning. Why was she crying? It didn't matter, she couldn't stop the tears that streamed down her cheeks. Her demons could no longer hold her back. She was in love.

Julia walked into her kitchen and stared at the phone. She desperately wanted to call him, to hear his voice, but knew she couldn't do that. "Nora would think I'd lost my marbles." She walked into the bedroom and fell on the bed. All she could think about was Josh and how desperately she wanted to be near him.

Josh made his way up the walk. He saw the curtains move in the window before Nora opened the door and walked onto the porch. She reached for one of the shopping bags. "Here, let me help you with that." Nora watched Julia drive away. "What happened? I thought she'd come in too. I picked up fried chicken from the Drive In. I've got plenty. She should have come in."

"I think she had things to do." Josh hoped his small fib would let Julia off the hook.

"Did you guys have a nice day?"

"We had a great time. I think we found where I could have been in an accident, which would explain how I ended up in County Park."

"Really, how did you find that?" Nora directed Josh down the hallway to a brightly lit kitchen.

"Wow!" Josh exclaimed. "This is beautiful."

Cabinets covered three walls. The low luster varnish finish brought out all the wonderful wood grain in the oak doors and drawers. Everything was accented with gold pin striping and gold tone hardware. The countertops were

134

rich looking, imitation marble Formica. The center island had three stools and a built in cook station. Copper kettles of various shapes and sizes hung on a rack overhead. On the back wall, a breakfast nook with windows on three sides overlooked the backyard.

"The outside is nice, but you wouldn't expect to see something like this inside." Josh continued to admire the room.

"That was my Duke," Nora said. "He completely remodeled the whole house. He made all the cabinets and hand rubbed the finish. He was a terrific carpenter. He built the breakfast nook, too. We would sit there every morning, have coffee and read the newspaper. God, I miss that man." Nora took a hankie from her apron pocket and wiped her eyes.

"He sure did a wonderful job. The layout, the color, the finish, they are all so beautiful."

"Duke never used a blueprint. He would just visualize what he wanted and build it. He had a real flair for things and was such a stickler for detail."

Josh pulled out a stool and sat.

Nora opened the oven and brought out a big platter of fried chicken, French fries and biscuits. "I hope you're hungry because we've got a lot of food."

Josh was still full from the burger at Teddy's, but didn't want Nora to feel bad. He took a plate and filled it with some of everything. It was all tasty so it wasn't hard to clean his plate.

Nora nibbled on the chicken between trips to the refrigerator. She brought out ketchup, mustard, dill pickles, sweet pickles, even a bowl of fresh strawberries. Each time Josh assured her he was fine and didn't need anything more.

"You say you found the place where you might have had an accident."

"Yes, we drove on the highway above County Park. I've had these visions flashing through my mind and I recognized a tree from one of them. It's a really big pine and stands next to the road."

"I know exactly where that tree is." Nora said, putting stuff back in the refrigerator.

"I kept seeing this large deer and I think we found the spot where he came out of the woods. We figured Mary swerved to miss the deer and we crashed into this huge bank on the other side of the road."

"Who's Mary?"

"It's all part of these little clips or flashes I keep seeing in my head. I think she was driving the car."

"What happened to her? I don't remember an accident being reported. Why would she drive off and leave you? And how did you end up out of the car and down in County Park?"

"Good questions. I don't have any answers for that part of the story." Josh reached in his pocket and brought out the shiny chrome letter. "We found this embedded in the dirt. It could have come off the car."

"Do you have an idea of what kind of car it was?" Nora leaned over the counter to get a closer look at the letter.

"It could have come off any number of cars. When you think about all the cars made in the last ten years with an O in their name, the possibilities are endless. We may never figure that out."

Nora came around the counter. "Let me have a closer look at that?" She studied the letter. Taking off her apron, she grabbed a set of keys from a hook on the wall. "Come with me."

Josh followed Nora out the back door and to a garage about thirty feet behind the house. She opened the door, turned on the light and walked to the front of the green car parked there. Bending, she held the O next to the one

136

mounted on the car. "Look at this. I think we have a perfect match."

The shape, the size, everything was the same. Josh stood and read the name aloud. "AMBASSADOR. What kind of car is this?"

"It's a 1959 Rambler. It's my car. Every time I wash it I have to wipe around each of those letters. Your letter looked familiar."

"Wow, I can't believe it. I thought this was going to be so hard, but you've solved the mystery."

"Does that help you? Do you remember anything else about the car?" Nora asked.

"Not right off." Josh looked inside the car. I'm not sure. I think I was in a black car. Julia is not going to believe this. I can't wait to tell her."

They walked to the house. "Let me straighten up the kitchen and I will show you to the upstairs. There's a phone up there to call her."

Josh sat on his stool. "Take your time. I'll finish this piece of chicken."

Nora put the rest of the chicken in a bowl and covered it with foil. She put the biscuits in a paper bag, threw the fries in the garbage, and wiped down the counter. The chicken went in the refrigerator and the biscuits in the breadbox. "Okay, ready to see your new abode?"

Josh got up and dumped what was left on his plate in the garbage and put the plate on top of hers in the sink. "Is it okay that I leave this here?"

"That's fine. I'll wash them up later."

When they reached the foyer, Josh looked up at the staircase. It arched its way to the second floor with a curved wood banister and beautiful white spindles. "I'll bet Duke built this too."

"He did, made every bit of it himself. He got the idea from the staircase in 'Gone with the Wind.' The one where

Rhett Butler carries Scarlet O'Hara up the stairs. I guess to make mad passionate love to her."

"Maybe that's what Duke had in mind when he built it." Josh gave Nora a poke in the ribs.

She swatted his hand. "He would have had a coronary before he lugged me half way up." Nora took a tissue from her sleeve and dabbed her eyes. "It's a nice thought though."

At the top of the stairs was a small sitting area with a couch and a chair. A small table stood on either side of the couch, each holding a tiffany lamp with a white lace doily underneath to protect the wood finish.

Josh touched one of the shades, "More of Duke's handiwork?"

"He should have been an artist. He was so good with his hands, and he had such a fertile imagination." Nora opened the double doors ahead of them. "Here's the living area."

Josh walked into a large room with maple wood flooring. A couch and coffee table were centered over a colorful woven rug. Against the wall was a large console TV. "I usually have everything covered, but I took the sheets off before you got here. Most of this furniture came from his mom's home in New York. Duke had it sent out here after she died. He built this apartment just for her. She was going to come and live with us but passed before she had a chance to get here."

"This is really something. I'm thinking his mom would have loved living up here and she would have been very proud of her son's work."

"It's been empty all this time," Nora said. "Not too many people have ever been up here. We were private people and Duke wasn't much for entertaining. Pine Lake has a lot of small-minded people. They looked down on us, because we weren't married."

Nora wiped her eyes again and put the tissue back up her sleeve. "That didn't bother us. We had such a good thing between us. He said he didn't want to spoil a good thing by making it legal."

"I guess there is something to be said for illicit sex," Josh said.

"Oh, you are a rascal, aren't you?" Nora swiped the air in his direction. "In here you have a full kitchen. Not as big or grand as the one down stairs but it has everything you need. I plugged in the refrigerator earlier. It should be cold by now." She opened the door and placed her hand inside. "I put some sodas in here. So if you get thirsty, please help yourself."

"Duke really thought this out, didn't he?"

"I told you, he was a stickler for detail." Nora moved to the next door. It opened up to a large room with a canopy bed, a dresser, vanity and armoire. There was soft plush carpet on the floor and flowered drapes on the window. "This was going to be her bedroom. I apologize, it's a bit feminine."

"No problem, it's beautiful. I would be happy to have a cot in some small corner."

"Here's the bathroom" The light bounced off the white tile walls. A pedestal sink and oval mirror reflected the light back to the glass enclosed shower stall. A gleaming white toilet sat on a floor of white and black mosaic tile. "No one has ever stayed up here. Everything is still brand new." Nora said as she turned out the light.

"Will you adopt me? I could be happy living here forever?"

Nora laughed. "You're welcome to stay as long as you want to."

Josh gave Nora a big hug. "I can't thank you enough. This is so amazing and you are an amazing person for inviting me here, a perfect stranger."

"You ain't so perfect. Your memory stinks." Nora giggled.

"I'll guarantee you one thing, I will never forget the kindness you have shown me."

Nora blushed. "That door over there is the back stairway. It goes to the outside. We needed that in case of fire. I keep it locked, but you can use it to come and go if you want."

"That won't be necessary. I don't have a lot of places to come and go to."

"I'll show you where I hide a key. You can use the front door." Nora started down the stairs.

"That will be perfectly fine." Josh said, emphasizing the word perfectly. He hurried past her on the stairs. "I'm going to bring up my things."

Nora waited on the stairs. "Nice luggage."

"It was a gift from a very dear friend."

Nora laughed as she continued down the stairs.

It Ain't Rocket Science

Josh finished putting his things in the armoire and his toiletries in the bathroom. He pulled out the slip of paper with Julia's phone number from his pocket but decided to wait and tell her everything in the morning. He was sure she'd be asleep by now.

Walking into the bathroom he threw a large fluffy towel over the shower glass and turned on the water. His shoulders sagged as the water pounced on his back, over his shoulders, and down his chest. A lot had happened since this morning. Lathering up, he scrubbed every inch of his body and let the hot water soothe his tense muscles.

He toweled dry and wrapped himself in the soft terry. Combing through his hair he checked to see if it had grown enough to cover the scars.

The pajamas Nora gave him were still in the original package. He put on the shirt and pulled up the pants. "Sorry Duke," he said, looking up. "You might not have liked these silky things, but I think they are wonderful."

Pulling back the flowered bedspread he was pleased to see the sheets were white and not pink, or God forbid, floral. The bed was firm and the pillow was also to his liking. In the darkened room he replayed the day in his mind. He saw the many faces of Julia, the innocent look, the pout, and how her lips curled in the corners when she

141

smiled. Could life be so cruel as to keep them apart? He murmured a prayer. "Whatever my life was before, please don't let me hurt her."

The room was awash in sunlight when he rolled over and opened his eyes. He looked around and smiled, knowing it wasn't a dream. The room was not only real, but unbelievably real. The whole upstairs was beyond imagination. "Julia will not believe me when I tell her about this place," he said, sliding his legs off the side of the bed. "I should send a thank you note to the county guy for forcing me to leave The Glen."

Julia smiled as Josh jumped in the car.
   "Good Morning, Good Morning!" Josh said returning her smile. "Have I got news for you."
   "Holy Cow, what's got you in such a good mood this morning?"
   "First of all, I had a great night of sleep. Secondly, I know the make of car the letter came off of, and third, you have got to see Nora's upstairs. It's a full apartment. There's a living room and a full kitchen. The bedroom is huge with a canopy bed, and the bathroom looks like it came out of a magazine. Duke built it all for his mom, but she died before she had a chance to live in it."
   "Whoa. Slow down. You say you know the car?"
   "It's unbelievable," Josh said. "I get here and Nora has fried chicken and biscuits. She was expecting you to come in."
   "I probably should have. Was she upset?"
   "I told her you had things to do. She was good with that."
   "So how did you find out about the letter?" Julia asked.
   "We're eating chicken and I told Nora about finding the place on the highway. I show her the letter. She looks

142

at it for a minute or two and then takes me out to her garage. She has a 1959 Rambler Ambassador and the letter is a perfect match to the one on her car. Of all the cars it could have come off, she's got the right one in her garage."

"Are you sure?" Julia asked.

"Positive."

"Is knowing the car going to help us?" Julia pulled the shifting lever into low gear and let out the clutch.

"I'm not sure, but it's a piece of the puzzle."

Julia pulled in front of the liquor store and shut off the engine. "Are you ready for this?"

"I think I got this liquor store business figured out. It's like you said, the customer comes in, takes a bottle off the shelf, hands me the money and leaves. Done deal. Nothing hard about that." Josh waited for her reaction.

Julia chuckled. "Do you want me to go in with you?"

"That's okay, I'll be fine."

"Then have a great day and I'll pick you up when I'm done at the hospital, probably about 4:30."

"Thanks for the ride." Josh got out and watched her drive away before going inside.

The front door opened into what was probably the original living room. A cash register sat on a glass display case to Josh's immediate left. Shelves of hard liquor lined both walls. The center of the room was stacked shoulder high with cases of beer and wine with narrow walkways between them. On the right and through an archway, stood a smaller room, possibly a den or dining room in the original floor plan. It was crowded with racks of bait, tackle, and fishing gear. Lighted beer signs hung from the ceiling and colorful price cards were scattered everywhere. The glass case under the cash register contained an array of candy bars, peanuts and chips.

"Anybody here?" Josh shouted.

A head poked up from behind some beer cases. "Be

143

right with you." The man made his way up one of the aisles. "What can I help you with?"

"Is Doug here? I was supposed to come in this morning to learn about the business."

"You're Julia's friend. I'm Fred, Doug's uncle. Doug had a guide job this morning, but asked me to show you around. Have you ever worked in a liquor store?"

"I don't know," Josh said. "I'm not sure what experience I have, but I'm willing to learn."

"It ain't rocket science. People come in, they get what they want and you collect the money."

Josh chuckled. "Seems everyone has the same simplified version of how a liquor store operates."

"What?"

"Nothing, I was just..."

Fred had already moved down an aisle. "C'mon I'll show you around. Our biggest seller is beer — Milwaukee favorites, Schlitz, Blatz, Pabst and Miller High Life. Locals buy beer. Lakeshore and tourists buy the liquor and wine."

Fred opened a large door. "This is the walk-in cooler."

The room was overfilled with cases of beer and an assortment of quarter barrels. Cases of wine stood four high on the opposite wall.

"Wow! You got a lot of inventory," Josh observed.

"Yeah, most of it will go during the 4th of July weekend. It's the most business we'll do all summer," Fred said. "Lucky you, you'll be here right in the thick of things."

Fred continued to show Josh around the store, stopping to talk about the specials they had on different items. "I know this all sounds pretty confusing, but don't worry, you'll pick it up."

Josh wasn't all that sure, there seemed to be a lot to remember.

Fred led the way into the room with the bait and tackle. "This room is a whole different animal. Fishermen will chew your ear off. They'll ask a million questions and waste a lot of your time over a twenty-five cent can of worms. Speaking of worms, night crawlers are thirty cents a can," he said holding up a Campbell's soup can. "The minnow tanks are out back. Chubs go for half a buck a dozen. Shiners, seventy-five cents."

"What's the difference?" Josh asked.

"Chubs are the bigger ones, good for northern pike. Shiners are better for walleye."

"When they ask about the fishing what do we tell them?"

"They'll want to know what's biting, where they're biting and what they're biting on. I suggest to them if they want to know all that they should go talk to the fish."

Fred laughed. "Hell, it's anybody's guess. It's a big lake. One day they are biting by the inlet and the next by Sandstone bluff. It don't matter. Whatever they buy I tell them the locals are having good luck with that. When they catch fish it was a good tip, when they don't, they figure the locals knew something they didn't. Either way I'm off the hook. C'mon, I'll show you how the cash register works."

Operating the cash register came easy for Josh. He learned how to add and subtract items and how to ring up a total sale.

A young man set two six packs of Blatz on the counter.

"There you go," Fred said. "Ring up your first sale."

"What do we charge for a six pack?"

"Ninety-nine cents for Blatz," Fred said, pointing to a sign in the back.

"Your total with tax is $2.03," Josh said, picking up the five dollar bill the man laid on the counter. "Going fishing? Got plenty of bait?"

The young man hesitated. "What are walleyes biting on? We've got worms. Are they biting on something else?"

145

"Locals are using minnows. Shiners are seventy-five a dozen." Josh waited.

"Gimme a dozen," the guy said.

"Better take two, the walleyes have been hitting and you wouldn't want to run out."

"Ok, make it two."

"Fred, could you get this young man two dozen of our finest shiners?" Josh looked out the window and saw a girl sitting in the guy's truck. "Wife?" Josh asked.

"Girlfriend. It's her first time fishing. She's not too hyped up about it."

"Tell you what," Josh reached under the counter. "Take her a couple Hershey bars. It will make everything alright."

The young man nodded.

Josh put two bars on top of the beer. "That will make it an even four dollars."

Fred handed the boy the minnows on his way out the door.

Josh and Fred watched the girl smile as the guy handed her the candy bars.

"How do you know the walleyes are biting?" Fred asked.

"Don't, but I'm hoping today is the day they do." Josh straightened things around the cash register. "Besides, it doubled the sale."

"Are you sure you've never done this before?" Fred asked. "I think you have a very bright future in the business."

The morning saw a steady stream of customers come through the door. Fred helped people with their purchases and let Josh handle the cash register. After each sale Josh marked down the item and the price on a sheet of paper. It was easier to check his list for prices than to yell at Fred.

Whenever he had a little time Josh looked around and

added items to his list.

"Are you hungry?" Fred asked.

Josh looked at the clock. "Wow! Where did the morning go?"

"I keep bread and lunch meat in the cooler. I can make us a ham and cheese sandwich."

"That would be great."

Fred brought up the sandwiches and pulled out a beer case to sit on. "I brought us a couple of Cokes too."

Josh took a big bite of his sandwich and found a case to sit on.

"We'll probably have to eat fast. Customers always seem to know when I'm eating." Like clockwork, two fellows came through the door. Josh got up. "Thanks for the sandwich. I'll finish it by the register."

Fred grumbled. "Sometime I would like to eat my sandwich slow enough to taste the meat." He finished his Coke. "I am real happy you're here. I wasn't looking forward to handling all the holiday business by myself."

"It's sort of fun and interesting."

"We'll wait and see if you think it's fun and interesting when we get through the week." Fred chuckled and walked to the back of the store.

Business remained steady. Josh got into the flow of things and felt at ease behind the counter. He laughed and made small talk with the customers on everything from fishing to the weather.

One lady teased Fred. "It's nice to have this personable young man behind the counter instead of your grouchy face." Fred didn't miss a beat. "Well Harriet, it's customers like you that make me grouchy." They both had a good laugh.

A few customers made the association that he was the one that had spent time in a coma. Josh downplayed it, saying he felt fine and was happy to be up and about.

The afternoon went by quickly. Josh lost track of time until he looked up and saw Julia by the counter.

"Well, how was your first day on the job?"

"It went fine," Josh said. "We've been busy all day."

"This guy is a Whiz-bang," Fred said. "He could probably sell snowballs to the Eskimos."

"Once I got comfortable with the cash register, it was just being myself. It was sort of fun." Josh turned to Fred. "Is it alright if I leave?"

"Sure. Doug should be back by five. It's his turn to close. Same time tomorrow?"

"Sure, if it's good with my chauffeur?"

"He'll be here," Julia said. "Thanks for helping him today."

"Strictly a selfish act," Fred said. "The quicker he's trained the sooner I get a vacation."

Josh followed Julia out the door. "See you tomorrow."

Dinner at Nora's

"Nora invited us for dinner tonight," Julia said and started the car.

"That's great. I can show you the upstairs." Josh shuffled papers on his lap.

"What's that, did Fred give you homework?"

"Homework? Very funny. No, I kept track of the prices we charge for things. I'm going to arrange them in alphabetical order and make a price sheet."

"You've really gotten into this working business."

"I had a good time," he said, sliding close to her and kissing her on the neck. "And I've got you to thank for it."

She pushed him away. "You want someone to see you?"

"Just wanted to say thank you," he said with a sheepish grin.

Julia pulled in front of Nora's place and turned off the engine. Josh made no move to get out.

"Is there a problem?" she asked.

Josh leaned forward and kissed her on the cheek, then drew himself nearer. Julia closed her eyes as their lips pressed gently together. His tongue slipped into her opened mouth and his hand move up her arm. She breathed deeply as his fingers danced lightly across her breast. Impulsively, she pulled his hand away and looked at the house. "If Nora sees us making out in the car she'll never let me live it down. C'mon, let's go in." Julia checked herself in the rear view mirror, then pulled a handkerchief from her pocket and wiped the lipstick off his mouth.

She couldn't help but wonder if she would ever be able to give her love freely and totally. "Now don't say anything," she pleaded. "You know, about what we were doing."

"My lips are sealed ... sealed with a kiss." Josh made a gesture of zipping his lips closed. On the porch, Josh reached for the knob.

"What are you doing? You can't just go walking in."

"Of course I can. I live here. Nora told me I could come and go as I please, so I'm coming." He opened the door and extended his hand for her to enter. "We're here," he yelled. The smell of roasted beef filled the hallway. "It sure smells good in here," he said walking into the kitchen.

Nora came around the island. "I'm glad you guys came early. I've got a bottle of sparkling burgundy chilling in the refrigerator. It's supposed to go with red meat." She brought out the bottle and handed it to Josh. "Will you do the honors?" Motioning to Julia, "There's some wine glasses in that cupboard."

Josh peeled the foil and unwound the wire. The cork came out with a loud pop. "What are we celebrating?" he asked as he pour them each a glass.

Nora raised her glass. "You coming back to life."

"And getting through his first day on the job," Julia offered. The three clinked glasses and took a collective sip of the wine.

"Is dinner ready?" Josh asked. "Do I have time to show Julia the upstairs?"

Nora peeked in the oven. "The roast needs at least another half hour. Give her the tour."

Julia's reaction to the swooping staircase mirrored

150

Josh's. "This is beautiful."

"Duke built it," Josh said. "Wait until you see the apartment."

Josh led her from room to room showing off the beautiful woodwork and wonderful craftsmanship. Julia especially liked the bedroom and chuckled when Josh told of being relieved to find plain white sheets on the bed. The kitchen, with the new appliances and the tiled bath, also brought a gasp from Julia. Josh had not exaggerated a bit.

"The furniture came from Duke's mom's place out east," he said. "Sit on the couch, I'll run down and get our wine."

Nora was seated at the counter, about to take a drink from her wine, when Josh bounded in. "You're one behind. I'm on my second glass."

"Julia loves the upstairs," he said, pouring a splash more in their glasses.

"You've got fifteen minutes."

Josh made short work of the stairs, taking two at a time. He walked into the room and slowed his pace.

"There are so many pretty things up here." Julia said taking a sip of wine. The pictures, the lamps, and I just love this beautiful rug on the floor."

"I know. I have to keep pinching myself to make sure I'm not dreaming." Josh sat on the edge of the couch. "When I woke four days ago I had nothing. Now, here I sit. I've got clothes, money, and a fantastic place to live." Holding his glass to her's, "and I've got someone I care for a great deal."

"You could wake up tomorrow and remember everything; our lives could change in a heartbeat." Julia stared into her glass and swirled the wine.

Josh slid back on the couch. "I know, it's not fair to you," he said softly. "I can't offer you any guarantees, but I want you to know, I think I fell in love with you before I

151

saw you. I fell in love with a voice, your voice."

"I can't bear the thought of losing you," she whispered, nestling her head on his shoulder. "What are we going to do?"

"It's tough. It would kill me if I ended up hurting you. There is no way to predict the future, or change the past, all we can control is today."

"I know." Tears streaked down her cheeks. "My heart tells me to go fast, fall in love, but my head says, slow down, you could get hurt. I don't know what to do."

"We don't have to resolve anything right now. Let's just enjoy the evening. C'mon, dinner is probably ready. We'll have lots of time to sort things out."

"Just a minute," Julia said. "Let me wash my face. Nora's going to see I've been crying." When she returned, she took his hand. "My biggest fear is if we get involved, you know, really involved, and it turns out you're married...I just don't know if I could deal with that."

Josh put his arm around her. "Let's leave all that for another day." He collected the glasses and they retreated down the stairs.

Nora was placing the roast on the table as they walked into the kitchen. "You're just in time." Looking at Julia, she slapped Josh on the arm with the hot pad. "What are you doing to her? Why has she been crying?" Josh shrugged his shoulders, feigning innocence. Nora threw up her hands. "I don't know why young love has to be so painful. Let's hope you two can find a way to work things out." She threw the hot pad on the counter. "Let's eat before it gets cold."

The roast was delicious, moist and tender, the mashed potatoes creamy, and the gravy rich in beef flavor. Green beans and applesauce complimented the meal.

Josh controlled most of the conversation, relating his adventures of the day at the liquor store. Nora was up and down fussing over her meal. Julia remained quiet but smiled whenever it seemed appropriate.

Dessert was vanilla ice cream with fresh strawberry topping. Julia took a few spoonfuls before announcing she had to go. "Midnight will come quickly."

Josh walked her to the car. "Are you okay?"

"I'm fine, just a little tired." Josh held her door.

"Why don't I ask Nora to give me a ride to work in the morning? She can drop me off on her way to The Glen."

"That's fine. I'll call you tomorrow." Julia waved as she drove off. Watching him in her rear view mirror, she wondered why life had to be so complicated. Everything was fine while he was in the coma. There was no pressure, no expectations. If his family or someone would have come and taken him while he was still asleep, she wouldn't have had a problem with it. His waking changed everything. She loved him from the moment he spoke her name and now couldn't bear the thought of losing him.

With Brad out of her life she had feelings of need and desire she had suppressed for too long. She wanted desperately to be intimate with him, to experience the joy of love when two people join as one. She wondered if she would be able to handle giving up her virginity, and he returning to his prior life with another woman. She shuddered at the thought. Now was not the time to decide, she'd leave that decision for tomorrow. Right now, she needed sleep.

Its All the Unknowns

Josh walked into the kitchen as Nora gathered up the dishes.

"You two having a problem?" she asked.

"It's all the unknowns." Josh sat at the counter. "To be safe I think we need to keep things from getting too serious before we know who I am and where I came from. The last thing I want to do is hurt her."

"A good idea. You could remember everything and be gone. She'd be left here at the mercy of the wagging tongues of Pine Lake. I can personally attest to how cruel they can be." Nora threw the washcloth in the sink. "I doubt Julia has thick enough skin to deal with it."

"We'll get things straightened out tomorrow. Speaking of tomorrow, could you drop me off at the liquor store in the morning on your way to The Glen?"

"Just be ready to go at seven thirty." Nora turned out the kitchen light.

"One more thing, do you have a typewriter?"

"Typewriter? Are you writing a book?" Nora chuckled. "Do you know how to type?"

"I'm sure I can hit the letters one at a time. I want to make a price list for the liquor store."

"It so happens I have one. It's in the closet at the top of the stairs. There should be paper on one of the shelves."

Josh put a hand on Nora's shoulder. "Thanks for everything, the clothes, the food, a place to live. I hope to be able to repay you someday."

"Don't be silly. This has been fun for me too. I enjoy having someone in the house." Nora took the hankie from her sleeve and wiped her eyes. "I know Duke would be happy to finally have someone living upstairs."

"I'll be ready at 7:30." He gave Nora a hug and bounded up the stairs. The typewriter and paper were where she said. He set the typewriter on the coffee table and fed a sheet of paper into the rollers. Looking at the keys, his fingers naturally fell on the middle row. He checked the first item on his list, and without thinking, his fingers danced across the keyboard. There it was, his first item, typed in beautiful black on white. "How do you like that?" he said aloud. "I can type." It was close to eleven when he finished.

Josh was sitting at the kitchen counter eating a bowl of cereal when Nora walked in. "My, you must have got up with the chickens. Do you want coffee? I can make some."

"Don't bother. I poured myself a glass of orange juice."

"I don't usually make coffee in the morning when I work," Nora said. "The cooks at The Glen make the best coffee." Nora poured herself some juice. "You be sure to smooth things out with Julia. I hate seeing her upset."

"I will. The last thing I want to do is hurt her."

It was seven thirty when they walked out the back door. Nora showed him a potted geranium on the first step of the porch. "I keep a key to the house underneath it. There's also a geranium on the front step with a key under it."

The drive to the liquor store took less than ten minutes. Josh was about to get out of the car when Nora grabbed his arm. "Don't forget. Talk to Julia."

"I will, I promise. Thanks for the ride."

155

It's A Price List

Fred stood by the cash register taking care of a customer when Josh walked in. "How much did I tell you we get for a case of Schlitz Shorty's?" Fred asked.

Josh looked at his freshly typed sheets. "Thirty six bottles to a case, four-fifty."

Fred rang up the sale and helped the lady take her purchases to her car. Returning to the counter, "Thanks. I've got so many prices rambling through my head sometimes I just draw a blank. Did you read that off your paper?"

"It's a price list." Josh handed the sheets to Fred.

"This is really something."

Josh put the list next to the cash register. "We can keep it right here for easy reference."

"You're still missing some items," Fred said. "I'll jot them down and you can add them later."

"What do you want me to do today?"

"If I'm ever going to get a vacation I still have to teach you how to clean minnow tanks, restock the cooler, re-package worms and stuff like that, but let's wait with that until next week. Since you've got your price list I think it will work best if we do it like yesterday. You run the cash register and I'll be the gopher." Fred chuckled. "You know, go for this and go for that."

Business picked up quickly and a steady stream of customers came through the door. Josh's price list was invaluable.

Mid-morning Fred came to the front of the store carrying a couple of cream sodas. Handing one to Josh, he said, "It's none of my business, but don't you remember anything about what happened to you?" They both pulled out a beer case and took a breather.

"It would make things a whole lot easier if I could. I remember everything since waking up. I get these visions that flash through my mind, but they're just a snipping of this and that. Nothing makes sense. There's a possibility I might have been in a car accident."

"I don't recall any accidents the night you were found."

"That's the mystery. If there was, what happened to the car?" Josh jumped up when Doug came through the front door.

"Hey Doug," Fred said, stacking the case back in place. "Josh and I were just taking a break. It's been real busy and Josh has been doing a bang-up job running the cash register."

Doug looked at Josh and gave no indication of what he was thinking. He turn to Fred, "I just came to get the scrub bucket. I had a bunch of college fraternity boys out for what was supposed to be an all-day fish. They started drinking straight shots of Jack Daniel's at seven this morning. By nine most of them were puking over the railing. Nobody was watching the poles. I got tired of it and brought them in. One snot-nose kid wanted his money back. I told him he'd get it as soon as he cleaned up the boat. They poured him into the car and took off."

Fred ran to the back and returned with the bucket and mop.

Doug finally acknowledged Josh's presence. "I'm happy to hear things are going well," he said. "I have

157

to admit, when Julia asked me to give you a job I was skeptical. As you've probably guessed, I would do almost anything for that girl."

"I appreciate you giving me a chance."

Doug went behind the counter and opened the cash drawer. Grabbing a zippered bank bag from the shelf he took the excess cash from the register and put in the bag. He tossed it to Fred. "Put this on ice." He hesitated when he spied Josh's price list. "What's this?"

"It's a price list," Fred said, before Josh had a chance to answer. "The guy works one day and he comes in this morning with this price list. He made it himself."

Doug studied the list. "Have you checked these prices?"

"He was missing some things, mostly odd stuff that we don't sell a lot of," Fred said. "I'm writing them down for him."

"Is this all we are charging for Johnny Walker Black Label?" Doug asked. "I bought three bottles the other day and I think I paid darn near that much for them."

"I took the price off the one bottle that was left on the shelf," Fred said.

"Hell, that bottle was probably left from when dad ran the place. We've got to check these prices. We are probably losing our shirt on a lot of this stuff." He tossed the price list on the counter and brushed past Josh. "Do you know anything about pricing? You know, percentages and stuff?"

"Maybe, I'm still learning about myself. Last night I found I could type."

"We need to talk about this." Doug grabbed mop and pail, and scooted out the door.

Josh took a deep breath. A warm burst of satisfaction came over him. Numbers and formulas began flowing through his mind. Josh scribbled some test numbers on his paper. Rechecking his calculations, he smiled. "Yep, I

158

know how to do that."

The back door bell rang and Fred went to check on it. He returned a few minutes later and handed Josh a yellow sheet. "Bonanza Beverage just delivered our order. Put this in the box under the register." Josh glanced at the invoice before placing it in the box.

The first moment he didn't have a customer waiting, Josh reached down and took the invoice from the box. He wrote down the cost of each item. Checking his price list and using his test formula, he jotted the percentage of markup on each item. He folded the paper and put it in his pocket.

Josh looked at the clock. Julia would be coming soon. He hadn't given much thought to what he would say to her. He knew it was best if they didn't get too involved, but how long do they wait? What happens if his situation never gets resolved?

A Look Inside the Icehouse

Josh saw Doug's white pickup drive past and pull up next to the icehouse. He hadn't had time to form an opinion of the guy, other than he was pretty straight forward. Julia had made a point to describe them as being just friends, but it was clearly evident the boss man had the sweets for her. Josh couldn't help but wonder if he had come between them.

Josh had been intrigued with the icehouse, since first seeing it from across the bay. Seeing it up close only piqued him more. The front was a massive wall of wood timbers framed by large oak trees on each side. The timbers were weathered and split giving the building a rustic appearance. It looked old, yet timeless.

Doug came storming up from the back. "Grab that box from under the counter," he said, pointing at Josh.

Josh set the box on the counter.

Doug removed the cover and began sifting through the papers. "Here it is, I knew it. I paid six-fifty apiece for those bottles of Black Label." He scanned Josh's price list, "And we're selling it for eight bucks. We're not making squat on them."

"You're making less than twenty percent," Josh said.

"Twenty percent! I know we can't put a high markup on beer, but we should make at least sixty percent on booze. Fred, have we sold any of that Walker Black, yet?"

"No, they're still here."

"Put them in the office until we can figure out what we should charge for them." Doug said, breathing a sigh of relief.

"If you want a sixty percent markup it should sell for close to eleven dollars," Josh said, scribbling on the paper.

"Are you sure? What are you, some kind of math genius?"

"Six dollars and fifty cents multiplied by one point six is ten dollars and forty cents. I just rounded it up to eleven." Josh showed Doug the paper. "I also ran the numbers on the delivery you got today. You're selling everything below forty percent. You're only making twenty-six percent on the vodka."

"That's gaud awful. How quickly can you work your magic on the rest of the liquor?" Doug pleaded. "I want to check pricing on everything."

"All I need are the invoices to see what you've paid for things."

Doug pointed to the bait shop. "I know I do fine with that stuff. I double everything. If it cost me fifty cents I sell it for a dollar. If it cost me a dollar, I sell it for two. Dang it, I wish I would have taken an accounting class in high school." Doug rubbed his chin. "We need to get the right prices on everything. When can we start?"

"Any time I guess." Josh said.

"This box only goes back to February or March," Doug said. If we have to go further back, we'll have to go out to the icehouse."

"It's a beautiful structure," Josh said. "I'd love to see the inside."

"If we need more invoices you'll get your wish. It's junky. I just use it for storage. It made my grandfather a lot of money, but now it's sort of a white elephant."

161

Josh looked at the clock. Julia should be home from the hospital. "Would you mind if I made a phone call?"

"Use the phone in the office." Doug motioned to the back. "Fred, come up here and help me sort out these invoices."

Julia answered on the third ring.

"Hi, how was your day?" he said. There was a hesitation. "How did it go at The Glen?"

"It went alright." She said, lacking emotion. "It's just so different now that you're not there. It's not as much fun."

"How did it go at the hospital?" Josh hoped to get a more cheerful answer.

"It went fine. I guess I'm a little burnt out. I'm really looking forward to the weekend."

"I'm not sure if I'm working this weekend," Josh said. "Right now Doug has me on a project of re-pricing his liquor inventory. I think he wants to get this done today."

"Do you know how to do that?"

"It took a few minutes to come up with the formula, but it's pretty simple. He and Fred are sorting invoices right now to get what he's paying for things. It'll probably take a couple of hours to go over everything." Josh hesitated. "I was hoping we would have a chance to talk. You know, about us."

"Before you say another word, I don't care what happens," Julia blurted. "I love you and will do anything you want. I just want to be with you." Her voice cracked.

Josh was stunned.

"Did you hear me, Josh? I love you."

"Julia, dear sweet Julia, any man would consider himself the luckiest man in the world to have you say that to them, but we face so many unknowns. It would kill me if you were hurt in any way. Can't we just be friends, at least until we know who I am?" Josh heard her crying on the other end of the line.

"I am so mixed up," she sobbed. "First, I think you want me and now you just want to be friends."

"I do want you," he said softly. "More than you know, but it would be too cruel to get involved and then have to give you up." The line went silent. "I really should get back to work. But, please, let's give it more time. If we are meant to be together we'll have a lifetime to make it right."

"Do you want me to give you a ride to Nora's?" Her voice was barely audible.

"No, I don't know how long this is going to take. I'll talk Doug or Fred into giving me a ride. I'll call you tomorrow, okay?" Josh barely heard her weak response. He slowly replaced the receiver and slumped in the chair. His vision of her, the one where she is smiling and laughing changed abruptly to one of her with tears in her eyes, and his heart ached.

Josh sat up when Doug walked into the office. "We've got the invoices all sorted back to March, but we'll need to go to the icehouse for some of the slow moving stuff. C'mon, you said you wanted to see it."

Doug took keys from his pocket, unlocked and pushed open the large sliding doors. The building was deceptively large. The walls rose twenty feet. Just below the ceiling, light flooded in through large openings along all four walls.

It was impossible not to notice all the clutter. Stacks of boxes stood against the wall. Odd lot furniture, shelving of various sizes and discarded cardboard displays were scattered about. Doug hit the light switch and a half-dozen fluorescent fixtures flickered, lighting a number of areas around the room. Off to one side, a sleek red sailboat sat on a trailer. Its mast and boom cradled on sawhorses.

"Is this your boat?" Josh walked closer.

"Yes, I have been working on it for the last three months. It has to be ready for the big trophy race on the

163

fourth."

Josh ran his fingers along the bow. "Nice paint job."

"That's the new urethane paint. It gives a really hard smooth finish. I've been so busy with the store and guiding I haven't had time to work on it. I still have to put all the hardware on and get it rigged. Do you sail?"

"I don't know, it's like finding I can type, I won't know about a lot of things until I try them."

"Well, maybe we can give it a try some day." Doug grabbed a box from one of the stacks.

"That would be great." Josh walked to the center of the building. "I really like this building. It has so much character. I'm surprised you haven't found a good use for it."

Doug set the box on the floor. "I've had people interested in it. The guys at the marina pester me to let them use it for boat storage, but they don't want to pay diddly. A guy from Middletown wanted to put a box factory in here, but when he found out how much it would cost to bring in three phase electricity to run his machines, plus the sewer and water, he backed off real quick. He told me his startup cost would be over thirty grand. That's been the big drawback. No matter what you would want to put in here it's going to cost a pretty penny to bring in utilities and get it to pass a commercial inspection."

"How big is it?" Josh asked. "What's the square footage?"

"It's eighty wide, one twenty long and twenty feet high." Doug continued his verbal tour. "It's always cool in here. Those openings around the ceiling let the warm air rise and go out. In its ice storage days those openings let the moisture escape from the melting ice. I had to put screens up there to keep the birds and squirrels out."

Josh looked to the lighted area across from the boat. Dozens of large framed photographs hung on the wall.

Many of them were of men in all sorts of dated clothing standing by the icehouse. "I love these old photos. These must be from when they harvested the ice."

"Grandpa was a camera nut. He took pictures of everything—did his own enlarging, too. There are boxes and boxes of his old photographs in the attic above the store. He took pictures of everything and everyone. I think he took the only known photo of Chief Hightower in full Indian garb. There's also some of Snowball, the chief's daughter, when she was about fifteen. Hightower was chief of the Winnebago's. They inhabited this area before the white man showed up. The chief died in thirty-nine trying to swim across the Fox River. Some say he was drunk. Not a smart thing to do, for a man in his eighties."

"These photos are great. Your grandfather must have had a good camera. They are so sharp and clear."

"He also took 8mm movies of every big event that happened in this town from 1946 until just before he died."

"I'd love to see more of his photos."

"Yeah, but right now we better get back in the shop and get this pricing business taken care of."

165

A New Set of Wheels

Walking to the door Josh caught sight of what appeared to be a bicycle partially hidden by a cardboard beer sign. He pushed the sign aside, grabbed the seat and stood it up. The tires were flat, but it appeared to be in working order.

"That's the bike from my carefree youth, Doug said. "I rode that thing over just about every inch of ground in this town. It's a Schwinn. Best bike ever made."

Josh brushed the dust off the seat and handlebars. "Any chance I could borrow it? I could get around pretty good if you'd let me."

Josh felt uneasy when Doug didn't answer right away.

"Of course you can," Doug finally said. "Bring it over by the compressor. I hope the tires will still hold air." He flipped the compressor switch. "It'll take a few minutes to build pressure. Sorry for hesitating. I'm a little sentimental about that bike. I don't know if anyone else has ever ridden her."

"I'll be careful."

Doug gave each tire a shot of air, gripping the tire to make sure he didn't over fill them. Satisfied, he handed the bike to Josh. "Just keep her under forty."

"I can't thank you enough," Josh said, with a huge smile on his face. "Now I won't have to bother Nora or

166

Julia to give me a ride everywhere." Josh wheeled the bike out the door.

"Are you sure you know how to ride a bike?" Doug's voice cracked and his eyebrows curled into a worried look.

"If I can type, I'm sure I can ride a bike."

"I sure hope so."

Josh wheeled the bike behind the store just as Fred walked out the back door. "The front is locked. I left the lights on," Fred said. "I've got a hot date with a barstool at Teddy's. I'll see you guys tomorrow."

"Thanks," Doug said. "Hopefully we will have this pricing business figured out by then."

Josh added his good night as Fred jumped in his truck.

Doug laughed. "Fred sells booze and beer all day long and then to relax he goes and sits on a barstool and drinks the stuff. To each his own I guess."

Doug set the box on the counter, grabbed a handful of papers and began sorting invoices.

Josh took an invoice and determined the selling price on each item listed. He wrote the new price next to the current price on his list. It was soon apparent the current prices were well below Doug's desired markup. "Have you ever thought about moving the liquor store over to the icehouse?" Josh asked. "You'd have a lot more room over there. You could expand the business by selling things like caps, T-shirts, and souvenirs. What about offering more fishing items, like rods, reels, tackle boxes, life preservers — stuff like that?"

"What a fantastic idea," Doug said, with mocked excitement. "Now all we need to find is a guy with an extra thirty thousand who wants to be in the liquor store business. Seriously, I couldn't afford to do anything like that." Doug shook his head as he looked over the prices on Josh's sheet. "This should have been done a long time ago. Some of these prices have to be from when dad ran

167

the store." Doug rubbed his chin. "I can't raise everything to these prices. People, especially the locals, would have a conniption fit."

"Raise the ones that are really off, then once a week or so change a few more," Josh offered. "The beer prices aren't too bad. Leave them be for now. You can always take them up a nickel or a dime at a time and most people would never notice."

"The hell you say. I raised night crawlers ten cents a dozen at the beginning of summer and you would have thought the world was coming to an end. You can't get anything past these locals. They'll squeeze a penny until Abe squeals." Doug tossed the price list on the counter. "I sure wish you would have come along a couple of years ago."

"I got here as quick as I could."

Doug did a double take. "That's a good one. It's one thing with the locals, but I sure wish I could have been charging the Lakeshore crowd these higher prices for the last couple of years. It wouldn't hurt them a bit, but it would have made a big difference in the business." Doug turned off the lights. "That's enough of this for tonight. It's eight o'clock. Let's get our butts out of here."

Outside, Doug watched Josh throw his leg over the bar and sit on the bike. "Geez, it just dawned on me. You don't have a social security card, do you?"

It took a moment for that to register with Josh.

"How am I gonna pay you?" Doug hesitated. "Do you have to be someplace?"

"Not really. I talked to Julia earlier. She was going to bed. I can come and go at Nora's. What did you have in mind?"

"Jim Farley will probably be at Teddy's. He's an attorney. Not the courtroom kind, he does wills, land deals, and stuff like that, but he's a walking law encyclopedia.

168

He's always quoting from some off the wall ruling in a far-fetched case. He would be the guy to talk to about getting you a name and a social security number. Should we see if we can find him?"

"We could try," Josh said.

"Do you know your way to Teddy's from here, or do you want to throw the bike in the back of the truck?"

"I'm anxious to give the bike a whirl." Josh gave himself a push forward and began pedaling. The first few yards were a little shaky, but he steadied himself and soon was pedaling up the street.

What's in A Name?

Doug waited in front of Teddy's for Josh to ride up. Josh came cruising, with a smile on his face. He jumped off and leaned the bike against the side of the building.

"That was a blast. Thanks again for letting me borrow it." Josh turned. "Will it be alright here?"

"Yeah, no one will bother it." Doug led Josh into the tavern. "Has Jim Farley been in tonight?"

The bartender pointed. "He's in the back eating."

Doug walked up to a middle-aged man sitting at a table by the window. "Jim, how's it going?" By the man's expression, it was apparent he didn't recognize Doug.

"It's Doug Foster. I got a question for you."

Jim set down his fork, folded his napkin and placed it beside his plate. "Hypothetical or actual?" he asked poking his glasses up on his nose.

"What do you mean?" Doug asked.

"If it's hypothetical, we can just chat. If it's an actual question that requires a legal opinion, I will have to put you on the clock."

"It's hypothetical. Let say, a guy is in a coma. He wakes up, but doesn't remember anything. He's using the name Josh but that's it. How would he get a last name and a social security card so he could get a job and get paid?"

Jim took off his glasses, set them on the table, and

motioned the men to sit. "At the end of the civil war you had a similar situation. Almost all the slaves that were set free only had a first name. It was the name given to them by the plantation owners. Most couldn't read or write, but in order to own property, or to be placed on the census rolls, they had to have a surname."

Doug looked at Josh and raised an eyebrow. Josh caught Doug's meaning, this was going to take some time.

Jim adjusted himself in his chair and looked at Josh. "I'm assuming this is the young man that was in a coma. Am I correct?"

Josh nodded.

"Okay then, where was I? Oh yes, a lot of the slaves took the name of their master or the name of the plantation they came from." Jim hesitated. "Do you know why?"

The guys shook their heads.

"Many didn't really believe they were being set free and if they were going to be enslaved again, they wanted people to know what plantation they came from. Some took a name representing an occupation or skill they had, like Smith for blacksmith or Carpenter. Others took well-known names like Washington, Jefferson and Lincoln. It took a few generations for some to fully establish a family name."

"It'll take that long?" Doug asked. "What's he supposed to do in the meantime?" Josh slouched in his chair.

"That was the 1860's," Jim said. "In the modern legal system, changing a name, or in the case of your young friend, coming up with a new name is relatively easy, and thereby making it possible to apply for a social security card."

"How easy?" Doug asked.

"First, you fill out a request a name change form. There are always forms to fill out. You pay a small filing fee, go before the circuit judge and with the bang of his gavel, you have a new name. It also has to be published three times in the local paper before its official."

"What if I do this and then remember my real name?" Josh asked.

"Simple," Jim said putting his glasses on and picking up his fork. "You fill out the same form and request your name to be changed to your new name, which in your case will be your old name." Jim pointed his fork at Josh. "You'll have to pay another filing fee, there's always a fee." Jim stabbed his fork into his mashed potatoes. "If you'd like some help with the form, stop by the office anytime."

"Thanks, he will be in to see you after the fourth." Doug pushed Josh towards the bar. "Want a beer to celebrate?" They took turns patting each other on the back. Doug grabbed the first available stool and ordered a couple of draft beers. Josh sat next to him.

"What are you guys up to?" Fred said, dragging a stool to be near them.

"Jim Farley just told us how Josh can get a last name and social security card." Doug lifted his glass. "What say we drink to that?" All three raised their glasses and took a drink.

"Have you thought of a name yet?" Fred asked.

"Don't have a clue." Josh said. "It's a big decision. I'll probably take my time and hope I remember who I am before it becomes necessary to go through with it."

"We can keep track of your hours for now," Doug offered. "But sooner or later, you are going to need some kind of identification. If I were you, I'd start thinking of a name." Doug ran his finger across the name printed on his beer glass. "How about Josh Blatz?"

Josh smiled and shook his head. "I know you're trying to be helpful, but seriously, this is going to take some thought." Josh swallowed the last of his beer.

"Have another?" Doug asked.

"Thanks, but I'm on a bicycle, remember?"

"Right, no more for you," Doug said. "Remember what I said, keep her under forty." Josh pushed the air as Doug and Fred broke in laughter.

"I'll see you guys tomorrow," Josh said walking to the door.

"Thanks for your help tonight," Doug yelled.

Josh backed the bike away from the building. Putting a foot on the pedal, he gave a small push and threw his leg over the seat. He pedaled up the street breathing in the cool night air. His spirit soared with the satisfaction of knowing he could ride a bike.

The black sky was alive with twinkling stars. He wondered if he should have handled things differently with Julia. She was ready to give herself to him. He was the one who suggested they not get physically involved until they knew more about his past. The prospects of her being hurt seemed high no matter what avenue they chose.

The porch light was on at Nora's. He carried the bike onto the porch, took the key from under the geranium plant, and let himself in. The stove light cast a soft glow in the kitchen. On the counter a note from Nora said there was food in the refrigerator. She also questioned if he had patched things up with Julia and if he needed a ride in the morning. Be ready by seven thirty, she wrote. He turned off the light and headed upstairs.

Nora was in the kitchen looking at the newspaper munching on a piece of toast when Josh walked in.

"Good Morning, Sunshine," she said. Opening the refrigerator, she brought out a glass of orange juice and set it in front of him. "I made coffee, would you like some?"

"I'd love a cup."

"How about an egg?" Nora poured his coffee.

"Just a couple pieces of toast will be fine." Josh took a

173

sip of coffee and gave a satisfying hum.

Nora buttered the toast, and pushed the honey and jelly in his direction.

"You're spoiling me, waiting on me like this," Josh said.

"I used to wait on Duke every morning, I miss that." Nora placed her dish in the sink. "Did you get things straightened out with Julia?"

"We talked on the phone. I might have made things worse. I'm going over to her place this morning to smooth things out."

"Don't you be a stinker. That girl has it bad for you and if you hurt her I'll...I'll bop you on the head."

"I'm trying my best not to hurt her, but she could be hurt no matter what we do."

"I agree, but sometimes you have to go with your heart, not your head." Nora tossed her apron over her chair. "I'm sure you two will find a way to work things out."

"I hope so." Josh put the last bite of toast in his mouth and put his dish in the sink.

"Do you want me to drop you off by Julia's place?"

"That won't be necessary, I've got my own wheels," Josh announced proudly.

"Wheels? What kind of wheels?"

"Doug let me borrow his bike, it's been sitting in the icehouse. I rode it home last night. It's out on the front porch."

"You're full of surprises, aren't you?"

"Don't say anything to Julia. I want to surprise her. I'm going over there to wait for her to come home."

Josh carried the bike off the porch and hopped on. The morning air was fresh and he took a deep breath. He felt empowered and welcomed the burst of adrenalin from the exercise. Riding up to Julia's back door, he put the kickstand down and took a seat on the porch step. It wasn't long before Julia's car came driving up the street. She parked in her normal spot and turned off the engine, but made no move to get out.

He stood, opened his arms, and smiled. "Welcome home."

"Don't tell me you rode over here on that bicycle." she said, sliding out of the car.

"I did," he said proudly. "It's Doug's. He let me borrow it."

Julia hesitated, then ran, throwing her arms around him. "I'm sorry," she said, looking sad.

Josh put his finger on her lips. "Don't. You have nothing to be sorry for. We are caught in a crazy situation and have to find our way through it. Let's enjoy the time we have together and if things happen, they happen."

She nestled her head on his chest. "Oh, Josh, I had a terrible night at work. I was so worried you were upset with me."

"I could never be upset with you," he said softly. "Listen, I really should get to the liquor store, but I have so much to tell you. Can we get together for lunch? Maybe we could meet somewhere?"

"I'll make some sandwiches. We can picnic in the park by the band shell." A feeling of excitement made her giggle with delight.

"I'll meet you there at noon." Josh planted a quick kiss on her cheek.

Julia grabbed him by the shirt collar and pulled him back. "You think you can get away with just a peck on the cheek?" She kissed him hard, then laughed.

A Picnic in the Park

Josh rode around to the back of the liquor store and leaned the bike against the building.

"I was wondering if you were coming in," Fred said. "I thought maybe you ran into a ditch somewhere."

"I had some personal business to take care of. Is Doug here?"

"He drove to the office supply store in Middletown to get one of those guns that spits out the little price labels. We have to put a price sticker on each bottle. Doug figures people will be less apt to notice a price change that way."

"I need to ask him if I can take a long lunch today."

"He should be back by then. I think he was planning on putting the finishing touches on the boat. You know tomorrow is the big race."

"It's a nice looking boat."

"It looks good, but its wood. I'm afraid he might have a hard time keeping up with the newer fiberglass boats."

"Sometimes, it's enough just to be out there competing," Josh said. "Enjoying a day of sailing."

"We're talking about Doug. He wants to beat the pants off those Lakeshore guys and will be very disappointed if he doesn't."

"Want me to run the register again?" Josh asked on his way to the front of the store.

176

"It's worked for two days. I don't see any reason to change things now."

Josh kept checking the clock. He didn't want to be late for his date with Julia, but he didn't want to run out and leave Fred alone in the store. Doug came through the door a few minutes before noon.

Josh spoke up. "Would it be alright if I took a long lunch?"

Doug shot him a puzzled look. "What's up? You got a hot date or something?"

"As a matter of fact I do...with Julia. We're meeting in the park." Doug's hesitation made Josh wonder.

"Sure, just get back as soon as you can. I've got a lot of work on the boat and will have to wait until you come back."

Josh ran to the back of the store, almost knocking Fred over on the way. He grabbed the bike and took off running before leaping on.

Julia was waiting by a picnic table near the water. Josh leaned the bike against the table. "Been waiting long?"

"Just got here." Julia opened a sack and laid out the things she brought for the picnic. "So what is all the good news you're wanting to tell me?"

"Doug and I talked to Jim Farley at Teddy's last night. He's an attorney. According to Jim, it's easy to legally change your name, or in my case get a name."

"You can just pick any name?"

"Yes, and I'll have to come up with a birth date, too."

"So, how old are you?" Julia asked playfully.

"Do you want me to be older than you or younger? Some women like younger men."

"Don't be silly. I don't want people thinking I robbed the cradle. I was born in forty. You need to be born in 1938 or maybe even thirty-seven."

Josh scratched his chin. "What day did I come out of

177

the coma?"

Julia had to think for a moment. "June twenty fifth."

"I guess I can also use The Glen as my birth place. June 25, 1938. Pine Lake, Wisconsin."

"What about Glen?" Julia asked. "What about using Glen as your last name? You could add a second "n" and spell it G-l-e-n-n. Josh Glenn."

Josh mouthed the words. "Josh Glenn. I like it. Will you go with me to fill out the paperwork?"

"Sure, but what happens if you go through all this and then remember who you are?"

"You go back into court and change your name back to your real one. It's probably not the best situation, but it will allow me to do things like get a driver's license, a social security card, and open up a checking account."

She assumed he would also need that information to get a marriage license. She pictured the words, Julia Glenn. She liked the thought. "Speaking of your real name, have you remembered anything more about the car, the accident, or Mary?"

"No, but I did find out a few things about myself."

"Like what?"

"I can type. I can ride a bike, and I think I'm pretty good with numbers," Josh said, taking a bite of his sandwich. "I'm learning more about myself every day."

"I have a feeling that one of these things will trigger something about your past."

"That would really be something." He finished his sandwich. "I should get back to work. Doug's waiting. He wants to work on the boat."

"Are you going to be late? Will I see you later?"

"I'm not sure."

"That's okay, just come over when you are done. I'll wait for you."

He leaned over and gave her a quick peck on the cheek.

178

"Is that all I get for fixing you this nice picnic lunch?" she pouted.

"I'll make it up to you later." He gave the bike a push and hopped on.

"You'd better!" She watched as he glided down the street. He turned once to give her a final wave.

The store was crowded with people when Josh got back. Fred was at the cash register. "Am I glad to see you! Take over here and I'll check on those people in the bait room."

"Where's Doug?"

"He couldn't wait. He's in the icehouse working on his boat."

Josh and Fred ran their tails off taking care of the crush of people who were stocking up for the big holiday weekend. At five, when for some odd reason there were no customers in the store, Doug strolled up to the front counter. "Things been slow this afternoon?"

Josh looked at Fred. "He's kidding, right? This is the first break we've had in three hours. It's been a zoo in here."

"Well, I've got a hell of a mess in the icehouse too," Doug said. "I'm having a hard time rounding up the hardware and rigging for the boat. When we had all that rain in the spring the icehouse flooded and we had to re-box everything. Now it's all mixed up. I have to open every box. It's going to take hours. If I don't stay with it, I'll never be ready for the race tomorrow. I know I'm supposed to take over the store now, but will you guys cover for me? Fred? Josh?"

Josh nodded. Fred nodded too, but not before letting Doug know that he was normally off on Friday nights and this was going to be a big sacrifice. Fred was still grumbling as he walked back to the cooler.

"Just keep it open until eight," Doug said, as he turned to leave.

The evening dragged on with just a smattering of customers. It was barely past seven forty five when Fred came to the front. "Everyone's celebrating the holiday already. We're getting out of here before we get any last minute drunks in here. He turned the lock on the door and snapped off the open sign. "I'm at least two beers behind at Teddy's."

The two walked out the back door. "Tell Doug I said good night," Fred yelled, as he jumped into his truck.

"Will do," Josh said walking to the icehouse.

Josh Gives Doug A Hand With the Boat

Doug was sitting in the boat screwing a pulley to the deck. "Will you see if you can find me another piece just like this?" Doug asked, holding up a part.

Josh looked around. "Where would I find it?"

"It's got to be in one of those boxes." Doug pointed to a dozen or so opened boxes.

Josh took the piece and began going through each box. He found what he thought was a match and brought it to Doug.

"No, this is for the same side. I need the opposite piece. The one that goes on the other side of the boat. It would be backwards to this. Actually I need two of them."

Josh went back and searched through several boxes before finding the parts. "The store's locked up, except the back door," Josh said. "And Fred said good night."

"Did you guys take the money out of the register?"

"No, we didn't."

"There are bank bags on the shelf behind the cash register. Would you go in and take out all the big bills, put them in the bag, and put it in the cooler?" Doug said, not taking his eyes off the part he was working on. "The bag goes in the cigar box on the top shelf in the far left corner of the cooler."

181

Josh hesitated, but then went and did as instructed. When he returned he stood by the boat.

"Did you find the cigar box?"

"Yeah, but that's an awful lot of money. Maybe I shouldn't know where you hide it."

"Are you going to steal it?"

"No, of course not."

"Then what's the problem?"

"I guess there isn't any."

"You got somewhere to go?" Doug asked as he flipped the screwdriver around in his hand. "I sure could use some help with this."

"Julia is sort of waiting up for me."

Doug jumped off the boat. "Would you go through those boxes and bring out all the metal pieces that look like they might go on the boat. I'll be right back."

Josh started picking through the boxes. He set each piece he found on the deck, placing matching pieces side by side.

Doug came back with a big smile on his face. "I called in a marker. Julia's coming down. I helped her when she first came to town and I told her I really needed your help. I also told her I would pay for a pizza if she would stop and pick it up from Teddy's."

Doug climbed on the boat and looked at the parts Josh had laid there. "This is great. Have you found any cable?"

"No, but there is one box with a lot of rope in it."

"Good, we'll need that too."

For the next hour Josh went through each box bringing out any parts he thought might go on the boat. "I still haven't found any cable."

"There's got to be cable. They're the stays that hold up the mast," Doug said. "Look in that stack of boxes over there. I thought that was all paperwork, but maybe some of the boat stuff ended up over there."

182

Josh started opening boxes. The first half dozen were filled with paper. The last box from the stack felt different, not as heavy. He opened it, sighed, then yelled to Doug. "Here's the cable."

Doug pulled out the cable and started untangling the strands. "This is a side stay. Put it by the mast." Untangling another strand, he handed it to Josh. "That's the front stay and this last one has to be the other side stay."

Doug hooked the stays to the top of the mast. "I think we should stand this baby up and see what we've got. The bottom of the mast goes on the little knob just ahead of the cockpit."

Josh followed Doug onto the boat and stood on the back deck. Doug positioned the mast on the knob. "Ok, lift her up," he yelled. "Hold it steady." Doug knelt and hooked the side stays to the rails on each side and the front stay to the bow. "Okay, you can let go." Josh released his grip and the mast stood straight and tall.

Doug eyed it up and looked at the front stay. "There are seven adjustment holes. I don't remember what hole we used. I guess we'll just leave it hooked in the center hole until Johnny has a chance to look at it. We can change that tomorrow."

The boys were admiring their handiwork when Julia walked in carrying a pizza box. She went straight to Josh and gave him a quick kiss.

"If you are giving those out, I'll take one." Doug said.

Julia stuck out her tongue and handed him the pizza.

"Well, what do you think?" Doug pointed to the boat. "She's finally coming together."

"Nothing like waiting until the last minute," Julia said.

"Josh, you want to go in and get us a couple of beers?" Doug said. "Julia, what do you want?"

"I'll have a beer, too."

Doug pulled some of the chairs off the stack of odd lot

furniture. Josh returned with the beers. They each took a slice of pizza, clinked their bottles in a toast to the boat, and sat to eat.

Doug handed Julia a crumpled twenty. "Here, this is for the pizza."

"That's way too much," she protested. "It was only six dollars."

"Yeah, but that's also for coming down here and letting Josh stay to help me. I would have been here half the night without his help."

"Is the Kinard kid still going to sail with you?" Julia asked.

"Yeah, I talked to him the day before yesterday. We're meeting by the marina at seven. It will give us a chance to give the boat a little shake down before the race."

"You should have had this boat done weeks ago," Julia scolded. "Then you would have had a chance to practice with him a few times."

"I know, time just got away from me, but she's ready now and we are going out tomorrow to kick some butt." Doug stood. "Anyone want another beer?"

Josh raised his empty bottle.

Julia waved hers. "No more for me."

Doug grabbed the bottles and headed to the store.

"He sure is on an emotional high," Josh said.

"I just hope he won't be too disappointed. He's up against some stiff competition with that Lakeshore bunch." Julia walked over to the tool bench. "Did you see the picture of the girl he's got taped up here? I asked him about it, but he wouldn't say much."

Josh walked over and looked at the photo. "She's pretty."

"Sure, but who is she?"

"I think you've got a little nose problem," Josh teased.

Julia walked away. "Don't be silly. I'm just curious."

Doug handed Josh a beer. "Here's to Julia, the sweetest girl in Pine Lake."

Josh raised his beer and smiled at Julia. "I'll drink to that."

Julia fanned the air. "I'll let you two schoolboys get back to playing boats." Then to Josh, "Are you going to stop by before going back to Nora's?"

"Sure, we should be done here in another hour or so."

Julia puckered her lips and kissed the air in Josh's direction.

"Thanks for coming down." Doug said. They both watched her walk away. "She is a great gal and you're not a bad guy. I just hope your situation doesn't break her heart."

"I'm trying not to let that happen."

Doug took a swallow of beer. "Let's take the mast down and get everything ready to take her out of here in the morning."

"Who's Kinard?"

"He's a Lakeshore kid and a hell of a sailor. A few years ago he beat everybody. He turned twenty-one, made some bad decisions, and got himself in trouble with the law. His folks threw him out. He's been living in a converted machine shed by the river with a couple of other guys. I'm hoping with him on the tiller we have a chance to win this thing tomorrow."

Working in tandem they quickly had the boat secured to the trailer. Doug turned out the lights and Josh pushed the one door closed. Doug closed the other and secured the padlock. Walking to the back entrance of the store Doug gave Josh a pat on the shoulder. "Thanks for helping me. I would've been up the creek without your help. It was a lot more fun having you here."

Josh stood up the bike. "I had a good time, too. Thanks for the beer and pizza."

185

"You got time for one more? I'm keyed up, I need another beer and I hate drinking by myself."

"I told Julia it would probably be about an hour. I guess I could stay for one more."

The neon beer signs cast a colorful glow in the store. "Don't turn on the lights. I don't want people thinking we're open." Doug said as he handed Josh a cold one.

"What are we drinking to now?" Josh asked.

"Let's drink to America. Tomorrow is her birthday. God bless the USA."

"Have I come between you and Julia?" Josh said.

"It's not like that." Doug waved his bottle. "When she came to town I pushed the boyfriend thing, but we never got past being good friends and I'm okay with that. She was dealing with stuff from Florida, and losing mom and dad the way I did left us both with trust issues. I guess I'm a little surprised she's hooked on you."

Josh saw the faraway look in Doug's eyes. "I would think you would have lots of girls chasing after you."

"The store and guide business keeps me busy. I never had time to chase girls in school. I was always working. The few girls I did like teamed up with other guys, mostly jocks." Doug took a long swig of beer. "There was one girl, she was Lakeshore. We met at the county fair. She was from Chicago. We hit it off right away." Doug cleared his throat. "Her name was Peggy. Peggy Floyd."

"What happened to her?"

"Gone," Doug said. "I went out to their place on the lake the next day and they were gone, the whole darned family. I tried to track her down. Apparently her dad had a string of jewelry stores and got caught fencing stolen jewelry. He went to jail and the family just disappeared from the face of the earth."

"And you haven't seen her since?"

"Nope." Doug squinted to hide the tear in the corner of

his eye. "It's been five years, and to this day when I pick up the mail I keep hoping to get a letter from her."

"Is that her picture taped to your workbench?"

"Yep, that's her. It's a school picture. She gave it to me that day at the fair."

"Man, you need to find this girl," Josh said. "If you've been carrying a torch for her for five years she had to be really special."

"She was. We only had that one afternoon. I'd love to find her, but I don't have a clue of where to start looking." Josh felt the anguish in Doug's voice.

"You mentioned your dad and the business. Was this your family business?"

"It's a long story, are you sure you want to hear it? It will take more than this one beer to tell it all."

Josh nodded. "I'll drink slowly."

Doug opened them each another beer. "Growing up I thought I had the ideal life, and then my mother walked out the door and never came back."

"How old were you?"

"Ten, and for the longest time I blamed myself for her leaving. Then when dad started drinking I was afraid he would leave me, too."

Josh put his empty on the floor and took a drink of his fresh one.

"I did everything I could to help in the business. It didn't leave much time for school. I never got to play sports, and I missed my junior prom. It wasn't all bad. I do have some happy memories with my Dad before he got lost in the bottle. When he passed, all of a sudden I had this business to run. I knew how to stock shelves, clean the minnow tank, and take care of customers, but didn't know diddly squat about running a business. I just showed up each day and did my best to keep everything going."

"Are you comfortable with how things are now?"

187

"They're getting better, but it's like this pricing thing." Doug's tone became more assertive, less reflective. "I need to get on top of things, not just assume everything is alright."

"I can write out the formulas. It will help you price any product or service you have." Josh chugged his beer. "I should get my buns out of here. I told Julia I would stop by."

"I'm sorry I kept you so long." Doug tossed his empty in the trash.

Plans For the Fourth

Julia's house was dark. Josh put down the kickstand and walked around to the bedroom window. The curtains fluttered in the breeze. "Julia," he whispered. "Julia, are you awake?"

Julia's face appeared in the darkened window. "What the dickens are you doing out there? You want someone to think you're a peeping Tom? What happened to you? I got tired of waiting and went to bed."

"Sorry. Doug and I sort of…got carried away."

"I'm in my pajamas. Come back tomorrow. Wait, I was thinking we could go to the Middletown flea market in the morning, and maybe a swim in the afternoon. You don't have to work, do you?"

"No, we can spend the whole day together."

"That'll be wonderful. Now get out of here before someone calls the cops."

Josh woke with a dry mouth and a sharp pain above his right eye. Nora was about to leave the house when he stumbled down the stairs.

"You're early today," he said.

"George, our Alzheimer patient, passed away early this morning. The coroner will be there and I'll have a mountain of paperwork. You got plans for today?"

189

"Julia and I are spending the day together. I think she has it all planned out."

"That's great, you guys have fun. There's some sweet rolls on the counter. I've got to run."

The coffee pot was still hot. Josh poured a cup and grabbed a roll on his way upstairs.

The Fourth of July celebration was always the big social happening of the summer. This year's schedule kicked off with sailboat races beginning at nine in the morning. Each boat class had a designated start time with competitions ending in the early afternoon.

Traditionally, many of the yacht club members hosted twilight cocktail parties. These were lavish affairs featuring live music and a big spread of hors d'oeuvres. The club president usually went overboard and added iced shrimp, caviar and other pricey delicacies. And of course, the liquor flowed freely. It was rich people trying to impress other rich people. Seldom would anyone from town receive an invitation to one of these fancy shindigs.

The celebration would wind up with a big dance at the Country Club. The club had booked a seven-piece dance band, but if things went according to past years, by the time eight o'clock rolled around a lot of the Lakeshore crowd would be too drunk to stand, much less dance. So, for the townspeople, the dance was the highlight of their holiday celebration. Along with the music and dancing people would be treated to a terrific fireworks show, all compliments of the Pine Lake Yacht Club.

The snipe is the smallest sailing class to race on the lake. It's a two-man boat with a skipper on the tiller and mainsail, and crew of one to pull jib and add ballast. Doug's snipe wasn't a bad boat. In fact, prior to people switching to the lighter fiberglass boats, it had been one of the fastest on the lake.

190

Doug didn't sleep well. He raced all night in his dreams. He also made a couple of bathroom runs because of all the beer he and Josh drank. At six o'clock, he gave up and got out of bed. Throwing on shorts and t-shirt he stumbled down the stairs.

Sliding the doors back on the icehouse, he stood looking at the bright red boat. She looked fast just sitting on the trailer. Once the hitch was secure, the safety chains hooked, he checked to make sure the trailer lights worked. He slowly brought the boat out into the sunlight. His fingertips tingled with excitement as he shut and locked the icehouse doors.

Doug had openly admitted his lack of sailing experience hurt him last year. He took a lot of ribbing about his last place finishes. Undaunted, he was determined to do better this year.

The boat looked unbelievably beautiful. The urethane paint created a hard, smooth finish that rivaled the finish on the fiberglass boats. Doug hoped that translated into more speed. He was also counting on Johnny Kinard to make a difference.

On the way to the marina he stopped at the bakery to pick up a donut and a cup of coffee. He was happy to see there were only three boats in line waiting to launch. "This is great, we will be out on the water in no time." He checked his watch. "Johnny should be here at any minute."

July fourth was easily the craziest day on Pine Lake. If the weather was good the old-timers exaggerated by saying there were so many boats on the lake, a person could literally walk across the lake, stepping from one boat to another.

Doug gave his watch another glance. It was five minutes to seven. He was about to take a swig of coffee when a young man came up to the truck.

191

"Are you Doug?"

"Yeah, what's up?" Doug looked past the boy to see if anyone was with him.

"Johnny won't be here," the fellow said. "He's in jail."

"What!" Doug jumped out of the truck. "What the hell did he do?"

The boy took a step back. "He was arrested for selling marijuana."

"Shit! Now what am I going to do?" Doug shouted. He banged his fist on the hood of the truck. "Is this some kind of joke?"

The boy took another step backwards and shook his head.

"What's the matter with that stupid ass? You Lakeshore kids grow up with everything, money, girls, cars, and then go around selling weed like some ghetto punks." Doug threw up his hands in disgust. The kid must have figured it was time to leave and took off running.

Doug jumped in the truck, threw the shift lever in drive and sped off with the tires squealing. The boat and trailer bounced behind him.

Julia sat at the table sipping coffee. Although she was up early, she was still in her pajamas and robe. She hadn't taken the time to brush her teeth or comb her hair. Her interest at the moment was scanning the sales ads in the newspaper. Maybe after they were done at the flea market there would be time to do a little shopping before heading out to the lake.

She heard a knock and turned to see Josh through the screen door. He came in before she could make a mad dash to the bedroom. She quickly tightened the robe around herself.

Josh threw his swimming suit on the counter and poured himself a cup of coffee. "Have you done something

192

different with your hair?" He asked as he leaned over and kissed the top of her head.

"Don't be a smarty pants. I wasn't expecting you to get here this early. Are we still going to Middletown?"

"Sure, it should be fun."

"What were you thinking last night? You're lucky no one saw you prowling around. You could have gotten yourself arrested."

Josh laughed. "You said you'd wait up for me. I had to make sure you were alright."

"That's a lot of bull. I think you and Doug had a few extra beers."

Josh didn't respond. The TV was on in the living room so he walked in and sat down. Ole Crooked Nose was forecasting a nice day, but said things could change rather abruptly. A low-pressure system could roll through and cool things down around noon. This would also bring a shift in the wind from the southwest to straight west.

"You might want to bring a sweater or sweatshirt when we go to the lake," he called to Julia. "It could cool off a bit around lunchtime."

"Thanks," Julia acknowledged without taking her head out of the newspaper. Emptying her cup, she got up for a refill. She had barely returned to her chair when Doug came busting through the door. It scared Julia and she nearly fell backwards off the chair. Her flailing arm knocked over the cup, spilling coffee on the paper.

"Holy Bajeebas!" Julia jumped to her feet. "Doug, you don't just come barging into a person's house that way." She grabbed a washcloth from the sink and wiped up the mess. "Don't you believe in knocking?"

"I'm sorry, but I need your help." Doug said between breaths.

"Help with what?"

"You have to come and sail with me. Kinard got himself

193

thrown in jail."

"Are you out of your mind?" Julia threw the soiled cloth in the sink. "I don't know a darn thing about sailing."

"It'll be okay, I can tell you what to do. I just need another person in the boat."

"When?"

"Right now," Doug shot back. "I've told everyone that I would be sailing today. If I'm not out there it will be embarrassing as hell."

"Look at me, I'm in my pajamas and my hair is a fright. I can't go out there looking like this."

Josh heard the commotion and walked into the kitchen. "What's going on?"

Doug showed his surprised to see Josh and looked at Julia.

She understood the look and quickly explained. "It's not what you think. He got here five minutes before you did." Turning to Josh, "Doug's sailor boy got thrown in the slammer and now he wants me to sail with him today." Julia was about to laugh at the sheer thought of it.

"Sounds like fun," Josh said. "Are you going to do it?

"He wants to go right now. Look what I look like," she said grabbing a few stands of her hair.

"It's a boat race," Doug blurted, "not a beauty contest."

"Well, I'm not going looking like this." She pointed at Josh, "Why don't you take him?"

"Wanna go?" Doug asked.

"Why not? It sounds like fun." Josh quickly turned to Julia. "Is that alright with you?"

"That's great, go." Julia's saw her plans for the day go down the drain. "You guys go have fun. Win the big race."

It Looked Like
an Old Keystone Cops Movie

Josh grabbed his bathing suit off the counter, and the two of them went out the door running and jumping like two young kids leaving school for summer vacation.

Doug put the pedal to the metal and sped off towards the marina. "Don't worry, I'll tell you what to do," he said. "Right now I don't care what happens, I just want to be out there. He pounded his fist on the dashboard and shouted to some people standing on the sidewalk. "WE'RE GOING TO BE IN THE BIG RACE!" Doug threw Josh's bathing suit at him. "You might want to put this on. You're probably going to get a little wet today."

Josh kicked off his shoes and unbuckled his belt. Looking around to see if anyone was watching, he slid off his pants and underwear and pulled on his swim trunks.

"Leave your shoes off. You can be in the water to grab the boat as it comes off the trailer." Approaching the marina, Doug yelled, "we caught a break, there are only three boats ahead of us." Doug pulled in line and nervously tapped his fingers on the steering wheel. "I've been dreaming about this for a whole year. He punched Josh on the shoulder. "You might get your face on Television, I heard Channel Three is coming down."

Even with just three boats, it still took an excruciatingly

long time for each boater to clear the ramp. Doug kept looking at his watch. "C'mon, c'mon." He pounded on the steering wheel. "Move it, move it." Checking his watch again, "we're going to have a hard time getting out there on time."

The ramp finally cleared. Doug wheeled the truck around and backed up. Josh went into the water, steadied the boat as it came off the trailer and held it to the pier. Doug parked the truck and came running back carrying the sail bag. Tossing the bag in the boat he grabbed the front rope and threw a couple half hitches around the post to secure the boat to the pier. "We have to work fast, jump up on the rear deck and start lifting the mast."

Josh came up quickly, and so did the mast. The boys repeated the way they raised it last night with Josh holding it steady while Doug fastened the stays. Doug pulled the sails from the bag and they both started inserting the wood battens. Doug fastened the jib to the front stem and hooked the clasps to the front stay. Attaching the halyard he hoisted the jib. Picking up the main sail he ran the bottom down the rail of the boom and tied it off. Feeding the leading edge into the grooved mast, he commanded Josh to hook the halyard and pull it up. The sails flapped in the breeze. Doug threw a line to Josh. "Here, attach this to the bottom of the jib." Doug untangled another line and fed it through the pulleys on the boom to secure the main sail. In a continued motion he reached forward and dropped the centerboard. Sitting next to the tiller, he began drawing in the main sail. "I guess we're ready. Untie us and give us a push away from the pier."

Josh was quick and nimble as he pushed the boat away. Jumping onboard, he took a seat forward in the cockpit.

Doug steered to open water. "Grab that line on the bottom of the jib. Put it through that pulley. Yes…that one on the left, and pull it tight. That's it…great. Slack off

196

just a bit...good...that's good." Doug trimmed the main. The boat immediately moved forward, gliding smoothly through the water.

The area in front of the marina was like a scene from an old-time Keystone Cops movie. Powerboats were going in every direction. Doug tried his best to navigate out of the congestion.

"Buoy!" Josh shouted.

"Where?"

"On your left. Ease off downwind and you should clear it."

Doug eased the bow right and watched the buoy pass less than a foot away. The speedboats continued to churn up the water and bounce the red boat around. "We've got forty minutes to race time. Unless these dodos give us a break we won't even be out of the bay by then."

"Why don't you get out of the channel? Sail to the far shore over there."

"Can't, it's too weedy, we'll get hung up."

Josh secured the jib line in a cleat and grabbed the centerboard. He lifted it so just a very small portion was left beneath the boat.

"Don't do that. Without a centerboard we'll just slide sideways."

"There's enough board to keep us straight. It'll get us past the weeds," Josh said. "Once we're over there we'll have the wind in our back and can run downwind until we get out on the lake."

Doug was surprised when it went just as Josh said. Reaching the far shore, Doug pushed the tiller hard and came about. Josh pulled the gaffe pole from inside the boat, hooked it to the bottom of the jib, and pushed the sail out to the left. He told Doug to push the boom out to the right. The wind quickly filled both sails and they headed straight out to the lake.

197

Josh pulled the centerboard completely up and sat on the rear deck across from Doug. "Don't need a centerboard now. We'll just skim across the water as fast as the wind takes us."

"I thought you said you've never sailed before," Doug said, surprised by what he had just witnessed.

"I feel right at home. Maybe it's like riding a bike, some things you never forget."

Trouble Ahead

The snipes gathered around the starting line. The games to outmaneuver one another had already begun. Each boat tried to force the other to yield the right of way for a better position at the start. As Doug joined the group, the trash talk began coming his way. Slurs like slowpoke, loser, and townie came in rapid succession.

"I see your fan club was able to make it," Josh said loud enough for the nearby boats to hear.

"Don't egg them on," Doug pleaded. "This is probably going to be brutal enough."

"Yield!" A boat came barreling at them from starboard. Doug pushed the tiller, turning to port, as the two boats narrowly missed colliding.

"I'm getting out of here," Doug said. "I'll let these assholes fight it out to see who gets off the line first. We'll circle around and try to time it so we are hard on the wind when the gun goes off. We may not be in the first group off the starting line, but we should be charging up their butts when the gun sounds."

Josh studied the mast. "I don't think we have enough rake, the mast is too upright. It should be leaning back more. We'd get more forward push if we move that front stay to the back adjustment hole."

"Remember, I just guessed at using the center hole. We

can't do anything about it now."

"How much time do we have?" Josh asked.

"The two minute warning should go off at any time. I hope you're not thinking about dropping…we could lose the whole danged thing in the water and be in a hell of a mess."

"We can do this. Even if we lose a little time now, the extra push should help us in the long run."

Doug fidgeted. "If we lose the thing our day is over."

"Just point the boat into the wind. I'll drop the main and you grab the mast. If we leave the jib up it will help to pull the mast forward and give me enough slack so I can loosen the pin and move it to the back hole. The mast may get heavy, but you will have to push it forward until I can change the pin."

"Do you really think it will make that much difference?" Doug said, wiping the sweat from his forehead.

"Maybe the difference between winning and losing," Josh said.

The look on Doug's face signaled he was unsure of making the move.

"It's your call, Captain."

The judge's cannon fired the two minute warning.

Doug looked at Josh and then at the other boats. "Oh hell, this is nuts, but let's do it."

Josh loosened the halyard and pulled down the main sail.

"I hope you're right," Doug said. "If we drop the mast in the water we're screwed."

When the sail came down the cat calls began anew. "Got a problem over there, Dougie-boy? Maybe it's time to pull the plug and let her sink."

"Don't listen to them. We can do this," Josh said in a confident tone. "Grab the mast and push it forward."

As soon as Doug had the mast firmly in his grip, Josh

dove on his belly and unfastened the front pin. "Push it forward. I need more slack."

Doug pushed with all his might. "You better get that thing secured. I don't know how much longer I can hold it."

"Okay, I got the pin out. Now, hold it until I get it in the back hole."

Doug could feel his strength draining. "Hurry up, I'm losing it."

"Got it!" Josh yelled. "We're good. Let go and hoist the main."

"Holy crap. We did it," Doug yelled. He grabbed the halyard and pulled as fast as he could. The main went up and he quickly fastened the halyard to the mast. Josh jumped in the cockpit and set the jib. Doug reeled in the main. The sail ballooned out and the boat literally jumped forward.

"Prepare to come about," Doug yelled, as he pushed on the tiller. Josh responded by bringing the jib to the opposite side. Doug looked at the judges boat and then at his watch. "This is going to be close. We're about fifty yards from the starting line and the gun should go off at any time." No sooner had the words left his mouth when a puff of smoke blew from the bow of the judge's boat. The delayed report of the cannon shot followed.

"That's it," Doug said. "We got a lot of ground to make up."

"We'll do it," Josh said. "Hold it right there." The sleek red boat cut sharply through the water as the wood creaked and groaned under the stress of the wind. Doug let out a whoop as they crossed the starting line. Two boats circled the buoy. "They must have jumped the gun and have to restart. Look at that," Doug squealed. "We're already ahead of two boats."

"Watch your telltales," Josh yelled.

201

"What?"

"The telltales. Those little strings on the sail. They tell you how the wind is coming off the sail. See, they're drooping. Bring her into the wind just a little bit more." The mast bent and creaked as the boat accelerated. "You want them to flow straight to the back of the boat."

"I never knew what they were for," Doug admitted. "I don't know if you know what the hell you are doing or just acting on instinct, but keep it up." Doug leaned out, grabbed a handful of water and splashed it on his face. His heart was beating a hundred miles an hour. "I thought for sure we were going to drop the mast in the water, but look at us now." He leaned out and looked ahead. "We're on a better line than those next two boats. I think we're gaining on them."

Josh looked at the buoy off in the distance. "I think the way the boat is handling the wind we should come about before they do, and stay on the windward side of them. If we can get close enough we can steal their wind and beat them to the buoy."

"When should we do it?" Doug asked.

"Right now." The boys moved in harmony and made a fast turn.

"Look," Doug said. "One of them is coming about too. I think he knows what we're up to."

"If you can hold this line I still think we've got him," Josh said pulling the jib in a bit. "Don't worry about the other one. He'll have a lot of water to make up."

Doug kept his eyes on the strings fluttering in the wind. As they approached the buoy things began to tighten. The other boat moved up wind trying to force Doug to break off. "I don't know if we're going to make it," Doug said. "I don't think I can hold this line. We may have to drop behind them."

"Don't, keep it steady." Josh gently worked the jib to

202

get as much out of it as he could. "We just need to get our nose in front of them and we can force them to yield."

The boats were less than ten yards apart and quickly closing in on the buoy. Josh wasn't sure if they were ahead or not but yelled anyway. "Yield! We have the right of way."

"Bullshit," came the reply. The boats were on a collision course unless someone gave way. Doug looked at Josh.

Josh held out his hand. "Keep it steady," he whispered. "Keep it right here." He kept his eyes on the other skipper. The boats were just five feet apart.

"You son-of-bitch." The kid yelled as he broke off and gave way.

Doug rounded the buoy and headed down the next leg. "That's four," he coughed. "We're beating four boats." His mouth was so dry he couldn't spit if he wanted to.

"The next ones might be a little harder to catch." Josh looked at the field in front of them. "We still have seven boats ahead of us. We might have to gamble a bit if we want to make up some ground."

Doug looked back at the other boats as they came around the buoy. "How did you know he wasn't going to just run into us?"

"I didn't. I figured him to be about seventeen and was hoping he would be too scared to go home and have to tell his dad he wrecked the boat."

"Well, you scared the crap out of me."

"Are we out here to win?"

Doug set his jaw. "You bet we are."

"Well, then let's pick off a few more on this leg. Josh looked across the water. "We are too close to shore. It looks like there's better wind farther out." He looked at Doug. "It's a gamble but I think we would do better out there."

"You've been right so far. Let's come about and find some good wind."

They made the turn, and soon Doug felt the wind push hard against the boom. The boat hiked on its side. Doug tightened the main. Those little strings streamed in a straight line to the back of the boat. "We've got wind now!"

Josh kept his eye on the other boats. Five of them stayed their course. Two broke off and mimicked Doug. "We got two boats coming out to our party," Josh said. "The other five are playing follow the leader and I don't think the leader knows where he's going."

"I can't believe it," Doug shrieked. "This is so damn much fun."

Josh looked at the buoy in the distance. "I think we can make it with one less tack than those five over there. It'll be close, but it will save us a lot of time and space."

Again, Josh was right. The only boats to round the buoy ahead of them were the two boats that came out with them. The extra tack the five boats had to make left a big gap between Doug and them.

"It looks like a three boat race now," Josh said.

"Yeah, but that's Morton and Schaefer, probably the two best sailors on the lake. I doubt if they are going to make any mistakes and give us a chance to catch them."

Josh watched the other boats slowly widen the gap between them. All three made the right moves at the right times. "Maybe third place is the best we can do."

"We've come so far," Doug lamented. "Third place is nice, best I've ever done, but can't you pull one more rabbit out of your bag of tricks? It would be so cool to beat these guys."

Josh watched the newer boats continue to increase their lead and saw Doug's shoulders droop. "It going to take some kind of miracle to pull this off." Doug's disappointment showed.

A splash of water hit Josh in the face. He wiped it away

and studied the waves. "What time is it?"

Doug looked at his watch. "Five to twelve, why?"

Josh continued watching the water. The waves went one way, but the wind made droplets of water dance in the air. He looked at the tree tops on the distant shore. They seemed to be undecided on which way to bend. The lead boats both turned and headed down on a long tact that would bring them back to the finish line. "How much faith do you have in Ole Crooked Nose?"

"Who?" Doug looked puzzled.

"The weatherman on Channel 3. His weather report this morning had a front coming through about noon with the wind changing from southwest to straight west. If that's true, and that change is happening right now, those guys will be out of position to get back to the starting line. Watch the water. See how the wind is licking the tips of the waves and making those drops of water dance.

"I see it, but what do we do?" Doug asked.

"If we stay on this line, take it all the way to the far shore, we have a chance to turn and take it hard on the wind, all the way to the finish line. Those guys will be stuck down there and have to come back here in order to get to the finish line."

"What if this weather guy is wrong and the wind doesn't change?"

"Then we'll probably go from third to last. We could end up looking mighty silly." Josh could see Doug struggled with the decision. "We don't have to do it. We can follow them and take a solid third."

Doug rubbed his chin. "All last year I've had to put up with their jokes and razzing. If you're right, I can shut them up once and for all." He sat up straight. "Where do you want me to point this thing? Loosing is no big deal. I've lost before, but if we've got a chance to win we're taking it."

205

"See that boathouse with the red roof. Aim right for it."

When they got to the far shore, like clockwork, the wind had completely shifted. They came about and Doug tightened the sail. The beautiful red boat leaned over and lunged forward. She cut through the water and picked up speed with every gust.

Josh pointed to the other boats. "They must have realized the wind shift and cut their run short. They're coming back, but I think they are still too far out of position to mount a serious challenge to us."

The people who came out in their powerboats to watch the races suddenly realized what was happening. They began cruising alongside as the red boat streaked to the finish line. Doug recognized many of the townspeople as they yelled and screamed with delight. Josh saw Julia waving her scarf and jumping up and down on the deck of a pontoon boat.

The red boat crossed the finish line as the cannon on the judge's boat gave them a thunderous salute. Doug turned the boat upwind and let the sails go limp. He jumped up and hugged Josh. "We did it, man, we did it." He then raised his arms in triumph as a gesture to the people in the powerboats. They in return, yelled, screamed, and blew their boat horns in celebration.

Josh watched as each of the other boats crossed the finish line. One by one they pounded the side of their boats as a tribute to the victors. Josh gave each one a wave of appreciation.

The pontoon boat came alongside, and Josh tied the sailboat to the rail. Julia leaned over the rail and gave him a big kiss. "That was wonderful," she squealed. "I'm so glad I was here to see this." She kissed him again.

"Whose boat is this?" Josh asked. "How did you end up out here?"

Julia had to pause to catch her breath. "I went to put

206

gas in my car so we could go to Middletown later and all these people were at the station buying beer and snacks. The TV crew from Channel three had rented the pontoon to film the races and invited a bunch of us townspeople along." Julia jumped up and down. "I still can't believe you guys won. How did you do it?"

"A tip from an old friend of yours."

"A friend of mine?"

"Ol' Crooked Nose, the weather guy on TV?" Josh laugh. "It's a long story. I'll tell you all about it later." He climbed up on the pontoon as Julia wrapped her arms around his neck. He leaned over and gave her a long passionate kiss.

The TV cameraman circled Doug, trying to capture the excitement. Someone handed Doug a beer, and another poured one over his head. Josh grabbed Doug's sleeve. "You want to go back with these people? Julia and I can bring the sailboat."

Doug quickly agreed. This was a once in a lifetime thing and he didn't want to miss a minute of it.

Josh grabbed Julia's hand. "C'mon, let's get out of here." He helped her down onto the sailboat, untied and pushed it away. He sat her down, put the tiller in one hand and the rope to the main sail in the other.

"What are you doing? I don't know how to sail this thing."

"Just hold it steady." He lowered the jib, unhooked it, and put it under the deck. "We don't need the jib to get back to the marina," he said, taking the tiller. He moved her forward and pulled in the main. It ballooned out and the boat moved forward with ease.

"What do you want me to do?"

He smiled. "You just sit there and look pretty."

"What happened out there? Was it fun?" Her finger drew circles on his chest.

"It was a blast. Doug and I make a pretty good team. He had to make some pretty tough decisions. Lucky for us, it all went our way."

"Were you able to help?"

"I helped a little. One thing is for sure, this isn't the first time I've sailed."

"This town is going to go wild. A town kid winning the Fourth of July trophy. That has never happened before."

They lazily rode the wind. Julia lay on the deck, dragged her fingers in the water and enjoyed the serenity of the afternoon. Without warning, Josh tightened the main sail. "Let's have some fun." The boat immediately leaned over and picked up speed.

Julia jumped up, grabbing the edge of the cockpit with one hand and Josh's leg with the other. "What are you doing?"

Josh pulled the main tighter. The boat leaned more and went even faster.

"Don't tip us over!" Julia screamed as they both leaned backward to counterbalance the force of the wind. Once Julia realized that they weren't going to tip over she relaxed and enjoyed the ride.

Josh eased off the sail as they passed the buoy marking the channel to the marina.

"Sailing is fun," Julia said. "I'm sorry now that I didn't take Doug's offer to go sailing with him last year."

"It gets in your blood," Josh said. "I'm happy I was here to give you your first ride. Maybe Doug will let us use the boat and we can do it again sometime?"

Julia brushed her fingers through her hair. "I'd love that. So, what are we going to do the rest of the day?" She poked him in the ribs. "Are you going to ask me to the dance tonight? They have a great band lined up."

"Julia, my princess," he said. "Will you do me the honor of accompanying me to the ball this evening?"

208

"Oh, Prince Charming, I would be delighted. Should I wear my glass slippers?"

"That could be dangerous," he said, continuing the fun. "I have a habit of stepping on people's toes when I dance." Julia laughed.

When they reached the marina, Josh brought the boat up to the pier and quickly dropped the sail. Doug came out of the marina office with a beer in his hand, followed by three other guys. "These two are going to take care of the boat. Fred will let them in the icehouse. This other guy is going to give us a ride to Teddy's. There is one big celebration already in progress."

Josh looked at Julia. "Is that alright with you?"

Julia really didn't want to go, but nodded her approval anyway.

A Trip to the Middletown Flea Market

Teddy's bar was rocking, and the music and noise could be heard blocks away. A local winning this race was a huge event and everyone wanted to be part of the celebration.

When Doug walked through the door the place erupted in a deafening round of applause. Everyone wanted to shake his hand and pat him on the back.

"Speech," came a cry from the back of the room. Someone pushed a chair next to Doug while others lifted him on it. Another loud cheer erupted. Doug waved his arms and the room went silent.

"This is unbelievable," Doug began. "I can't tell you what a feeling it was as we came down to the finish line, and having all your boats running alongside. Winning this race, and getting my name on the fourth of July trophy, is probably the best thing to ever happen to me." The crowd clapped loudly.

Josh and Julia had followed Doug into Teddy's, but moved off to the side and stood in the far corner. Doug searched the crowd. He pointed to Josh, "And, there's the guy I owe it all to."

Josh waved and pointed back at Doug.

"His name is Josh. You may know him as the guy that

spent time in a coma. He is still struggling to remember things about himself, but today he remembered one thing. He's a sailor. He was the one that came up with the final strategy that allowed us to beat Morton and Schaefer on that last leg. C'mon up here, Josh."

Josh shook his head and waved him off.

"You want to hear from him don't you?" Doug asked the crowd. The chanting started. "Josh! Josh! Josh!" Josh was pushed to the center of the room and lifted onto a chair next to Doug. The applause reached a new crescendo. The two men hugged and Doug waved the crowd to quiet down.

"Doug is being way too modest," Josh said. "He made all the tough decisions out there. We had a solid third place finish locked up, but he risked it all for a chance to win. If we didn't get that wind shift we probably would have come in last." Josh grabbed Doug's hand and raised it in the air. "Here's your hero."

The crowd exploded in another round of whooping and hollering. The boys hugged again before Josh jumped off his chair and worked his way back to Julia.

She met him halfway. "These people will remember this day for a long, long time. This sailing thing has been dominated by Lakeshore people for as long as anyone can remember. For a couple of townies to go out there and win the biggest race of the season is truly unbelievable."

Josh pushed her out the front door. "Let's get out of here. It's too noisy. Where did you leave your car?"

Julia pointed up the street. "It's behind the Shell station." She was about to take off and make a foot race of it, but Josh grabbed her by the belt and pulled her to a stop.

"Whoa, not so fast. Let's be sensible and walk to the car."

"Are you afraid you might lose a race to a girl?"

211

Josh smiled. "One big race is enough. Are we still going to Middletown?"

"Yes, let's, and maybe I can find a dress for the dance tonight."

On the way to Middletown, Josh slid over and sat next to Julia.

"What are you doing? Guys don't sit in the middle, she said. "Get over in your own seat.

"Geez, winning the big race doesn't get you much," he said, sliding over to the passenger seat.

"Your prize is a funnel cake. They have a stand at the flea market that makes them. I get one every time I go."

"No trophy, no big kiss, just a funnel cake?"

"You'll love it. They drizzle donut batter into hot oil and sprinkle it with powdered sugar. It's absolutely delicious."

Finding a parking stall near the market was normally a challenge. Luckily, a car backed out as they drove up.

Julia danced two to three steps ahead of Josh. "C'mon, is that as fast as you can walk?"

Tables of merchandise were scattered throughout the park. Some had scads of one item, like shirts or dresses, while others had a potpourri of both new and used things. Julia passed all of them until she reached the one selling the funnel cakes. She quickly ordered two with lots of sugar.

Josh tried to pick up the powdery tart, but quickly dropped it back on the plate. "Dang, that's hot. You should have warned me."

"You have to pull it apart and eat small bites."

"It would have been nice to tell me that before I burned my fingers." He put a piece in his mouth.

Julia waited for his reaction. "Good, huh?"

Josh smiled and nodded his satisfaction. Looking around, "are you shopping for a dress here?"

"Don't be silly. If I want to go as a gypsy princess, here

would be fine. We have to go to Penney's down on Main Street." Julia ate her last morsel and threw the paper plate in the trash.

Josh did the same. "That was really good."

"Did you want to look around some more?" she asked. "I just wanted a funnel cake."

"I'm good. Let's go to Penney's."

On the way to the car Josh recognized the man walking toward them. "Dr. Erickson. It's me, Josh."

The doctor's face lit up. "Josh, how are you doing?"

"You remember Julia?" Josh pulled Julia to his side.

"I do, from The Glen."

"Do you like coming to the swap meet?" Julia asked.

"My wife drags me down here every once in a while. She's around here someplace." He turned his attention to Josh. "Have you remembered anything more about yourself?"

"Not really, but I'm learning things about myself. I can type, ride a bicycle, and today I found that I know how to sail."

"He and a guy from town won the snipe race this morning." Julia said.

The doctor smiled. "That's quite an accomplishment."

"I get these memory flashes in my head. I'm pretty sure I was in an automobile accident, but there's no accident report and no vehicle. It could be just a fabrication of my mind."

"That's interesting," the doctor said. "You will probably continue to find out things about yourself. As far as remembering your past, something may trigger your mind and all of sudden everything could come back to you."

"I hope so," Josh said.

"But, in the meantime continue what you are doing, live, make friends, and win sailboat races. With head

213

injuries there are no guarantees. This could be your life, and if I were you, I would live it." The doctor bid them good-bye.

Josh watched the doctor disappear in the crowd. "It would be great to have my memory back, but maybe that's too much to hope for."

A New Dress For Julia

Walking into Penney's, Julia went directly to the sale rack. Summer dresses were 50% off. She pushed back each hanger, taking a moment or two to study each dress. Now and then she took a hanger from the rack and held the dress up to herself. Each time she looked for Josh's reaction. His expression told her he didn't care for anything she showed him so far.

She was near the end of the selection when she pulled out a sundress with a full skirt and spaghetti straps. It had yellow, pink, and purple flowers in a muted print on white shiny fabric. She held it to herself and looked at Josh.

Josh's face lit up. "I like that one."

"I'm going to try it on."

Josh waited. Soon Julia appeared carrying the dress. Josh shot her an inquisitive look.

Julia walked past him with a broad smile on her face. She paid and started for the door.

"How come you didn't come out and show me the dress?" Josh asked.

Julia kept walking. "Because I want it to be a surprise."

"It was the nicest one. I can't believe nobody bought that dress." Josh said.

"I haven't had a party dress since high school. I can't wait to wear it."

On the way back to Pine Lake they decided to forget swimming and take it easy. Julia dropped Josh off at Nora's.

"What time should I be over to your place?" he asked, before closing the car door.

"We don't want to be the first ones there. How about eight o'clock?"

Josh nodded and stepped away from the car.

Julia blew him a kiss and drove off.

Julia kicked off her shoes, took the dress out of the bag, and put it on a hanger. She fanned out the skirt. "This is going to look so good with a crinoline underneath it." The slip hung on the last hanger in the closet and the strapless bra she wore to a wedding a few years ago lay in the bottom of a dresser drawer. She laid them both on the bed. Taking off her clothes, she wrapped up in her robe. With a towel in one hand, and shampoo in the other, she danced her way to the kitchen. She felt like a schoolgirl going to the prom.

With her hair wrapped in the towel, she skipped her way to the bathroom. For the next couple of hours she fussed over herself, putting sponge rollers in her hair, shaving her legs, polishing her nails, and plucking her eyebrows. She even found time for a short nap.

It was a little after six when she donned her cap and stepped into the shower. She continued to sing parts of the Beatles' songs she knew, even while toweling dry and putting on her makeup. Donning fresh underwear, she bent and hooked the bra behind her. Her eyes weren't the only thing that looked big when she looked in the mirror. The bra pushed her breasts up creating an ample amount of cleavage. It was apparent she had put on a little weight since she last wore it. The gossip ladies would probably have a field day if she showed up at the dance looking like a hussy.

She took the dress off the hanger and slipped it over her head. The bodice was cut straight across, and thanks to the bra, she seemed to blossom forth across her chest. She slipped the spaghetti straps over her shoulders and tied the ribbon belt in a bow behind her. She stepped into the crinoline slip and spun around watching the skirt twirl around her. A big smile crossed her face as she looked in the mirror. Gossip be damned, she liked it. Her stomach was a bundle of nerves, but she relished the feeling of a moon-struck schoolgirl getting ready for a big date.

Periodically she checked the clock to make sure she was on schedule as she puttered and primped while dreaming about the music, the dancing, and what the evening had in store for her and Josh.

*E*arlier, Josh had retrieved the key from under the geranium plant. "Nora?" He called out. "Anybody home?" He walked into the kitchen, found pen and paper and wrote Nora a note letting her know he was taking a nap. Upstairs, he stripped to his underwear and climbed into bed.

It was one of those naps where you think you only slept for a short period of time. Josh stretched and glanced at the clock. It was ten minutes after seven. He sprang from the bed. He'd slept for almost three hours. The shower was quick and efficient. Shaving took a mere three minutes, and brushing his teeth took even less.

His outfit selection was limited. He laid the navy slacks on the bed and choose a white short-sleeved shirt with navy trim on the collar and cuffs. "Shoes!" He looked at the white tennis shoes he had been wearing since leaving The Glen. Not your typical dance shoes, but that's all he had. Taking them into the bathroom he scrubbed them as best he could. He combed his hair, swiped on deodorant, and added a splash of aftershave. Dressed, he descended the stairs two at a time.

Josh checked the note he left for Nora. On the bottom she had scribbled, "Went to dinner with friends. Congratulations on the sailing". He added the word "Thanks," and hurried out the door.

The Yacht Club Dance

Julia had just finished putting a splash of perfume by each ear and in the crease between her breasts. She was putting on lipstick when she heard the knock on her back door. Her prince was right on time. She took one last look and went to let him in.

Josh's eyes grew as big as saucers. He took a step back. "Wow!" he said, first looking at her hair, then at the dress, and then at the top of her dress. "You look absolutely beautiful."

Julia twirled around letting the dress flare out.

"I'll need a baseball bat to beat the guys off when you walk into the dance."

Julia giggled with delight. "Do you like the dress?"

"A whole lot more with you in it." Josh said. "I like your hair too. How did you get it so curly and wavy?"

"Sponge rollers." She flashed the bright red polished nails in front of his eyes.

"Nice, and the My Sin, too."

Julia put her hands on her hips. "Are you some kind of authority on ladies' perfume?"

"Don't know. I just know the scent."

Maybe from a wife or girlfriend? She bit her lip, not wanting talk of her perfume to spoil the evening. This was their night and she was going to enjoy every minute. "Are we ready to go?"

"At your beck and call, my fair princess." He Jumped ahead and opened her car door.

"Thank you gallant prince." She giggled as she got in the car.

When they got to the country club the parking lot was full. They parked on the grass near the first tee and had quite a walk to the clubhouse. Julia did a few dance steps as the orchestra music filled the air. The main entrance opened into a large lobby with a giant chandelier hanging in the middle of the room. The dining room had been converted into a ballroom complete with mirrored ball that illuminated the room with dizzying refracted diamond sparkles that flowed endlessly across the walls, floor and ceiling. The band in light blue tuxedoes, occupied the tiered stage against the far wall while people sat at candle-lit tables lining the perimeter of the room. A few couples stepped merrily across the temporary dance floor.

Doug's laugh could be heard above the others coming from the bar room. Standing in the midst of a group of guys, Doug stopped mid-sentence when the couple walked into the room. "Josh, Julia, come over here."

All eyes were on Julia, mostly on one particular part of her. Julia could feel their stares and moved behind Josh. Doug's eyes widened also, bloodshot as they were from an afternoon of drinking, but quickly turned his attention to Josh. "Look, here's our trophy." Doug pointed to the large silver cup standing on the bar.

No one looked at the shiny cup. All eyes seemed glued to Julia's chest. She gave Josh's arm a tug.

Josh moved to shield Julia from prying eyes.

"They handed out trophies at six o'clock over at Morton's place. I got a big round of applause. A lot of those Lakeshore people are pretty nice." Doug said, as he wobbled and used the bar to steady himself.

Julia pulled on Josh's arm.

"That's great," Josh said. "You guys have a great time. We're going to do a little dancing."

Someone handed Doug a beer and the cheers went up once again.

"I guess that was a little bit uncomfortable for you," Josh said, as they made their exit.

Julia nodded. "I'm sure tongues will wag in the morning."

"Don't let those nitwits spoil your evening. You look gorgeous. C'mon, let's dance."

"Are you sure you know how?"

"We're about to find out."

Stepping on the dance floor, he hesitated. She grabbed his left hand and put his right hand on her hip. She waited for the downbeat and moved her left foot back as her left hand drew his right foot forward matching her move. He followed her lead for the first three or four steps before he squeezed her hand, drew her hips in close, and moved her across the floor. She held her breath as he twirled her under his arm. He was light on his feet and his hands guided her in the direction he wanted to go.

"You are unbelievable," she said, as he dipped her slightly.

"Fun isn't it. I'm a dancing sailor." The band switched from the two-step to a waltz. He hesitated a moment, then raised her hand high.

"Oh geez, I don't know if I know how to waltz." The words barely broke from her lips before he had them gliding across the floor. Her dress flowed with the music.

Following a final dip, Julia pulled him to the table. "You type, you ride a bike, you sail, and now you dance like Fred Astaire. What are you going to do next, save the planet?"

A broad smile crossed his face. "My feet just took over."

The cocktail waitress came by. "Would you like something to drink?"

"I'll have a whiskey sour." Julia said. The waitress wrote it down and looked at Josh.

221

"Bring me a big bottle of Blatz."

No matter what the band played, the two-step, waltz, jitterbug, Josh could dance them all. Julia liked the slow dances. He would hold her tight and she could just melt in his arms.

At 10 o'clock the band leader announced they were taking a break for the big fireworks show. Josh and Julia ordered another drink and went out on the patio. They found two chaise lounge chairs, put the backs down flat, and pushed them together. They lay side by side and watched the colorful displays burst overhead. In between canon blasts Julia rolled onto his chair and laid across his chest. She pressed her lips to his, sticking her tongue deep into his mouth and then retreating as his tongue followed hers back. With fireworks exploding overhead she felt the sparks of passion surge through her body. She rolled to the side and he leaned on his elbow to make room for her on the chair.

She took a deep breath as his fingertips slowly and tenderly move in circles, first on the top of one breast then to the other. Julia had to fight to control the emotions that almost consumed her.

The firework show ended and the music again drifted out into the night air. She and Josh stayed on the patio, their lips never far apart.

It was close to midnight when they finally got off the chairs. Julia patted the loose straggles of hair into place. She straightened her dress, giving the top a pull upward. She straightened the shoulder straps. "I may have put on a pound or two since the last time I wore this bra."

"You don't hear me complaining, do you? I think you look great."

"Oh, you do, do you?" She poked him in the ribs as they walked back into the club.

The Night Was Young

The band leader announced the final dance. Julia grabbed Josh's hand and pulled him to the middle of the dance floor. Putting her arm around his neck she twirled the back of his hair with her finger. Josh drew her close. She nestled her head on his chest and breathed in the moist aroma that was uniquely his.

The soft melody of HARBOR LIGHTS filled the room. Josh moved her slowly side-to-side as he gently pressed his cheek in her hair. The sparkles of light from the mirrored ball danced over the crowded floor. Each couple, as if on cue, stopped at various intervals during the song and left the floor. Julia and Josh were alone, and continued dancing even as the band members began packing up their instruments.

Josh put his arm behind Julia's waist and dipped her so low her hair almost touched the floor. He held her there for the longest moment before bringing her upright.

"Thank you, my prince." She whispered. "It has been a fairytale evening."

"Don't tell me this is where you turn into a pumpkin?"

She pushed him away. "You are such a poop."

They walked into the foyer. Doug's voice could again be heard coming from the bar. Julia pulled on Josh's arm. "Let's just go."

Josh smiled as they went out the front door.

On the way to the car Julia pointed to the sky. "Look, a falling star!" A white light streaked across the sky. "Did you make a wish?"

"A wish?"

"If you see a falling star and you make a wish it's supposed to come true," Julia said with childlike excitement.

"Okay."

Julia turned and skipped backwards in front of him. "Okay what? Did you make a wish or not?"

"Yes, I made a wish."

"What did you wish for?" She circled behind him and tickled his ribs.

Josh pushed her hands away. "If I tell you, it won't come true."

"Was I a part of it? Was I?" Julia pestered.

"No, I don't think so," he said in mocked confusion.

"Liar, liar," she said, jumping up on his back and kissing his neck.

"Okay. Okay. I wished you didn't weigh so much." Julia jumped down, swatted him on the back, and took off running. "Race you to the car!"

Josh didn't take the challenge.

"You are so slow," she said, leaning against the car as he walked up.

"And you are nothing but a big cheater." Josh gave her a spank on her bottom.

"Ooooh, now we're going to play rough." She tried to tickle his ribs.

He held her hands. "Let's be serious. Are you okay to drive?" he asked, as he opened her door.

Julia slid behind the wheel. "I only had those two drinks, and the dancing took care of them."

Driving through town. Josh realized they weren't

224

going in the direction of her place. "Where are we going?"

"For a ride. The night is still young."

Josh pointed to the clock on the dashboard. "You do realize it's one o'clock in the morning?"

Julia drove past The Glen and turned into the entrance to County Park. She continued on the winding road down to the swimming beach parking lot.

Jumping from the car she skipped across the footbridge to the deserted small island beach. She turned to see if he was coming before walking to the end of the pier and sitting on the bench.

Josh seemed to be enjoying the surreal beauty of the night and took his time joining her. The moon was rising, sending its light dancing across the water. He took a deep breath of cool night air before sitting next to her.

"Isn't it a gorgeous night?" Julia laid her head back and looked up at the stars. "When we saw the falling star, I wished the night would never end. What did you wish for?"

Josh seemed lost in his own world. "It's a beautiful night, and it was a wonderful day. The boat race, the flea market, the fireworks, the dance... it was all wonderful."

Julia rested her head on his shoulder. "Josh, I'm afraid."

"Afraid of what?"

"You know, what it will be like if you start remembering. Things could be a lot different for us. That's why I wished tonight would never end."

Silently, they both stared off into the night.

Julia took his hand. "What did you wish for? Why won't you tell me?"

"I wished I could remember," he said. "I want to know who I am and where I came from so I can bring you into my life and know I won't be hurting you."

"It was me."

"It was you what?" Josh said.

225

"I was the one they caught hiding in your room," she said.

Josh spun around on the bench. "You, but why?"

"I know this sounds silly, but it's like destiny brought you here and we were meant to find each other. For some odd reason, from the moment you were found, I've been attracted to you. I can't explain why I went to the hospital that day—curious maybe—I just had to see what you looked like."

"I guess I'm a little surprised, too, at how quickly you've captured my heart."

Julia stood. "Stay right here. I'll be right back."

Josh watched as she disappeared down the pier. He closed his eyes. Immediately his mind bombarded him with images. Buildings and houses flashed by. Faces, young and old, appeared momentarily, and then faded. Everything came at him so fast there was no way to make sense of it.

He jumped when a wet hand grabbed his ankle. Looking down, he saw Julia's head sticking out of the water. "What are you doing down there?" His eyes searched to see the rest of her.

"Swimming," she said with a broad smile.

"Have you got a bathing suit on?" His voice rising an octave.

"Don't be silly. Where would I get a bathing suit?" She dove beneath the surface exposing her bare behind. Coming up, she swam towards the raft. "Are you coming in? The water is beautiful."

"This is crazy," he said, pulling at his shoelaces.

Julia was already near the raft by the time Josh shed the last of his clothes. Diving into the water, he came up quickly. "Wow!" The cold water momentarily took his breath away. He swam a few strokes before realizing he hadn't given a thought to whether or not he could swim.

226

The strokes came easy and natural.

Julia swam to the far side of the raft. He could see her between the barrels that kept the platform afloat. It turned into a cat and mouse game. When he went right, she went left. She seemed to anticipate his every move. Suddenly, it was quiet. Julia looked both ways and squealed when Josh came up from under the water. He put his hands on her waist. She smiled, pursed her lips, and slowly brought her head towards him.

He knew he'd been suckered when as soon as he closed his eyes she pulled free and slipped deep into the water. It was his turn to wonder where she would come up. The water dripped as she climbed the ladder on the other side of the float. He pulled himself up, resting his arms on the deck. He watched the silhouette of her naked body as she walked to the center and laid down.

Reaching the ladder, he climbed and laid beside her. Her body heaved with long hard breaths. The moonlight glistened off the beads of water that rolled off her breast. She shivered as a breeze caused her nipples to blossom. Josh raised onto his elbow, bent over and kissed them, letting his tongue roll around each nipple. His hand rubbed across her tummy and inched lower.

Without warning, Julia bolted up sending Josh over on his back. "Someone's coming!" she exclaimed in a loud whisper and rolled off the side of the raft. Josh stayed still as headlights fanned across the water. The raft was tilted enough to conceal him as the lights passed over. He raised his head enough to see the car pull alongside Julia's. It was a white or cream-colored four-door sedan. Josh slipped backwards off the raft just as the car's spotlight cut a bright swath through the night. The beam searched every part of the pier, beach, and water. Josh could see Julia hiding beneath the pier, keeping a post between herself and the probing light. Josh made sure he too stayed out of sight.

Finally the car turned off the spot and left.

Julia had disappeared before Josh made it back to the pier. Moving quickly, he dressed and was walking off the pier when Julia stepped out from behind the snack house adjusting the straps on her dress.

"I think that would have moved to the top of the gossip list." Josh said.

"I don't know what made me do that. That could have been a disaster."

"Can you see the headlines in the paper? Local nurse and coma boy caught skinny dipping in the park." He laughed loudly.

"Don't laugh. It's not funny," she said. "I would have had to leave town if that got out." She grabbed his hand and literally dragged him to the car. "Let's just get out of here."

It wasn't until they were safely out of the park that Julia gave out a small giggle. She touched his arm. "That was close. You're right, the phone lines would have lit up big time. Those gossip ladies would have had a field day with it."

Julia stood on her doorstep. "Do you want to come..."

He put his finger to her lips, then, brushing a curl of hair from her cheek. "I think it would be best if we don't let our emotions take us over the edge."

"But," she protested.

"Me too. I want to as much as you, but not tonight. It will be wonderful when the time is right." He wiped a tear from her cheek as his other hand slipped from hers. He stepped backwards down the steps, kicked up the stand on the bike and said, "I'll call you in the morning."

Julia watched as he disappeared up the street. She went in, sat at the table, and buried her head in her hands. She cried, and cried hard. "Life is so cruel," she murmured. Her heart ached. She envisioned herself lying beside him in bed. She imagined his kiss, and fantasized their bodies coming together. The thought of losing him to a previous life quickly ended the spell. She wiped the tears from her eyes. Josh was right. They shouldn't do anything that could come back to haunt them later on.

She walked to the bedroom, washed up, and put on her pajamas. Her last thought before falling asleep was lying beside him on red satin sheets.

Josh pedaled up Nora's street. Just ahead, a cream colored four door sedan sat parked at the curb. He was sure it was the car from the park and took note of the Illinois license plate and the spotlight mounted above the outside mirror. The inside of the car was dark and Josh was not able to discern much of the man's features as he pedaled by. Leaning the bike against the porch post Josh took a step in the direction of the car, but halted when the headlights came on, momentarily blinding him. The car spun around and quickly disappeared down the street. Once the taillights were out of sight, Josh brought the bike onto the porch and used the key from under the geranium plant to let himself in. He brushed back the curtain on the door window making sure the car hadn't returned. He gave a small head shake, turned off the porch light and headed upstairs.

Sheriff Joe Apologizes

"Josh, are you awake?" It was Nora knocking on his door. "You've got a visitor. It's Sheriff Christenson. He's waiting downstairs for you."

Josh sat up out of a deep sleep. "Tell him I'll be right down." Josh hurriedly pulled his pants up over his pajamas and wondered what the sheriff could want? Maybe it had something to do with the guy in the cream colored car, or better yet, he may have new information about what happened to him. Josh splashed some water on his face, combed his hair and hurried downstairs.

Nora and the sheriff sat at the kitchen counter. Joe stood and set his coffee cup down when Josh came into the room. "You're a hard person to track down," the sheriff said. "I looked everywhere for you yesterday."

"We were on the run pretty much the whole day."

The sheriff reached into his shirt pocket. "I brought you this." He handed Josh a slip of paper, a brownish stain covered most of the printing. Josh studied the paper before giving the sheriff a puzzled look.

"All your stuff came back from the crime lab in Madison. Apparently that slip of paper was in your shirt pocket. It appears the hospital didn't check the pockets when they cut the clothes off you. Your stuff came to us in a plastic bag, a big bloody mess, but we should have

230

checked the stuff before sending it to Madison. The lab did confirm the stain on the paper was your blood."

Josh read the words written on the paper. "Josh Bennett, 1521 Grove Street, Weston, Wisconsin." Josh looked at Joe. "Where's Weston?"

"It's about seventy miles north of here," the sheriff said.

"Josh Bennett. Is that your name?" Nora asked.

"I guess it could be," Josh said. "But Grove Street and Weston don't ring a bell.

The sheriff handed a key to Josh. "This was in one of your pants pockets. It appears to be a house key." The sheriff tipped his cap. "I'm truly sorry if this has delayed you in any way of finding out who you are. Since we have no evidence suggesting there was any criminal activity involved in your mishap, you are free to go there if you want."

Nora saw the sheriff to the door and returned to the kitchen. "I think we are finally getting someplace. You need to go to Weston to check on this."

"Do you have a map of Wisconsin?" Josh asked. "I'd like to see where this Weston is?"

"I've got one in the junk drawer."

Josh unfolded the map, and spread it on the counter. "Show me where Pine Lake is?"

Nora pointed to a spot on the map. "You kids must have had a good time last night. You had the local tongues wagging big time. I've already had two phone calls about it this morning."

"Oh, yeah. What were they saying?"

"That you two were dancing up a storm and making out on the patio."

"Guilty as charged," Josh said. "We had a wonderful time. Anything else?" He held his breath, hoping their later activity was not part of the scenario.

231

"You also made the six o'clock sports on channel three."

Josh looked up from the map. "What was that about?"

"They talked about the guy who awoke from a coma to help a local lad win the Fourth of July race. They interviewed Doug. He gave you a lot of the credit for the win."

"That win meant a lot to him, and I had a really good time." Josh returned to the map. He put his finger on Pine Lake and began searching north until he found Weston. "I wonder if Julia would like to take a ride."

"It would be a nice Sunday drive," Nora said. "Do you want to call her?"

"Maybe I'll just get dressed and go over there."

"Don't be silly. It's eight thirty in the morning. You have to give the poor girl a chance to get ready." Nora dialed the number and handed the phone to Josh. "Girls aren't like you guys. We need fifteen minutes to get ready to go to the grocery store."

Julia answered on the second ring.

"Good morning," Josh said brightly. "You dressed?" Josh's face flushed. "I didn't mean it like that."

Nora smiled and turned away.

Josh switched the phone to his other hand. "I was wondering if you would like to take a ride to Weston, Wisconsin. It's about seventy miles north of here...The sheriff was here this morning...It's a long story...I'll tell you all about it when I get there...Ten, that's great, see you then." He hung up the phone. "She's going to take me."

"I gathered that," Nora said. "Ten o'clock right? I told you she would need time to get ready. Would you like some breakfast? I had eggs."

"An egg sandwich would be great." Josh picked up the bloodstained paper and studied it.

Nora poured him a glass of juice and cracked two eggs

232

into the pan. "Want me to bust the yolks?"

"That's fine. You keep spoiling me. How is any girl I find going to measure up to you?"

Nora blushed. "If I was twenty years younger I'd be one of those girls trying to land you." Nora handed him the sandwich.

"Is that how it was with Duke?"

"He had other girls sniffing around him, but once I landed him he was mine forever." She used her hankie to brush the moisture from her eyes. "I'm anxious to hear what you find in Weston. It could open up your whole past."

"I hope you're right. I'll tell you all about it when we get back."

Josh made a quick trip through the bathroom and put on the clothes he wore to the dance. He picked up the envelope and thumbed through the bills. "I'll have to make sure I pay Julia for gas," he said, stuffing the envelope in his pocket.

Nora stood at the foot of the stairs. She handed him the map. "I hope you find what you are looking for."

Josh held up the key. "This could unlock the mystery of my past, but for the life of me I have no idea of what it's to."

A Ride to Weston

Josh pedaled up just as Julia walked out of the door. "I put a couple of sodas on the back seat. They're wrapped in a towel to keep them cold. Where did you say we're going?"

"Weston." Josh waved the paper in the air. "I'll tell you all about it on the way."

"So, which way are we heading?" she asked, while starting the car.

"Straight up Highway twenty-four."

It was a beautiful day, barely a cloud in the sky. Julia picked up the highway on the outskirts of town. "So what did the sheriff have to say?"

Josh handed her the bloodstained note. "My clothes came back from the lab in Madison. They found that in my shirt pocket. That's my blood on it.'

"Josh Bennett, is that you?" The car bounced as she momentarily drove off of the pavement. "Are you Josh Bennett?"

"It seems to be the logical conclusion."

"What do you mean? You're not sure? It came out of your pocket."

"Before we get ahead of ourselves, I'd like to go to the address on Grove Street and see if I remember anything."

Julia wondered what they would find on Grove Street.

234

He could be returning to a life that had been erased from his memory. She could lose the man she had fallen deeply in love with. The next hour or two would determine their fate. "I've never been up this way," she said, trying to keep the mood light. "This part of Wisconsin is so beautiful with its mixture of farms, woods and small towns."

Josh seemed deep in thought and just stared out the window. A cream car passed going in the opposite direction. Josh suddenly spun in his seat. "Did you see that car? Did it have Illinois license plates?"

"I don't know," Julia said, looking in the rear-view mirror. "I wasn't paying attention. Why would you ask that?"

"When I rode home last night, a cream colored car was parked on the street a little ways from Nora's place."

"It was close to three in the morning. What was he doing there?"

"Just sitting, I was going to check on him, but he took off."

"What did he look like? Have you ever seen him before?"

"No, but I think it was the same car that drove into the parking lot when we were...swimming."

Julia swallowed hard. "Did he have bleached blond hair?"

"It was dark inside the car, I couldn't get a good look. You know someone with bleached blond hair?"

Julia bit her lip. That was not a good thing to ask. "Nobody from Illinois," she said quickly. "What makes you think the car we just passed was the same car?"

"You don't see too many cream colored cars, and besides, that one also had a spotlight."

"You're spooking me out," Julia said. "There's a lot of nasty people in Chicago. That's where the mob is."

"Don't get carried away, I'm sure it's just a coincidence."

235

The sign said, Weston, twelve miles ahead. Josh moved in his seat and Julia too found a new position. An eerie silence ensued as each struggled with what they might find there.

On their initial pass through downtown neither saw Grove Street.

Julia made a U-turn. "Let's go back and ask someone."

"There was an A&W Root Beer stand on the way into town. We can have a root beer and ask the carhop where Grove Street is."

The root beer was cold and refreshing. Josh paid the girl and got the directions. The house on Grove Street was a one story with an attached garage. The shades were pulled and it was hard to determine if anyone was living there. Josh studied the house.

"Does it look familiar?" Julia finally asked.

"No, not at all." He sounded disappointed.

Josh reached into his pocket and pulled out the key Sheriff Joe gave him. "Do you think this key...?" He walked to the house with Julia in lock step behind him. After ringing the doorbell and knocking three times, Josh opened the screen door, slid the key into the lock and slowly turned it. The latch released. He turned the knob and pushed the door open. "Hello, anybody home?" He waited, then leaned forward and peered into the room. The house was fully furnished. Nothing new, but everything in reasonably good shape. Josh put one foot into the room and Julia pushed him the rest of the way in.

"I don't think anyone is living here," she said. "Look at the dust on the coffee table." She walked into the dining room and swiped her finger across the table making a long streak through the dust.

Josh studied each piece of furniture and every picture on the wall. The look on his face revealed he didn't recognize any of it.

Julia ventured into the kitchen. "Look, there's nothing in the refrigerator." She picked up a business card from the counter. "Here's a card from a Dan Kennedy, realtor."

Josh came into the kitchen and opened the door on his right. "This must be the pantry but there's nothing on the shelves." He went to the next door. "Garage, it's empty, too." He was about to close the door when he noticed a large yellow envelope lying on the floor near the overhead door. "There's a mail drop here," he said picking up the envelope. It was addressed to Josh Bennett, 1521 Grove Street, Weston, Wisconsin.

Julia came running. "Open it up." She reached for the envelope. "Let's see what's in it."

Josh pulled it away before she could grab it. He tapped the envelope in his hand.

"Aren't you going to open it? Don't you want to know what's in there?"

Josh felt the contents. "I guess, if I'm Josh Bennett, I have a right to open it." He tore it across the top, peered inside and quickly pressed it closed. "C'mon, let's go into the kitchen. You're not going to believe what is in here."

"Let me see. What is it?"

Josh emptied the contents on the kitchen table. Hundred dollar bills spilled out in a large pile, along with a piece of paper folded in half.

"Good Lord." Julia quickly gathered the bills and began counting. "There's five thousand dollars here." She said placing the last bill on a stack.

As Josh unfolded the paper, something fell to the table. It was a driver's license with his picture on it. "Look at this."

The picture and description matched perfectly. "That's you. That confirms it, you're Josh Bennett." Julia said clutching the money in both hands. "What did you do, rob a bank?"

Josh laughed. "Yeah, I robbed a bank and mailed the money to myself. Josh studied the envelope. "The return address is a P.O. Box. It's postmarked on April 18, Waukegan, Illinois."

"That would have been the day after you were found in the park." Julia said. "Maybe you are with the mob and it's a payoff for a job, or maybe you're on the lam, and you were supposed to hide out in this small town."

"I'm sure there is a logical explanation to all of this," he said.

"There are people who would kill for this kind of money." She dropped the money on the table and took a step back. "You're not...are you?"

Josh chuckled. "You've been watching too much Perry Mason." He read further. "Good luck, Josh. Be careful." It was signed Stuart. On the bottom, there was a phone number and the words, 'in an emergency call me.'

Julia read the note over Josh's shoulder. "Well, I think this IS an emergency. I think you should call him."

"I think...I would like to know more about this Stuart before I call him," Josh said. "Since I don't remember anything about this place, maybe we can find out more from that realtor, Dan Kennedy." He picked up the money, folded it over, and tried to put it in his pocket. "Here, put this in your purse," he said handing the wad to Julia.

Julia stepped back. "I'll be a nervous wreck walking around with five thousand dollars in my purse. What if I lose it?"

"You won't lose it. Just forget it's in there."

Julia put a death grip on her purse. "Easy for you to say."

The Truth About Grove Street

Josh read the card as they walked to the car. "His office is on Main Street. We must have passed it."

Kennedy's office stood on a corner and appeared to be a converted gas station. Josh tried the door and peered through the window. He strolled back to the car and surveyed the surrounding buildings. "Do you have any change? I need a dime."

Julia reached past the wad of bills and pulled a dime from the bottom of her purse. "Do you need any hundreds? I've got lots of those. She choked back a laugh.

Josh smiled and shook his head. Walking to a nearby phone booth, he took the card and dialed the number. The bell jingled as the coin dropped through. Julia watched as Josh became animated on the phone.

"He's coming down to the office." Josh said, returning to the car. "The house is a rental. The guy hesitated when I told him my name. He said, he expected me a couple of months ago. He acknowledged this whole rental process was a bit strange, everything was handled over the phone."

"Do you think this guy is on the level? What if he's a front for…you know who." Julia patted the side of her purse. "This whole thing has mob written all over it."

"He thinks there were two woman involved, couldn't remember names, but offered to show me the file."

A man in a '62 Dodge Coronet pulled up to the building. A graying man in his fifties stepped out of the car.

Josh waited for Julia to get out of the car. "Are you coming?"

Julia scooted to his side.

The man introduced himself and extended his hand. "May I call you Josh? I'm glad you finally showed up. Will the two of you be moving in now?"

"Probably not. Did I happen to mention the reason I was coming up here?"

"We never spoke. I dealt with a lady." He looked at Julia. "Are you Mary?"

Julia shook her head and stepped behind Josh.

The realtor opened the office door and invited them in. "The three months are just about up so I can't refund any rent money, but since you've haven't occupied the place I will send back your cleaning and security deposits.

"Actually, I'm only here for the day. I spent some time in a coma and am trying to put the pieces of my life back together. I was hoping we could get things cleared up today."

"Have a seat. I'll get that folder." The man retreated to the back office.

Julia stiffened. "Did you hear that, he spoke to Mary?"

"I heard. Please, just relax?"

The man returned carrying a manila folder. "I spoke to a Mary. Funny, I didn't write down a last name. The money order came overnight by UPS. It was a month-to-month rental, so we didn't need signatures. The strange part, I had a woman come in a few days before that, asking to see some rentals. I showed her a few places including the one on Grove and two days later this Mary calls and wants to rent fifteen twenty-one, sight unseen. I figured the first woman was looking at places for this Mary."

"Do you have the other woman's name?" Josh asked.

"Hmm, I don't see it. I know she gave me her name. Wait, here it is, Rachel Benson. She's a local gal. I've seen her in the grocery store a couple of times."

"Did you keep the envelope that the money order came in? Do you remember where it came from?"

The man opened the folder to show it only contained the one sheet of paper.

"I think it came from Illinois." A lot of people from Illinois vacation up here and some of them don't want people to know where they are. I just figured you were one of them."

Josh stood. "Thanks for all your trouble."

"If you wait a moment, I'll get you a check for the deposits, it'll save me a five cent stamp." The man went to the back office.

"Maybe we should just get out of here." Julia whispered. Josh put his finger to his lips.

"The check is for a thousand dollars," he said. "Five hundred for cleaning and five hundred for the security deposit." The man saw Julia's eyebrows raise. "I know it seems high, but we have to charge those kinds of prices because some people will tear a place apart or leave it in a total mess. Who should I make the check to?"

"Could you make it out to Julia Parsons," Josh said. "I'm switching banks and I haven't had a chance to set up a new account. It will save me a lot of problems."

The realtor wrote Julia's name on the check and handed it to Josh. Josh handed the check to Julia. "Here, dear, put this in your purse for safekeeping."

The man laughed. "Same thing in my house. My wife handles the money." The realtor walked them to the door. "If you ever decide to spend some time up here please give me a call. We've got a lot of nice places to rent."

"We'll do that." Josh said.

The realtor stopped. "Oh, there's one other thing. A

241

fellow stopped by the office a few times wondering if I had heard from you. He didn't leave a name or number, so I can't tell you any more than that."

"Was he driving a cream colored four door sedan?" Josh asked.

"Yes, so you know who I mean?"

"I've got a pretty good idea." Josh saw the look on Julia's face and ushered her out the door.

"Now I've got six thousand dollars in this purse," she said as they both got in the car. "I'm ready to have a heart attack. Why in the world did you have him make the check out to me?"

"I'm not quite ready for Josh Bennett to surface. Cashing a big check is a sure way to get people talking."

"What are we going to do about the guy in the cream colored car?"

Josh tapped his knee. "Apparently he's been here and knows me. I'm just not sure if that's a good thing or a bad thing.

Julia peeked into her purse to make sure the money was still there. "What do we do now?" Julia put the key in the ignition.

"Wait, let him drive away." They waved as the realtor drove up the street. Josh got out and went back to the phone booth. Looking in the phonebook, his finger stopped in the middle of the page. He came back to the car. "Remember this address, 2247 West River Road."

Julia took a pen and small tablet from her purse. "Rachel Benson?"

Puppies For Sale

"We need to come up with a reason to go see this Rachel," Josh said. "We need to know her connection to Mary."

"What if...?"

Josh cut her off. "There's probably a logical explanation to all of this and has nothing to do with the mob. Pull over, let's ask this man where River Road is."

The man pointed. "At the bend. This street turns into River Road."

They rounded the bend and Josh pointed to Julia's side of the car. "There it is."

Julia pulled to the curb.

The house needed paint, the bushes were overgrown, and the yard was filled with plants and flowers of every variety. Some were planted in the ground while others were in pots, cans, pails and containers of every shape and size. There was an older model car on the gravel driveway and a caramel colored dog lounged on the porch.

"A typical mob hideout," Josh said, a smile gathered from the corners of his mouth.

"Very funny," Julia said, punching him on the shoulder. "What do we do now?"

"I'm wondering what to say when I go to the door."

Just then a woman came out and walked up to the

roadway. She glanced at Julia's car before bending down and picking up a sign that had fallen over. She leaned it against the mailbox.

"Look at that, she's got puppies, for sale," Josh said, as the woman went back into the house, taking the dog with her.

Josh got out of the car. "C'mon."

Julia caught up. "What are you going to say to her?"

"I'm going to ask if we can see the puppies."

The woman, in her middle thirties, opened the door but held the screen closed. Her unattractive appearance had more to do with grooming than genes. Combing her hair, adding some makeup and lipstick would have made a huge improvement. Her wrinkled clothes was probably whatever came out of the wash basket.

"We were wondering if we could see the puppies," Josh said. "What kind are they?"

"Cockapoo, a cross between cocker spaniel and poodle." A half dozen little balls of fluff ran wildly around her feet. "Let me get them corralled in the kitchen and I will let you in."

Julia rushed to pick up one of the pups. "They are so cute. How much are you asking for them?"

"One fifty, both the bitch and male have papers," the lady said. "You can reserve one now and pick it up in two weeks. I would need a fifty-dollar deposit. The tan one and the runt are already spoken for." The woman sat on the couch. "Where are you from?"

"Pine Lake." Julia said before Josh had a chance to answer.

"Actually, I'm from Waukegan," Josh said waiting to see if there was any reaction from the woman. "I'm visiting friends in Pine Lake." Josh ignored Julia's puzzled look. "Have you ever been to Waukegan?"

"I was there two months ago for a funeral. A cousin of

244

mine was killed in a car accident."

"I'm sorry to hear that." Josh saw the expression on Julia's face and nodded slightly hoping to thwart a reaction. "Losing a loved one that way is hard, it's so abrupt. Was your cousin from Waukegan?" Josh waited a moment. "What was her name, maybe I knew her?"

"Mary Manchester," the lady said. "Her mom and my mom are sisters."

"Did the accident happen in Waukegan?" Josh asked.

"It happened three miles south of here," the woman said. "Please, I don't want to talk about it anymore. It's still too painful. Would you like to reserve a puppy?"

Josh wanted to ask more questions, but didn't want to tip his hand. "I guess we will have to think about it, right, Julia?"

Julia set the puppy down. "They are cute, but Josh is right. We will have to think about it."

The lady handed Josh a business card. "Let me know what you decide."

Josh and Julia hurried to the car. "I'm sure this Mary is the one I was with. There are just too many pieces of the puzzle that fit. We need to find out more about the accident."

"What about the library?" Julia said. "When I was on the debate team we did a lot of our research at the library. I spent hours looking at microfilm. If they have a library, we can look up past editions of the local paper. I'm sure the accident would have been written up in the newspaper."

On their first pass through town, Julia spotted the green library sign hanging on a light pole. It pointed to a large red brick building with white pillars on either side of the entrance.

"Let's hope they are open on Sundays," Josh said, grabbing Julia's hand and rushing up the steps.

Julia stopped at the front counter and quickly ran to

245

the room on the left. "The reference area is over here." She looked around. "I don't see a microfilm projector. We could be in trouble." She returned to the front counter and came back with a sad look on her face. "They don't microfilm." Josh felt color drain from his face. "But they do save a copy of the local paper." She squealed. "They're over here in this file cabinet."

"You stinker!" Josh said. "You really had me going."

Julia opened the top drawer. "It's a weekly paper so we don't have that many to go through." She leafed through the papers checking the dates. "The paper comes out on Thursdays. You were found Friday night, April 17th, so we need to start checking the April 23rd edition."

Josh looked over her shoulder as Julia searched for the correct edition.

"Hurry up, will you," he said, leaning on her back.

Julia poked her elbow into his stomach. "I'm going as fast as I can. Here it is." She pulled it out and brought it over to the table.

Josh scanned the front page. "Look at this," he said, pointing to a small article in the lower right hand corner of the page.

Julia read the headline. "GIRL KILLED IN HEAD ON CRASH." She pointed to the name Mary Manchester in the first paragraph.

Josh read the article, saying the important details out loud. "Early Saturday morning...April 18th...an Illinois girl...25 years old...crossed the medium ... hit by 18 wheel semi." Josh straightened and took a deep breath.

Julia finished the article. "The truck driver was unhurt and cleared in mishap. The investigation is ongoing to determine if drugs or alcohol were involved. The car was a 1959 Rambler Ambassador registered to Charles Manchester ...Waukegan, Illinois."

"This is all further proof that she and I are connected

in this mystery, Josh said. "The day, the time frame, the car, Waukegan. There are just too many things that fit for it not to be."

Julia scoured the rest of the article. "There's no mention of a husband in the list of survivors."

Josh was somewhat relieved hearing that, but was sure Julia was more so. "Now we know why she never came back for me," Josh said. "I feel bad that in some way I might be responsible for her death."

"You can't think that way. You could have been killed yourself. You could have been in the car when it hit that semi."

"We have to go back and talk to Rachel and hope she can shed more light on the situation." He looked to see if anyone was looking before tearing out the article and putting it in his pocket.

"Are you sure you want to talk to her again?" Julia said. "What if...?"

"The mob? Rachel? Are you kidding? Look at the way she's dressed. Look at the house. People in the mob don't live like that. We have to go see her."

*T*he woman was shocked to see them on her doorstep. "That was quick, did you decide on a puppy?"

"No." Josh said. "But we need to talk. My name is Josh Bennett. Does that name mean anything to you?"

"No, should it?" Rachel opened the screen door.

Josh stepped in and handed her the newspaper article. "This is about Mary, I believe I was in the car with her that evening."

The woman stiffened and took a step backwards.

"I don't mean to frighten you. It's a strange story, but please, just listen to what I have to say."

The woman sat and Josh joined her on the couch.

"I was in a coma in Pine Lake for almost two months.

247

I was found unconscious in the park the night Mary was in the accident up here. I don't remember much about that night or anything about my life before waking up." Josh dug the blood-stained piece of paper from his shirt pocket. "This and a key were the only things I had on me. The key opened the door to the house on Grove Street, which led us to the realtor, Dan Kennedy. He said he showed some rental properties to you."

Rachel's eyes widened.

"Did Mary ask you to look at rental homes?"

"Yes," she said. "I hadn't heard from her in two or three years. Then, out of the blue, she calls and says she was looking to rent a furnished place for a friend, and would I look for something in Weston. I met with Mr. Kennedy and when Mary called the next day and I told her about the Grove Street house. She called two days later and said she was driving up and was looking forward to a visit."

Julia jumped into the conversation. "Did she mention she was bringing someone with her?"

"No, but she said not to mention she was coming to anyone." Rachel eyed Josh and cleared her throat. "What makes you think you were in the car with her?"

"He remembered the name Mary when he came out of the coma. I'm a nurse. I was in the room when he woke up." Julia said.

Josh held up his hand to quiet Julia. "I keep getting these images flashing through my mind. One is, I'm riding in a car and a deer jumps out in front of us. I'm yelling, 'Mary watch out!' We found the place where this might have happened and it's close to where I was found. The article said Mary was driving a Rambler Ambassador. Is that right?"

Rachel nodded. "A black one. It was her father's car. Her mom and dad were in Europe on a river cruise. No one knows why she took their car. She had a new Ford

248

Thunderbird of her own."

Josh took the chrome letter from his pocket. "What happened to the Rambler? Is it still around?"

"It sat for the longest time behind the Mobil gas station on Main. I think someone said they took it, or what was left of it, out to Abraham's Junkyard. I'm glad they finally moved it. I couldn't bear to look at it."

Josh showed Rachel the chrome letter and explained how and where they found it. "If this letter came off her car it would pretty much confirm what we have been saying and explain how I ended up in Pine Lake."

"Old man Abraham lives next to the yard. You probably passed it on your way into town," Rachel said.

"Mary told you she was looking forward to a visit," Josh said. "Did she say it just like that, a visit?

Rachel nodded. "I asked her what was bringing her to Weston. She said she would tell me about it when she got here."

"Mary rented 1521 Grove Street in my name. She sent a check for three months' rent to Mr. Kennedy. If she was coming for a visit, the house wouldn't have been for her," Josh sat back on the couch. "The one thing that bothers me is why she would drive off and leave me."

"Maybe she was hurt and tried to get here so I could help her," Rachel said. "The coroner's report showed she had internal bleeding that occurred prior to her being hit by the semi. They thought she might have been in a prior accident, but couldn't confirm that. The coroner figured she passed out or was unconscious before she hit the semi. He told us she probably never knew what hit her."

"I feel bad for you and her family. If we only knew the reason we were coming here." Josh asked.

"Did Mary have a husband?" Julia asked.

"No, she was single." Rachel wiped a tear on her sleeve.

"What kind of work did she do?" he asked. "Maybe I

249

worked with her."

"She graduated from Marquette law school in Milwaukee, I assume she was working as a lawyer."

"She was driving her father's car? What does he do?" Julia asked.

"He's a retired Presbyterian Minister. Mary was the pride of his life. He tried to find out why she was making the trip up here, but all they told him was that she had taken a few days off and was going to visit friends up north."

Josh gave Julia a menacing look. "Do her folks still live in Waukegan?"

"Yes, her dad was a pastor there for twenty-five years. He retired last year and the congregation gave them the European river cruise as a retirement gift."

"If we ever figure out what happened that night, I would like to give her folks any information I might have." Josh said. "Would you write down their address and phone number? I'd appreciate it."

Rachel took her tablet and wrote the information. "Nobody could tell them anything about why she was driving up here. I'm sure they have no idea you were with her."

Abrahams Junkyard

Returning to the car, Josh opened the door. "Was asking what Mary's father did a veiled attempt to connect this to the mob?"

Julia huffed. "Normal people don't send five thousand dollars cash in the mail. I still think there's some shady business going on here. And don't forget about the guy in the cream colored car."

"I suppose it would be foolish not to consider it a possibility. All we can hope for is, if the law is involved, I'm on the right side of it. We need to proceed cautiously until we are sure of what we are dealing with. If the mob is connected we could be in danger."

"I'm glad you are finally taking this seriously." Julia started the car. "At least we know you and Mary weren't married."

"I saw your cheesy smile. I never felt like she was my wife. Let's see if we can find the junkyard and get a look at Mary's car."

Julia retraced their route out of town. "Do you remember where we passed it?"

"There, on the left, I think that's it."

The yard was completely fenced with a large chain and padlock securing the gate. A dog the size of a small pony paced back and forth, barking his fool head off.

"Of course there's got to be a big dog guarding the place," Josh muttered, as Julia pulled to the gate.

A man in bib overalls stepped out of the nearby house.

Josh met him half way. "Hello, sorry to trouble you on a Sunday but I'm an insurance investigator. We were vacationing north of here and were on our way back to Waukegan." The man's expression didn't change. Josh kept rambling. "I got a call from my company. Some paperwork got screwed up and they want me to confirm the VIN number on the '59 Rambler the girl was killed in. The final check is being held up and the family really needs it for burial expenses and all. I was hoping I could see the car."

Josh waited. Still no reaction. It appeared the wheels were grinding in the man's head as he bent over to get a look at Julia sitting in the car.

"If it's too much trouble," Josh added. "I can drive all the way back up here tomorrow, but it sure would save the poor family from any more delays."

The dog continued to bark and jump at the fence. "The last time I checked on the car," Josh said, "it was still behind the Mobil station." *What is it with this guy, what's the big deal?* "When did they move it out here?" The wheels continued to churn in Josh's head. *Maybe I should just get in the car and get my ass out of here.*

"I guess it will be alright," the man finally said. "I wouldn't want the family to have to wait any longer. God knows they suffered enough. Wait here, I'll get my keys."

Josh went to the car. "I didn't know if this guy was going to sic the dog on us or what."

"Insurance investigator? You sure can tell some whoppers."

"C'mon, he is going to let us see the car."

The man came and began unlocking the gate. "You'd best wait here until I get Rex in the office. He don't take kindly to strangers." The man put the dog in the office and closed the door. The dog was not happy with the situation, and showed his displeasure going window to window barking like a crazy fool.

"He can't get out of there can he?" Josh asked.

The man yelled. "Rex! Shut up!" The dog slobbered on the window while continuing to growl angrily. "The car is all the way in the back next to the wrecker. If you don't mind, I'll wait here for you. I got a bum knee and it don't like me walking around on it too much. The young lady can wait here, too, if she wants."

"No, she'll want to come with me," Josh said. "We're newlyweds. This is our honeymoon and she just wants to be at my side no matter what I'm doing."

Julia smiled and nodded vigorously.

They hurried to the back of the yard. Julia couldn't stop laughing. "Newlyweds? Honeymoon? You are such a liar. I don't even remember being asked."

"Did you want to stay back there with the guy and Rex?"

"No way!"

As they came around the corner they saw the mangled mess. The whole front of the car was caved in. The engine had been pushed into the middle of the passenger compartment.

Josh walked slowly to the car. "No one could have survived a crash like that."

Julia stopped in her tracks. "I'm not coming any closer. It's too gruesome. That poor girl."

"The hood is gone, what happened to the hood?" Josh peered inside the car and then walked to the back. "Here it is, or what's left of it." He dragged it out. All but one letter were still mounted on the hood. "Look, the O is missing." He took the letter from his pocket and held it in place. "It's a perfect match."

253

"He put the hood back and grabbed Julia's hand. "C'mon, let's get out of here."

They ran out of the gate, waving and yelling their thanks to the man. Julia turned the key and hit the starter button. At the first sound of the engine firing she threw it into reverse. The car swung around violently. The tires spit stones as she floored it out of the driveway.

Josh looked at the man and waved.

The man shook his fist in return.

"I don't think Mr. Abraham is too happy with us," Josh said.

"There was hardly anything left of that car." Julia's voice cracked. "She must have been crushed to death, and you could have been in there too."

"I think Mary was hurt when we crashed by Pine Lake. The coroner said she was bleeding internally. Like Rachel said. Maybe she tried to make it here to get help."

"She could have gotten help in Pine Lake," Julia said. "Why would she leave you and drive another seventy miles to get help. Can you reach me a soda? There's a bottle opener in the glove box."

Josh reached over the seat and grabbed the two bottles. Opening one he handed it to Julia. "Maybe she didn't want to be found there, or with me?"

Julia took a drink. Her prolonged silence drew Josh's attention. "I know what's whirling around in that pretty little head of yours. You've got that mob thing going, don't you?"

"Well, you have to admit there are a lot of strange things going on here."

Josh reached into his pocket, brought out the note that came with the money and the paper with Mary's parent's information. "The decision now is to figure out who we contact first. I'm sure if we called this Stuart person we would find out real quick what is going on. But then, if your hunch is correct, we could be tipping our whereabouts to the wrong people. Maybe we should talk to Mary's folks first. If we know where she worked and things like that, it might tell us how to proceed." Josh tapped his fingers on his knee.

"So, what are you thinking?"

"Whether we need to drive to Waukegan and speak to them in person. I'm not sure a phone call is the way to handle this after all they've been through."

"I'm off tomorrow and we've got plenty of gas money." Julia slapped the side of her purse.

Josh chuckled. "I guess we do."

The rest of the ride to Pine Lake went by quickly. Josh looked at the dashboard clock. "Its five o'clock, do you want to stop at Teddy's and get something to eat?"

"I could go for some pizza," Julia said. "How about you?"

"Pizza it is."

Julia pulled to the curb in front of Teddy's "I don't think we should say anything about today." She lifted her purse. "Especially not about you know what."

Josh smiled.

A loud cheer went up and everyone started clapping as they walked into the tavern. Julia smiled. Josh was embarrassed.

Teddy pointed to the big trophy sitting on the back bar. "Winning that race is the best thing to happen in this town in a long time. Can I buy you guys a drink?"

Josh looked at Julia. "Would you like something?"

Julia nodded and they both took a seat at the bar.

"What will it be?" Teddy asked, setting a coaster in front of Julia.

"I'll have a whiskey sour."

Josh ordered a big bottle of Blatz. "I'm surprised Doug left the trophy behind. The last I saw him he wasn't letting go of it for love nor money."

255

"He might have had one too many last night. A couple of the guys took him home at closing time and put him to bed. I tried to hand him the trophy, but he said keep it, he'd pick it up later. I haven't seen him today."

"He probably has a massive hangover," Josh said. "We're having pizza, would you mind if we take the drinks and go in the back?"

"Go ahead. I'll have the waitress bring your drinks." Teddy said, motioning to the gal.

Julia ordered the pizza. "I think we ought to leave by six in the morning, if we want to avoid the morning traffic around Milwaukee," she suggested. "That would put us in Waukegan sometime between nine and ten. We have to be back by six or seven so I can get some sleep before going to work at midnight."

"I'll give Doug a call when I get to Nora's," Josh said. "I hope he won't be upset about me taking off work."

Teddy followed the waitress as she brought the pizza. "There was a guy in here earlier today, fishing for information. Wanted to know all about you, when you were found and stuff like that. I thought it was a little weird."

"Did he give you a name?" Josh asked.

"Nah, we were real busy, everyone was still celebrating your big victory. I did see him talking to some of the people at the bar."

"That's okay. I'll probably run into him sooner or later." Josh hoped Julia understood his small head shake and was happy when she smiled and took a bite of her pizza.

Putting the last morsel in his mouth, Josh tossed his napkin on his plate and push back from the table.

Julia folded her napkin and set it beside her plate. "It's obviously our guy in the cream colored car," she said. "What are we going to do about him?"

"If he intended to harm me," Josh said, trying to be reassuring. "I'm sure he's had many chances to do so. I think we should stick with our plan and drive to Waukegan in the morning."

Julia parked in front of Nora's. "Okay, I'm picking you up at six, right?"

"That'll be great. Are you sure, you don't want to come in. I'm sure Nora would like to see you."

"Maybe I should," Julia said. "I never had a chance to thank her for the day off."

Nora opened the door as they walked up the steps. "Here they are, the weary travelers. What did you find out? Did you just get back?"

"We stopped and had pizza at Teddy's," Josh said.

"I never thanked you for the day off," Julia said. "We're going to Waukegan in the morning, but we will be back in time for me to be at work at my regular time."

"You're going to Waukegan?" Nora gave them both a concerned look. "What did you find out in Weston?"

"A lot," Josh said, and proceeded to give Nora a blow-by-blow recap of the day's events. He told her about the house, but purposely left out the envelope full of money and the thousand-dollar check.

"I'm surprised how this all came together." Nora used her handkerchief to wipe her eyes. "It's so tragic about that poor girl."

The mood lightened as Julia repeated the fibs Josh told old man Abraham and how the chrome letter was the only one missing from the hood of Mary's car.

"So who are you going to see in Waukegan," Nora asked.

"Mary's folks live there. Her dad is a Presbyterian minister," Julia said. "We're hoping that he will help us figure out why Josh and his daughter were going to

257

Weston in the first place."

"That's a long way down there. Are you sure you can get down there and back, and still get to work," Nora asked with concern. "Let me get someone to cover your shift. This is important to Josh. You don't know where this will lead, or how much time it will take."

"I hate to miss work, but you're right. We are so close. We need to stay until we get this resolved."

"I'll make sure you're covered money-wise," Josh said.

Julia gave Nora a big hug. "Thanks for everything. I'm going home to take care of a few things so I'm ready to go in the morning." She gave Nora an extra squeeze.

"I just hope you guys find what you are looking for." Nora said.

Josh walked Julia to her car. "I want you to know how much I have enjoyed our time together. You are a very special person and regardless of what we find tomorrow, I hope it won't change a thing for us."

"Me too," she said. Opening her purse, she handed him the wad of bills. "Here, I don't want the responsibility of carrying this around in my purse any longer. Have you got a safe place to put it?"

"I forgot about this." Josh proceeded to stuff the money in his pocket.

Julia laughed at the big lump it made in his pants. "It should be safe in there. Nobody would ever suspect you were carrying a big wad of cash in your pocket."

Josh tried to pat it down. "Maybe people will think I am impressively endowed."

Julia laughed. "I guess that would be impressive if that was all you."

Josh made his eyebrows go up and down.

"In your dreams," she said and drove off.

Julia felt the tears coming. She wanted for him to know who he was, but dreaded the thought that it could lead to the end of their relationship. She felt torn between wanting the morning to come quickly, or not at all.

She put her purse on the kitchen table and unbuttoned her blouse as she walked to the bedroom. She looked at the bed and wondered if she would ever lie with him and snuggle in his arms?

A Letter to Julia

Josh walked slowly back to the house. He couldn't shake the questions that flooded his mind. Why was he and this Mary driving to Weston? What was the hurry, and why all the secrecy? Why did he need a house? Was he running away from something, or someone? Who was this Stuart person, and what was the money for?

Standing on the porch he thought about what he would say to Mary's parents and didn't hear Nora open the door.

"A lot of thoughts on your mind?"

"I was thinking of how to handle things tomorrow. I guess once we put the wheels in motion, good or bad, we will find out the truth."

"Nothing is written in stone. Go there with an open mind. If there is something that needs fixing, fix it."

"I've enjoyed my time here in Pine Lake and regardless of what or who I was before, I can choose to come back."

"Absolutely," Nora said, putting a hand on his shoulder. "Now, you better get your buns upstairs and get some sleep. You have a big day ahead of you."

Josh walked the stairs as Nora doused the lights. Sitting on the couch, he took a sheet of paper and began writing.

Dear Julia,
If you get this letter it will be because I am unable

260

to return to Pine Lake with you. If this happens, I want you to know that I am thankful for all the things you did for me, the fun we had and the joy you brought into my life. I have no idea where this money came from or who it belongs to, but I think it is only right that you get to enjoy some of it.
Love, Josh.

He took the money and check from Weston, plus the cash he got from the county, and counted out five, one hundred dollar bills. He folded the letter around the bills and wrote her name on the envelope. Taking another envelope, he wrote: Give to the county treasurer for payment of loan to Josh Bennett. Counting out two hundred fifty dollars, he put it in the envelope and licked it shut. He folded the rest of the money and put it in his pocket. He set the envelopes on the TV.

Julia was up at five. She'd taken the time before going to bed to lay out the outfit she planned to wear, baby blue blouse and white Bermuda shorts. After a quick shower and a light touch of makeup, she checked the clock while taking out the last of the sponge rollers. She brushed through her hair and generously sprayed it. "That's going to have to hold all day."

Picking up her everyday purse, she wrinkled her nose. She went to the closet and found a small blue purse that matched her blouse. It was evident not everything was going to transfer. Her billfold was almost as big as the small purse. She threw in her driver's license, a lipstick, a few tissues and put her billfold back into the old purse. She grabbed a sweater, her car keys, and went out the door.

As she drove up the street she wondered if she should have grabbed some cash. She looked at the dashboard clock and decided if she needed money Josh would have

261

to give her some.

Josh had tossed and turned most of the night. He was dressed and ready at five thirty. He picked up the envelopes and started down the stairs. The sweet aroma of freshly brewed coffee was heavy in the air. Nora sat at the counter stirring her cup. "Want some?" she said as he entered the room.

"Yes, please. It smells good."

"Are you ready for your big day?" She said, setting the cup in front of him.

"I hope so." He took a sip. "I didn't sleep for beans."

"Would you like me to fix you something to eat?"

"Maybe a piece of toast." Josh laid the envelopes on the counter by her cup.

"What's this?" she asked.

"Just in case, for whatever reason, I don't make it back here, would you please give one to Julia and the other to the county treasurer?"

Nora felt the envelope marked for the treasurer. "What's in here, money?"

"It's to pay back the loan he gave me."

Nora squeezed the one marked for Julia, "in here, too?"

Josh saw the look on Nora's face. "I guess you're wondering where the money came from?"

"My next question," Nora pushed the toast and a jar of jelly in front of him.

"We probably should have told you last night. In the house, the one in Weston, we found an envelope under the mail drop in the garage. It was sent from Waukegan. Josh reached into his pocket and pulled out the driver's license. "There was a lot of cash and this was in it, too."

She studied the license. "You look a little different, but that's definitely you. Josh Bennett, it's a nice name. Who sent it to you?"

Josh showed her the note. "It will be interesting to find out who Stuart is. The envelope was postmarked the day after I was found. The house was rented a few days before."

"You said there was money, how much?"

"Five-thousand, all in one-hundred dollar bills."

"Good Lord almighty." Nora choked. "That's a small fortune. What do you think it was for?"

"I don't have a clue," Josh said taking the note back. "I'm sure when we find out what the money was for, we'll have a direct link back to who I am."

Nora took the envelopes and put them in the cupboard. "Well, I'm not doing anything with these until I hear from you."

"Also, if I don't make it back, I want to thank you for everything you've done for me. If it wasn't for you, I'd still be running around in a hospital gown." He began peeling a bill from the wad. "I owe you a lot..."

"Put that money away. You don't owe me a thing. I've enjoyed having you, and I fully expect to see you back here."

The doorbell rang. Nora went and brought Julia to the kitchen. Josh jumped off his stool and gave Julia a hug and quick kiss.

Julia turned down Nora's offer of coffee. "I've got too many butterflies in my stomach."

"Me, too," Josh said. "We can catch something along the way." He gave Nora a hug. "It's time to get this show on the road."

What's in Waukegan?

"**W**ould it be alright if I tried driving?" Josh asked before they reached the car. "I have a license, you know."

"Are you sure you know how?"

"I have been watching you. If I have a problem we can switch."

Julia reluctantly agreed and cringed as Josh ground the gears on his first few shifts. Surprisingly, he became more fluid with each change after that. After directing him out of town she opened the map. "We stay on 37 until we come to highway 41. It will take us to Milwaukee, through Racine, Kenosha, and across the border into Waukegan."

"Do we have enough gas?"

Julia leaned over. "There's a gas station where we pick up 41. Let's stop there and pick up a sweet roll."

"Sounds good."

Once they gassed up, got a roll and coffee, and proceeded down 41, the miles passed quickly. The morning commute around Milwaukee offered no problems as traffic moved at normal speed.

"What are we going to do once we get to Waukegan, see Mary's parents?" Julia asked.

"I don't want to add to their grief or confuse them by saying I was in the car without having the reason of why

264

I was with her."

"True. So, what's your plan?"

"To find a telephone booth and call this Stuart. It may cause a firestorm, but we'll have to face that sooner or later. If things are good, fine, if not, we'll have to fix or deal with the consequences."

Julia couldn't shake the feeling of a mob connection. Fixing that might be tricky, depending on which side of the law Josh was on. Married was the scenario she feared most. Fixable, highly unlikely. She dreaded the thought, but had faced that possibility all along. "I agree. That way we will definitely find out who you are."

They passed through Kenosha and the state border came a few minutes later. Julia pointed out the Waukegan city limits sign. They had reached their destination. She put down the map. "You'll have to take it from here, I have no idea where to go."

Josh made a few turns, and soon, they were in the heart of the city.

"Do you know where you're going?"

"No, maybe instinctively." He parked the car in front of a large building in what appeared to be the heart of downtown.

Julia glanced around. "Does any of this look familiar?"

Josh studied each building, each sign, and each storefront. "I don't recognize anything, but I feel I have been here before. It's hard to describe."

"There is a phone booth over there if you want to call this guy, Stuart," Julia said. "No sense putting this off any longer."

Josh leaned over and kissed her on the cheek. "For good Luck."

She watched him drop in a coin and dial the number. He waited, then looking at Julia, he raised his hand and shook his head. She thought he was about to hang up the

265

receiver when he suddenly turned and began speaking. After a short exchange, he hung up and hurried back to the car.

"What did he say?" she asked

"It was a woman. She answered 'Stuart Brenaman's office, may I help you?' He was on a call but she asked if I could leave a message of why I called."

"What did you tell her?"

"I said I would call back. I didn't know what to say."

"Did you say his name was Brenaman?"

"Yes, Stuart Brenaman."

"Look at that." Julia pointed to a sign in the storefront window. In bold letters it read, RE-ELECT STUART BRENAMAN, LAKE COUNTY DISTRICT ATTORNEY.

Josh read the sign and then pointed down the street. On the building beyond the phone booth, above towering pillars, engraved in the stone mantel were the words, LAKE COUNTY. "I guess that's where his office would be."

"What are you going to do?" she asked, as he opened his door.

"Find his office and see what happens."

"I'm coming too." Julia ran to catch up. "Wait, we have to put money in the parking meter." Julia fumbled in her purse. "Josh, I don't have any money with me."

He handed her some change.

They held hands and climbed the wide stone steps together. The lobby was huge with marble floors and three large statues along one wall. On the opposite wall, a winding staircase led to the second floor. The ornate mural on the ceiling depicted early settlers trading with Indians.

Walking to the lighted directory of tenants and suite numbers Josh found Brenaman's office listed on the second floor. He took Julia's hand and ascended the stairs.

Josh hesitated at the door before walking in. The

woman at the desk was talking on the phone while busily writing on her spiral bound tablet. Without looking up, she raised her hand with one finger extended as if to say she would be with them in a minute. When she concluded her phone call, Josh moved forward. The lady looked up and her face went white. She jumped out of her chair and opened the gate leading to the back offices. "Come this way," she said as she scurried ahead of them.

Josh and Julia followed her into a large office with a dozen desks scattered throughout the room. One by one, people sat up in their chairs. All eyes were on the young couple. One man, carrying papers, was so engrossed he walked into a post, spilling his papers on the floor. The lady continued through the room as people got up from their desks and began following them.

Julia tugged on Josh's arm. "What's going on?"

Josh shrugged.

The woman entered a back office. A man, with his back to the door, talked on the telephone while looking out the window. The lady knocked hard and in rapid succession on the door jam. The man swung around in his chair. She stepped aside and the man looked at the couple. His face went from mildly inquisitive to utter shock. He dropped the receiver on the cradle and sprang to his feet. Rushing around the desk, "Josh! Josh!" he yelled. "My God, you're safe. You're alive." He gave Josh a big hug. "I can't believe it. What happened to you?"

Josh put up his hand. "Before we go any further, you have me at a disadvantage. You all seem to know me, but I don't know any of you."

The man stepped back. "Josh, you don't know...?"

"I was in a coma for nearly two months in Pine Lake, Wisconsin."

"A coma? Are you alright?"

"I'm fine now, except I don't remember much prior to

267

being found." Josh took Julia's hand. "This is Julia. She has been at my side the whole time. She's a nurse at the facility where I spent most of that time."

The man extended his hand to Julia. "I'm Stuart Brenaman, I'm the district attorney for Lake County."

"We saw your election poster in the store window," Julia said.

"Do I work for you?" Josh asked.

"Not exactly, we were working on a case together."

"So you know who I am?"

The DA paused. "You're Josh Forrester, CPA."

"Wait, I thought I was Josh Bennett." He reached in his pocket and brought out his driver's license.

The man looked at it and broke into a broad smile. "You must have made it to Weston."

"We were there yesterday," Josh confirmed. "That's how we found you."

"Where did you say you were, in the coma?"

"Pine Lake, it's about seventy miles south of Weston."

"And that's where you've been all this time?" Brenaman looked at one of his subordinates. "Didn't we check on that Pine Lake thing? I know we checked on every accident or event that happened in that whole area."

"We did," the man replied. Someone in the sheriff's office told us it was a party at a quarry and a person was hurt in a fall. We didn't pursue it any further."

Brenaman looked at Josh. "I guess we should have looked into that situation a little further. We did a lot of checking, but we had to be so careful not to expose the reason we were doing it. If the papers would have gotten the story there would have been a lot of the wrong people out there looking for you. Pete McFarland has been camped out in Weston since you disappeared."

"Does he drive a cream colored sedan?" Josh asked.

"You saw him? That's who I was talking to when you

came in the office. He thought he recognized you from a TV spot about a sailboat race or something. Was that you on the bicycle?"

Josh nodded. "I was going to talk to him but he drove off."

"When you didn't recognize him, he chose not to confront you. I told him yesterday to discreetly check on you. He drove to Pine Lake yesterday but couldn't find you.

"I'm sure I saw him on our way to Weston," Josh said. "We figured he was looking for us, but didn't know why."

"He talked to your landlady this morning but she wouldn't tell him anything."

Josh smiled. "That would be Nora. She's not easily intimidated."

Stuart tossed the license on the desk. "As you can see, crooks aren't the only ones that can make a good forgery." He opened the drawer and handed Josh a billfold. "We had to give you a new identity."

Josh opened the wallet and took out the driver's license. Swallowing deeply, he wiped the corner of his eye and read the information aloud. "Josh Forrester, born July 26, 1937." Showing the license to Julia, he said, "This is me. The real me."

Julia squeezed his hand.

"How did you find your way to Weston?" The DA asked.

Josh related the story of the blood stained paper. How they found the envelope and learned about Rachel Benson from the realtor, Dan Kennedy. He credited Julia for suggesting they go to the library where they found the newspaper account of Mary's accident."

Julia told of the antics that went on at Abraham's junkyard. Josh showed the chrome letter. "We found this embedded in a dirt bank near where I was found. When it matched the missing one on her car, we were sure I had been in the car with this Mary Manchester."

"That's a fine piece of investigative work," Stuart said. A spontaneous round of applause broke out.

"Now the big question," Josh asked. "Who is Mary Manchester and why were we going to Weston? Am I in some sort of trouble?"

"This is going to take some time. Let's get some chairs in here," Stuart said. "I've got to make a phone call."

People scurried to bring chairs into the room. A gal offered Josh and Julia something to drink as they sat and waited for Stuart to get off the phone.

Stuart turned a chair backwards and faced them. "First of all, you're not in any trouble, not anymore. Mary was my assistant, a dear sweet girl. She was taking you to Weston to hide you from some pretty unsavory people."

"Was it the mob?" Julia blurted.

"There was an underworld connection." Stuart said. "You did an audit of one of the big banks in Waukegan and turned up a huge money laundering scheme being operated by a crime family from Chicago. It also involved the president and a few officers at the bank. We made a bunch of arrests and wanted to use your report under the banner of your company without naming you directly. Lawyers for the accused filed to have the report disallowed. The judge was going to toss it unless the person who did the work testified to its validity. That meant our whole case would go up in smoke if you didn't take the stand. I left that decision to you. You were prepared to testify."

Stuart got up from his chair. "That's when all hell broke loose. Word on the street was, there was a contract out on you. We scrambled, we had to come up with a plan fast. We needed a place to hide you until the trial. Mary told us about Weston. She had a cousin there that could help us with the logistics. We didn't know who we could trust. I personally picked you up at your office and brought you here. We put you in a motel in Kenosha for a couple of days while we got things lined up. We couldn't take the chance of you going back to your place, so Mary went to the Sears store around the corner and bought you some clothes to travel in.

"Mary's parents were in Europe on some kind of cruise. She borrowed their car thinking someone might recognize hers."

"The Thunderbird?" Josh said

Stuart looked at Josh. "How did you know that?"

"Rachel Benson, Mary's cousin."

"We thought everything went fine until we found out two days later that Mary had died in an accident. Her brother called to tell me what had happened. When there was no mention of you we didn't know what to do. We couldn't send a bunch of people up there snooping around for fear of alerting the bad guys down here."

"So you didn't know about Mary until the Monday after?" Josh asked.

"Her folks got back a few days later. Her dad called me. I felt bad that I had to lie to him. I told him she had taken a few days off to visit some family and friends in Wisconsin. Here again, we were trying not to blow your cover."

Josh lowered his head. "So, her folks don't know I was with her."

"I took her dad to lunch on Friday and told him the whole story," Stuart said.

"So, does that mean I no longer have a target on my back?"

"That's true, when you disappeared we started putting pressure on people at the bank to try to save our case. One of the younger guys finally took our offer of immunity and spilled the beans on everyone. He verified all the figures

271

on your report and we got our conviction. The case ended Wednesday."

Stuart reached in the opened drawer and took out a watch and a ring of keys. "These are yours, too."

Josh put the watch on his wrist. He looked at the keys, but none looked familiar. "I'm glad you were able to complete your case without my testimony. I'm just sorry it cost Mary her life."

"We all are," Stuart said. "It was a tragic accident, but that's what is was, an accident. She was doing what she felt she needed to do. We're just glad that you're safe."

A commotion in the outer office caused everyone to look. "There's someone here I think you will be happy to see." Stuart said.

Josh and Julia stood. A young woman ran through the office towards them.

"Josh! Josh!" She yelled and threw her arms around him. Julia stepped back as she caught a whiff of the familiar My Sin fragrance. The girl sobbed and shook as she continued to hold onto Josh.

Julia couldn't help but noticed the wedding band. Her head started to pound, she felt dizzy, and her breathing became erratic. She collapsed on a chair as tears streamed down her cheeks.

The girl finally took her head off Josh's chest and saw the blank look on his face. "Josh! Don't you know me?" She looked into his eyes. "It's me, Jenny."

Josh closed his eyes and shook his head, his mind whirled as images bombarded his consciousness. He saw a boy and girl dancing, a man and a boy sailing and a boy with his hand on his chest reciting the pledge of allegiance. Seasons changed as if years were flying by. He opened his eyes and stared at the girl. A smile slowly came to his lips. "Jenny," he said, running his fingers over her cheeks and lips. He cupped her face in his hands and gave her a big kiss.

Julia felt her world crash around her. She buried her face in her hands and sobbed. Josh's hand drew her to her feet. "Julia, I want you to meet my sister, Jenny."

The girls fell into each other's arms. They hugged as their tears flowed freely. "I'm so happy to meet you," Julia sobbed.

"Me, too." Jenny wiped the tears off her cheeks.

Josh put his arms around both of them as the room exploded in a round of applause.

Julia had seen the way Josh looked at Jenny. "Do you remember her?"

Josh smiled. "I do. It's all coming back." He turned to Stuart. "It's not all there yet, but I do remember driving to Weston with Mary. When that deer jumped in front of the car, she swerved and we hit the wall of dirt. I guess we were both knocked unconscious. When I came to, Mary was slumped over the wheel. I saw a light off in the distance and went to get help."

"That must have been the parking lot light at The Glen," Julia said. "Remember, we could see it from where we found the letter? If you would have made it to The Glen, I would have been there to help you."

Josh nodded to her and turned back to Stuart. "You're right. She loved working for you. I'm sure she tried to make it to Weston to get help for both of us."

"Probably, hoping to get help before your identity and whereabouts were discovered," Stuart added.

"And it cost her her life." Josh said. "I must stop and see her folks. It may help them deal with their loss if I can tell them a little bit about the last hours of her life."

"I'm sure her dad and mom would love to hear from you."

Josh reached into his pocket and brought out the wad of money. "I guess this belongs to you."

"What is it?"

"It's the money you sent to Grove Street. It's a little short, I had a few expenses I had to take care of."

"You keep it. You earned it."

"This is a lot of money. Why did you send so much?"

"We had no idea how long you would have to stay there," Stuart said. "You needed food, new clothes and a car of some sort. We wanted to make sure you were covered."

"Don't we have to give it back to wherever it came from?"

"It came out of a fund where we put money confiscated in drug busts and other illegal activities. Getting it out is easy, trying to put it back requires a mountain of paperwork, especially now, since the case is closed. The best thing is for you to keep it."

"You're joking right?"

"No," Stuart said. "Seriously, with everything you have gone through, you've earned every penny. Case closed. He walked around his desk and sat. "So, what are you going to do now?"

"Take care of loose ends. I'll have to check with my firm to see what my employment status is. I'll also want to spend time with Jenny." Josh thought for a moment. "How did she know I was here?"

Stuart smiled.

"That was the phone call you made."

"She's the only one outside of this office that knew about our plan to send you to Weston. She was so good about it and understood that going public about your disappearance would only put you in jeopardy. It was really hard on her."

Stuart stood and extended his hand. "You take care of yourself and if you ever need…anything, just call. You've got my private number."

Josh took a slip of paper from Stuart's desk and wrote a name. "Maybe you could find this person for me. It's an eight year old jewelry fencing case out of Chicago.'

"I'll put someone on it." Stuart said.

"Are you girls ready to get out of here?" Josh said.

Jenny took Julia by the arm. "You guys are coming over to the house. Frank can put some steaks on the grill and we can spend time getting to know one another."

Lunch at the Blue Water Inn

"Jen, where are you parked?" Josh asked.

"I'm around the corner. Are you coming to the house now? I'm dying to hear how you two met and everything that's happened to you."

"I'd like to show Julia around a bit," Josh said. "How about we come over about four?"

"Okay. I'm sure you two have a lot to talk about. I'll stop and get some of your favorite slaw from Leo's deli." She gave him a quick peck on the cheek.

"I figured we needed some time to ourselves," Josh said, as they walked to the car.

"Thank you," Julia said weakly, "I'm emotionally drained."

"Let's go down by the lake. There's a great restaurant overlooking the marina. We can have lunch and relax. Is that alright with you?"

"Any place will be fine."

It was evident Josh knew his way as he drove through town. There was no hesitation, no look of doubt on his face.

"Do you remember everything? What triggered it?" Julia asked.

"I guess it was Jenny. Just seeing her, hearing her, smelling her perfume. It was like a thousand flash bulbs going off in my head. I thought I was watching a movie of my life going by in super-fast motion. I'm not sure of every detail, but I know who I am, where I live, where I work, it's all there. Dr. Erickson said it might happen that way, it was like someone flipped on a switch."

Julia read the sign in front of the restaurant. "Blue Water Inn, Established 1954, Serving the Finest Steaks and Seafood." It sat mid-way down a hill overlooking Lake Michigan. A large anchor sat in the middle of the circular flowerbed that split the walk to the entrance. The bed was alive in a colorful display of geraniums, pansies, and petunias. The restaurant's weathered board exterior was accented with ornate shutters painted light blue to match the roof trim. A doorman dressed in a naval uniform greeted them, and opened the heavy timber clad door.

Once inside, a man with slicked back silvery hair, a pencil-thin mustache, and wearing a tuxedo with shiny lapels approached, "Table for two, Mr. Forrester?"

"Thank you, Reneè." Josh also greeted the bartender by name before motioning Julia to follow the host. Renee' held a chair for Julia at a table by the window.

Julia sat, and immediately turned to watch the activity on the harbor below. People were scurrying around the hundreds of boats moored in the maze of docks and slips. There were sailboats, speedboats, and cabin cruisers, each one big or bigger than the next. "Wow, people must have a fortune in some of those boats."

"I'm sure some of them do." Josh greeted the waitress by her first name. She in turn questioned where he had been. Skipping the details, he basically told of being in an accident and spending time in a hospital.

Julia looked at the menu. "Expensive."

"They have a wonderful cold seafood platter with jumbo shrimp and crab salad on a bed of fresh greens," Josh said. "Would you like one?"

277

Julia nodded, put down the menu and gazed around the room.

The restaurant was elegant. The tables were covered with pale pink tablecloths, cloth napkins, crystal glassware and highly polished tableware. The diners were well dressed, the men in suits and the ladies smartly attired in tailored outfits. She turned to Josh and straightened the collar on her blouse. "I've never been in a place this fancy."

Josh gave the waitress their order. "It's a little over the top, but the food is wonderful and it's hard to beat the view. At night, with all the lights, it is even more beautiful and romantic."

The busboy came with a water pitcher and filled their glasses. Another waitress came to the table to express her happiness at seeing Josh again and two professional looking men approached to ask where he had been the past couple of months.

"You're a pretty popular fellow," Julia said. "I think everyone in the place knows you."

Josh's face flushed. "I come here a lot."

Julia continued to look out the window. Romantic setting, fancy meal, she bit her tongue but couldn't keep from posing the question. "Do you bring girls here?"

"I have, but mostly I come here for lunch with people from work." Josh fidgeted in his chair.

A third man came to the table. Josh stood and shook his hand. They exchanged pleasantries before Josh extended his hand towards Julia. "This is a dear friend of mine. She helped nurse me back to health."

The man leaned forward and shook Julia's hand. "It appears you've done a fine job, Josh has never looked so good." The man tapped Josh on the shoulder and winked. "Lucky dog," he said under his breath, as he walked away.

"Who was that?" Julia asked.

"President of the bank I deal with." Josh was happy to

see the waitress bring their food.

Julia put her fork into one of the giant prawns and held it up. "I didn't know you could get shrimp this big." She dipped it in the cocktail sauce and took a bite. "Oh, that's so delicious." Everything on her plate was delicious. She ate it all, including the sprig of parsley that was there for decoration.

They declined dessert, so the waitress set down a leather folder and gathered up the rest of the dishes. "It's nice to have you back, Mr. Forrester," she said as she backed away from the table.

"Thank you. It's good to be back." He opened the folder, scribbled some numbers and signed the check. He closed the folder and sat back in his chair.

"That's it? They let you just sign the check?" Julia asked.

Josh laughed. "It's not free, we have an account here. We send a check at the end of the month. How would you like to take a walk down on the pier and look at the boats?"

"I'd love to."

On the walk down Julia would point to a particular boat and ask about it. Josh would not only name the owner, but would give a little biographical information on him.

"Do you know all these people?"

"Some I know, and some I know of them." Josh steered her down a particular pier. At the third slip, he stopped and pointed to a large sailboat. "What do you think of this one?"

She read the name painted on the stern, "Totally Deductible." The hull was painted bright white, had teak decks, and well-polished hardware. She was looking up at the mast and rigging and didn't notice Josh stepping into the boat.

"What are you doing?" she said. "You shouldn't be in there."

279

"It's okay, I know the owner. C'mon I'll show you around."

"Josh, is this your boat?"

"Yes." he said with a smile. "Do you like it? Come aboard, I want to show it to you."

Josh helped her step onto the boat. "It's a twenty-nine foot Wayfarer Islander. I had it built in California. It has sleeping quarters fore and aft, a full galley and a nice sitting area." He took the keys that Brenaman had given him earlier and opened the cabin door. He stepped in and motioned her to follow.

They stood in the galley, complete with stove, sink, and refrigerator all neatly compacted along one side. "The booth is big enough to sit four people for dinner and makes into a bed at night." Walking ahead, he pointed to ladder steps going down to a sleeping compartment. The forward quarters has a full size mattress with its own compact shower and toilet. There are bunk beds in aft quarters.

Back on deck Josh sat along one side and Julia sat on the opposite side. "So this is how you knew so much about sailing."

"My father got me started when I was eight years old. We would sail every Sunday afternoon. His boat was a little bigger than Doug's."

"Does your father still sail with you?"

"Both my parents have been gone for a while. Mom's heart gave out, and it broke Dad's. He never got over her death. I was in my third year at Northwestern."

Julia focused on the small flag fluttering atop of the mast. "I used to think we had some big boats on Pine Lake, but we have nothing like this." Julia sighed. "I guess I never gave this part much thought, of what your life was like before you came to Pine Lake." She looked at him and wondered what happened to the person she had

280

come to know. "A few hours ago you were a man without a past,wearing hand-me-down clothes. Now, people are eager to shake your hand and you have the wherewithal to have a twenty-nine foot sailing yacht custom built for you."

"I guess it's pretty overwhelming."

"I just never expected this."

"Expected what?"

"That you were rich. My whole concern was that you were married or engaged."

"Well, I'm not married or engaged. Rich? Maybe by Pine Lake standards, but I'm still the person you helped nurse back to health." Josh offered his hand as they stepped out of the boat.

Him being rich was going to take some getting used to she thought as they walked up the hill.

"I want to swing by my apartment and check on a few things before we go over to Jenny's. Is that, okay?"

Julia nodded. Good Lord, an apartment too, what will that be like?

"It's only a few minutes from here," he said, driving out of the restaurant parking lot. At the top of the hill he turned and entered the underground parking garage of a large five-story building and parked next to a dusty '62 Corvette.

Julia looked out her window. "Yours?"

"I guess the dust gives it away. I hope it will start."

Julia followed Josh through a door and then into an elevator. Josh pushed the button for the fifth floor.

"You live on the top floor?" She had to hold back from saying what she was thinking. Of course he did. Why wouldn't he?

"There are four apartments on each floor. I have one that faces the lake," he said, getting off the elevator. He unlocked the door on his right. It swung open to a large

281

living area with wall to ceiling glass across the far wall.

The restaurant and harbor lay below. "You have a spectacular view from up here," she said. The room was decorated in soft autumn colors. The furniture looked new. On the right stood a bar with marble top, mirrored shelves, and four overstuffed stools. The assortment of cut glassware and ornate bottles sparkled under a large chandelier. The kitchen could have graced the pages of any home and garden magazine.

Julia wiped her finger across the table. "Do you have someone living with you?" she asked. "Somebody has been doing the dusting."

"We have cleaning people that come once a week. They keep the place ready to show at any time. Would you like to see the rest of the place?" He walked down the hall. "It's a two bedroom apartment, about eleven hundred square feet." Josh sounded like a real estate salesman. "The apartments facing east have a view of the lake. The ones facing west have a view of the city. All nineteen units are leased and there's a waiting list if one opens. Since all floor plans are basically the same, we use mine to show prospective clients."

"By we, do you mean you? Do you own this building?" Julia swallowed hard.

"Jenny and I. Thanks to Dad. He and mom had a grocery store on Grand Avenue for thirty-five years. They were pretty successful. Both were workaholics.

"Dad was always buying stock, but saw the craziness that was going on in the stock market and he cashed out before the crash in '29. During the depression he'd pick up small parcels of land and old buildings downtown, things people were about to lose to the banks. Dad would give them a small amount and take over the mortgages. He never went back into the stock market. He just kept buying and selling land and buildings."

"You own more buildings?"

"About forty, mostly downtown. There's been a resurgence in the past five years. The demand for retail and office space is strong. We keep remodeling and renting them. C'mon, I'll show you the rest of the apartment. This is the guest bedroom, it has its own private bath," he said, opening a door on the left.

Julia peeked through the doorway. Everything was neat and decorated like it came from the same magazine as the living room.

Opening double doors on the right, he walked ahead of her. "This is the master suite."

The other parts of the apartment were impressive, but Julia couldn't think of words to describe this room. The back wall had large windows on each side of French doors that went out onto a balcony. The brocade drapes hung ceiling to floor. Two large overstuffed chairs faced each other, flanked by tables and reading lamps.

"I've never seen a bed this big," she said, and bounced on the edge. The headboard was massive with matching carved wood end tables and brass lamps on either side.

"It's a California king." Josh opened the bathroom door. The vanity held double sinks with gilded oval mirrors on the wall. It had both a large tub and huge shower stall.

"Four people could shower in here all at once!" Julia said opening the glass door.

Josh laughed while moving to the next door. "This is the walk in closet. It's a real selling point. People love it."

The closet was as big as Julia's kitchen. It had double clothes bars, one high and one low along each wall. At the end was a large full size mirror with a built in chest of drawers on one side, and shelves loaded with shoes on the other. Julia walked to the chest. She opened the top one. It contained socks, all rolled and aligned by color, light to dark. She opened the second drawer. It contained boxer

283

shorts in a multitude of colors and patterns.

She picked up a pair and looked at the tag. "This one doesn't have your name on the label," she said.

"What?"

"The shorts you were wearing when they found you in Pine Lake had your name printed on the label."

"Oh, My Gosh, I forgot about that." Josh picked another pair from of the drawer. That one had the word Josh neatly hand printed on the label. "This is funny."

"Why would you print your name in your shorts? That's weird."

"I take my clothes to the Chinese laundry near work. And for a while, every week I'd come up missing a pair or two of my shorts. I wrote my name on the label hoping they could keep from losing them. They're silk and somewhat expensive. It turned out a boy working for them had a lucrative business selling them to his buddies at school."

Julia put the shorts back in the drawer. "It's a good thing you put your name on the label or we would have been calling you 'Fruit of the Loom.'"

It took Josh a moment to catch the joke. "They're actually from Bloomingdale's, but I guess that would have been just as funny." Josh laughed. Julia smiled.

"This is very impressive," Julia said. "Your father must have done a lot of wheeling and dealing to acquire a building like this."

"Actually it was all about timing. In the early fifties, the state was in the middle of building the toll way and needed a chunk of land he bought in the thirties for a major intersection and off ramp. They paid him a huge price. At the same time, this building was almost complete when the builder ran into some financial problems. Dad was able to buy and complete it for basically what the state paid him. The timing was perfect."

"How much does it cost to live here?"

"Well, I don't pay, but the units rent for four fifty. It brings in about nine thousand a month."

When they got down to the garage, Josh stepped over to the blue Corvette. "Let's see if it will start." He put the key in the ignition, pumped the accelerator a few times and turned the key. The starter growled and the engine fired. He let it idle for a minute and then stepped down the accelerator a few times. The engine responded instantly with a mild roar. He let it idle a few minutes and turned it off. "That's great! I'll have it washed and it'll be ready to go."

Dinner at Jennys

The drive to Jenny's took about twenty minutes. Julia stared out the window trying to sort the many thoughts floating around in her head. She no longer worried about another woman, but how was this money and lifestyle going to affect their relationship?

She sat forward when Josh turned into the driveway of a large two-story house. The yard was awash in color with flowers and plants of every variety. The bushes were trimmed and the grass freshly mowed and edged. Josh drove to the house on a large circular drive. "Here we are," he announced.

As they were exiting the car, the front door flew open and Jenny rushed out to greet them. "I'm so glad you are here. I've been dying to talk to you." She gave each a big hug. "C'mon, I made lemonade and baked some chocolate chip cookies. The steaks are marinating and I picked up some of Leo's coleslaw."

The house was not new, but well kept and neat as a pin. The walls were covered with oil paintings and photos. A large formal dining room with an elegantly carved table and eight high backed chairs, was to the left. The matching breakfront held beautifully decorated china, crystal glassware, and silver serving items. The living room was huge, with two couches, four overstuffed chairs and a variety of tables, both high and low. The white marble fireplace took most of the far wall, and to the right, book shelves covered floor to ceiling with every space filled.

"My goodness. Who reads all the books?" Julia asked. "You have more books than the Pine Lake Library."

"That's Frank," Jenny said. "I read some, but he's always got his nose in a book. Josh, why don't you pour us all a glass of lemonade while I show Julia the rest of the house."

Josh walked into the kitchen and took the lemonade out of the refrigerator. He put ice in the glasses Jenny had placed on the counter and poured them full. He took one of the glasses, walked to the adjoining sunroom, and sat on the wicker couch. The windows were open and a cool breeze brought with it the smell of fresh cut grass. He took a sip of the lemonade and wondered how he was going to fit in seeing Mary's folks, checking in at work and driving Julia back to Pine Lake. "Okay, smarty," he said aloud. "If you drive her there, how are you going to get back to Waukegan? A good question." He reached into his pocket and brought out the wad of money. He looked at the check from the realtor. He studied it for a moment. "I'm sure it came from the same place, so Stuart is not going to take it back.

He searched the kitchen and found a pen and notepad. He wrote a short message, put the check and note in an envelope and licked it shut. He walked outside and put it in the glove box of Julia's car. "I'll give it to her on the trip back to Pine Lake."

He went back to his place on the couch and took another sip of lemonade. He leaned back, slowly closed his eyes and drifted off to sleep.

Jenny's home was no less impressive than Josh's place. The furnishings were expensive looking and color

287

coordinated. Original oils hung on the walls and a variety of statuary adorned the shelves and tables. Nothing appeared out of place.

"You have a very beautiful home," Julia said as she followed Jenny down the stairs.

"It was my folk's," Jenny said. "I've redecorated the whole place so it really feels like my own."

Seeing Josh asleep on the porch, Jenny suggested they sit in the living room. Julia picked up one glass of lemonade and took a sip, as she walked to the fireplace. Looking at the pictures that lined the mantel, one caught her eye. Josh as a boy, wearing a tuxedo, top hat and cane, holding Jenny who was decked out in a satin dress and tiara.

"Did you guys take dance lessons?"

"Oh yeah," Jenny said. "That was mom's thing. Josh took tap and I took ballet. We both took ballroom. That picture is when we won the 1950 city juvenile ballroom championship. He was twelve and I was fourteen."

Julia giggled. "We went to the Yacht Club dance Saturday night, in Pine Lake. Josh surprised everyone with his dancing. He's a really good dancer and now I know why."

"I'm surprised," Jenny said. "He hated those lessons. I don't remember ever seeing him dance as an adult."

The next picture was of Jenny and a man with a butch haircut and full mustache. "Is this Frank?"

"Yes." Jenny picked up the picture. "This was taken the day we got engaged. Frank was a carpenter for one of Dad's contractors. My Father wasn't too thrilled about me dating him, but after we were married he and Frank got along real well."

"How long have you been married?"

Jenny set the picture back on the mantel. "Four years. We were only married a year when dad passed away. Josh was still in school. I was twenty-three and left with all of the property to manage. Frank was a big help. He handled the fixing and repair problems. We've remodeled most of our older buildings but they still require a lot of attention. Frank is in charge of property maintenance."

Julia looked up at the large wedding picture above the fireplace. "No children?"

"We've been trying, but no luck so far," Jenny swallowed hard, "I used to get depressed thinking about it."

"Maybe if you don't try so hard it will just happen." Julia turned as Josh walk into the room. "Did you have a nice snooze?"

"Felt good," Josh said. "What are you girls up to?"

Julia took the picture of him and Jenny. "Now we know why you are such a good dancer. You both look so cute in your dance outfits."

"She would have to show you that," he said, giving his sister a mock dirty look.

"Would anyone like a glass of wine before dinner?" Jenny said. "Josh, why don't you go out and get the charcoal lit. Frank might have been delayed at the office."

Julia followed Jenny to the kitchen. Jenny opened the cupboard and brought out a bottle of wine. "This Cabernet will go good with steak." She put the bottle on the counter and pulled a chair from the table. "I'll have Josh open it when he comes in. Come, sit here. You've got to tell me how you guys met."

Julia explained how and where Josh was found. She gave a brief description of his injuries, the time spent in the hospital and his arrival at The Glen. Julia confessed going to his room while he was in a coma and giving him therapy. They giggled as Julia recounted the night he came to, how he responded by wiggling his big toe. Jenny wiped away a tear when Julia told how Nora

289

gave him some of Duke's clothes and let him live in her upstairs. Jenny loved that he rode a bike and had a job in a liquor store.

"Have the two of you," Jenny started, "you know..."

Julia immediately picked up on what Jenny was asking. She thought about their dip in the lake, and later on her back porch when it felt like the natural thing to do. "No, we could have, but Josh was the sensible one. He said that until we knew more about him and his past, we shouldn't do anything we might regret later." Julia leaned close to Jenny. "If it were up to me, I would have given him anything he wanted." The girls straightened at the sound of the back door opening.

"The charcoal is lit," Josh said.

The girls stifled a laugh.

"What's so funny?"

"Oh, nothing." Jenny pushed the bottle of wine towards him. "Here, open this for us." She took a corkscrew from the drawer and handed it to him.

Josh opened the wine and poured some in three glasses. He handed one to Jenny, then picked up the other two. Handing one to Julia, he said, "I'd like to make a toast." He held his glass to Julia. "I want to thank you for never giving up on me. You have been a true friend and I think the world of you." He clinked his glass to hers and took a drink.

"Think the world of you?" Jenny teased. "That's something you would say to me, your sister. Are you having trouble using the "L-word?"

"Julia knows what I mean."

"Well then, say it." Jenny shot back not letting him off the hook.

Josh looked at Julia. "Can we continue this conversation at a later time, when we are alone?" Julia had no time to respond before Jenny spoke again.

"You men!" she exclaimed. "Why is it so hard for you to express yourself? I love you! I love you! I swear, hell will freeze over before you men get around to telling a girl how you feel about her."

Frank walked in from the garage. "And that goes for you, too!" Jenny said, pointing a finger at him.

"What did I do?" Frank asked.

Josh laughed. "Chief in big trouble. Squaw on warpath."

Jenny wasn't done. "This squaw wants a papoose."

"How much wine has she had?" Frank asked playfully.

Jenny took the platter of steaks out of the refrigerator and handed them to Frank. She gave him a kiss on the cheek and apologized for going off like a nutcase. "I was showing Julia the house and I was thinking how nice it would be to have children running around."

Frank set the platter on the counter. "Hello brother," he said, giving Josh a hug. "Jenny called and told me you were back. Who's the lovely lady?"

"I'd like you to meet Julia, Julia Parsons," Josh said, taking her hand. "She helped nurse me back to health."

Frank shook Julia's hand. "Be careful with this guy, he's quite a Casanova."

Josh shook his head and poured Frank a glass of wine. "C'mon, I'll help you cook up those steaks before you get me into trouble."

While Jenny continued preparing her meal, Julia picked up the story of how they learned about Weston and how it all led them to Waukegan and Stuart Brenaman. "When you came into Stuart's office and flew into Josh's arms, I thought for sure you were his wife."

Jenny smiled. "I guess I was pretty emotional, but he is the only family I've got. I was just so overwhelmed to see him."

"Then it was you're My Sin perfume, Josh freaked me out a couple of times when he identified it on me. He said

291

it was one of the things that triggered the return of his memory." Julia finished her glass of wine. Jenny picked up the bottle to pour her another glass. "Just a little bit, wine and I don't get along very well."

Before sitting down for the meal, Jenny offered a short prayer. "Lord, bless this food and thank you for bringing back Josh, and Julia."

The table discussion centered on the family business. Facts and figures, some almost unbelievable to Julia, were being tossed around. They not only talked thousands, but hundreds of thousands.

Frank talked about the condition of some of the properties while Jenny spoke of the financial concerns. She reminded Josh he had tax filings and reports to get out.

Julia paid more attention to her steak than the conversation. Finished, she pushed her plate forward and caught Josh's attention. "Could I see you in the living room?"

Josh followed her. "What's up?"

"I'm driving back to Pine Lake."

"When?"

"Now," she said. "It's five thirty, I can be home by ten."

"Why don't you wait until tomorrow," he pleaded. "I'll drive you."

"That's silly. How would you get back? Take a bus?"

"It's a long drive. Are you sure you can do it?"

Julia laughed. "I drove all the way from Florida. I know the way, and it's mostly highway driving. This way I can get a good night sleep and get back into my own routine. I have a life back there and you have a life here."

Josh seemed to search for words. "I feel terrible. There is so much I want to talk to you about, but I know people are counting on me to get things back in order."

"It's alright, I understand. I guess we always knew that things would change when we found out who you are.

We'll just have to wait and see how things work out." Julia bit her lip trying not to cry.

"Please stay the night. I don't feel right about you leaving this way," Josh said, taking her in his arms. He tried to kiss her, but she bowed her head.

"No, it's best if I go now." She grabbed her purse and ran out the front door.

The Long Ride Home

"Where's Julia?" Jenny asked when Josh walked into the kitchen alone.

"Gone."

"Why? Is it something we did?"

"It's nothing we did. It's who we are."

"Who we are?" Jenny repeated.

"Julia is a girl who works two jobs, makes a little over minimum wage, and barely scrapes by. She comes down here and what do I do? I take her to the Blue Water and everybody and his brother comes up to the table to shake my hand, including John Bundy, the president of the bank. Then I show her my custom-built sailboat, my fancy rooftop apartment and my Corvette sports car. She comes over here and sees how you live and we spend the whole meal in conversation about property and money. She wasn't ready to handle all of that."

"Josh, you have to do something. She's such a sweet girl and she has a real case for you," Jenny pleaded.

"I know, and I'm really fond... and I'm in love with her."

"Praise be to the saints. I can't believe you said that out loud," Jenny said.

"I was in love with her from the moment I woke up from the coma. It was just such a complicated matter. I tried to hold back, not wanting things to go too far. I was afraid of hurting her."

"You are not going to let her get away, are you?"

"I have to see what's happening at work and I want to talk to Mary's parents. Hopefully I can ease some of their pain."

"Those things can wait." Jenny said. "You need to get your buns up there and corral that girl."

"I will, but before I do, I have a few ideas I want to discuss with you and Frank regarding Pine Lake."

Josh poured a cup of coffee for each of them and the three sat at the counter. Josh outlined what he experienced and all the potential for business he saw in the small community. He spoke of finding a friend who he felt they could partner with to get things started.

Frank took Jenny's empty coffee cup. "Why don't you guys take it into the living room? I'll clean up the kitchen."

Jenny stood. "When were you planning to go to Pine Lake?"

"I was thinking Friday."

"If you lose that girl, you'll need your head examined," Jenny said.

Josh handed his empty cup to Frank. "Could you give me a ride to my place?"

"For the first time in a long time, I agree with everything Jenny is saying," Frank said. "I understand how Julia feels. You two can be a little overpowering at times."

"Just what do you mean by that?" Jenny said sharply.

"Nothing dear," Frank said. "C'mon Josh, let's get out of here before I dig myself a hole I'll never get out of.

Julia found her way out of town and headed up highway 41. The traffic around Milwaukee was light and she made it without a problem. She had cried herself out and now wondered if this was the end of the road for them. She had

295

prepared herself for any number of scenarios of how things would turn out, including if he were on the wrong side of the law. She thought of him being a number of things, but never thought of him as being rich. Not just a little rich, but richer than anyone she had ever met before. Their worlds weren't even in the same universe. She was small town, burgers and beer. He was big city, giant shrimp and crab salad. She scraped to pay her rent, while he and his sister collected rent on over forty properties. Her net worth included this eleven-year-old car, clothes and some second hand furniture. From the numbers they threw around, he had to be worth a million, or more.

The miles went by and every road sign brought her closer to home. She thought about her life in Pine Lake. It was comfortable. She liked her job. She enjoyed her friends and the people she worked with. Nobody had much, but everyone was reasonably happy.

Her thoughts soon shifted to Josh and the time she spent with him while he slept the days away. She smiled, remembering how good she felt giving him therapy.

The turnoff for highway thirty-seven was coming up, only forty miles to go. She glanced at the gas gauge. The needle was below the E. "Dear God," she exclaimed. "I don't have any money."

She made the turn and pulled into the gas station on the corner. "Darn it, I never should have changed purses." She frantically rummaged through her purse hoping to have overlooked some money, any kind of money, nickels, dimes, anything. Nope, not one red cent.

She reached over and opened the glove box. She didn't expect to find any money, but maybe something she could sell or trade for a couple gallons of gas. The glove box door dropped open as a high school kid came up to the car.

"What will it be, ma'am?"

Julia reached into the glove box, the white envelope

296

fell into her hand. She opened it and read what Josh had written:

Please apply to the Julia Parson's
College Scholarship Fund.

She recognized the realtor's check. She looked to see if there was anything else in the envelope.

Julia opened her window and held the check for the boy to see. "Can you cash this?"

The lad read the name and then the amount. "A thousand dollars! Are you crazy? I ain't got but thirty dollars in the register."

"I'm sorry this is all the money I have and I need at least three gallons of gas to get to Pine Lake. If you could trust me, I will send you the money in the morning."

The boy looked at Julia. "I'd git fired if I just gave you the gas. How 'bout I loan you a dollar and you can send it back to me."

"I will, I promise," she said.

The young man took a dollar from his pocket and handed it to her. He waited a second and then asked again. "What will it be, ma'am?"

She handed the dollar back. "A dollar's worth of regular, please."

When he finished pumping the gas she took his pen and wrote his information on the envelope. "Thank you so much. I promise I will send your money tomorrow."

Back in Pine Lake

Julia woke to the sound of someone knocking on her door.

"Did I wake you?" Nora said, opening the screen door and walking in.

"I got back late," Julia said, glancing at the clock.

"I picked up some coffee and sweet rolls," Nora said, setting a paper sack on the table. "I came by last night and saw your car. The house was dark, so I didn't stop. This guy stopped at the house soon after you left yesterday, asking all sorts of questions about Josh. What's going on? What did you find out?"

"You better sit down. You're not going to believe this."

Nora opened the bag and brought out two cups of coffee. "Did you find out who he was?"

"Yes, and a whole lot more." Julia took a sip of coffee. "His name isn't Bennett, its Forrester. Josh Forrester. He's a CPA and has a sister and brother-in-law. He's also rich!"

Nora choked on her coffee. "Rich? What do you mean, rich?"

"Rich, rich," Julia said. "Penthouse apartment, Corvette sports car, and twenty-nine foot sailboat rich. He and his sister own forty rental properties. One of them is a five story building with twenty luxury apartments."

"Good Lord, who would have thought that?"

"I was completely blindsided."

Nora took a bite of one of the sweet rolls. "You say his name is Forrester? What about the driver's license with Bennett?"

"A fake. They were trying to conceal his identity."

Nora raised an eyebrow. "Is he married?"

"No, and no girlfriend that I know of, although his brother-in-law called him a Casanova. His sister Jenny and her husband are really nice."

"How did you find out about all of this?"

"From Stuart Brenaman, the District Attorney in Waukegan. It was his phone number with the money. Josh was to be a witness in a mob run money laundering case. They put out a contract on Josh. The DA was trying to hide him up in Weston."

"They were trying to kill Josh?"

"Apparently the mob wanted to make sure he never made it to the witness stand."

Julia took another sip of her coffee. "That girl, Mary, worked for Stuart. After her accident, Stuart sent people to find out what happened to Josh. They couldn't go public or stir things up too much for fear of exposing Josh's whereabouts to the mob. Brenaman believes that was also the reason Mary took off and didn't try to get help here. Jenny didn't dare raise a ruckus for fear of putting her brother in danger."

"So, that's why no one came looking for him." Nora sipped her coffee.

"And get this, when they crashed here, Josh saw the light in The Glen's parking lot. That's where he was headed when they found him in the park. If he'd made it to The Glen, I would have been there to help him."

"And this whole saga of the last few months might never have happened."

Julia nodded. "Stuart said they heard about a person

299

in a coma up here, but when they called the sheriff's office they were told it was a partygoer, hurt in a quarry accident."

"Why in hell would they say something like that?" Nora bellowed. "It would have saved everyone a lot of trouble if the sheriff's office had told the truth." Nora looked at her watch. "I've got to get to The Glen, but I want to hear more of this. The big question, where is Josh now? Is he coming back?"

"I don't know," Julia said softly. "He has a life down there. He's got a job, family, and friends. He knows just about everyone in Waukegan. We were sitting in this fancy restaurant and everyone came up to shake his hand, including the president of the bank." Julia stood. "You wouldn't believe this restaurant, pink linen table cloths, crystal glasses, polished silverware, sitting on a hill overlooking the harbor. We had a shrimp and crab salad. I kid you not, the shrimp were bigger than my thumb." Julia's mood changed as she remembered the question. "No, I don't know if he will be coming back."

"He'll be back." Nora stood and threw her paper cup in the wastebasket. "I know he will. Are you working tonight?"

"Yeah. I'm going to loaf around the rest of the day and get my head on straight. I'll be there for my regular shift. Thanks, for the coffee. I'll eat the sweet roll after I clean up."

Nora started for the door. "You didn't say...did he get his memory back?"

"When Jenny showed up. Josh didn't recognize her at first, but then all of a sudden it all came back to him. When she came running up, shouting his name, I almost had a heart attack, I thought for sure she was his wife or girlfriend. When he introduced her as his sister, I lost it. I'm crying, she's crying, he's crying, it was all pretty emotional." Julia found a tissue and wiped her eyes.

"Get some rest, I can see this has taken a lot out of you," Nora said. "I'll see you tomorrow morning." Nora gave her a hug and went out the door.

Julia fell into the chair and wondered what she would do. She really didn't feel like doing anything. It was like she lost her rudder, her compass. Without Josh she felt adrift with no course to follow. She folded her arms on the table, closed her eyes and laid her head on her arms. She wanted to cry but no tears came. She had cried herself out. All she could think of were the times they spent together, beginning with the first day they brought him to The Glen. Her mind lingered on the evenings she sat with him, the night he woke up, the talks, the rides, and the picnic in the park. How would she ever get him out of her mind?

Half dazed, half asleep, she picked up the receiver on the second ring. "Hello."

"Julia, its Doug. Is Josh there?"

"No, he's in Waukegan."

There was a brief pause. "Is he coming back?"

"I don't know. It's a long story."

"Are you okay? Do you want me to come over?"

"No, don't do that. I'm fine. I'm still in my pajamas. I just need some time to get back into the swing of things."

"Lunch?" Doug asked. "Let's meet for lunch. I've got to find out what's going on. Fred still wants some time off. I was hoping Josh would be able to cover for him."

"I'll meet you at Teddy's at noon."

"Fred is going to have a hissy fit. Teddy's at noon. I'll see you there."

Julia hung up the phone and took a bite of the sweet roll as she walked to the bedroom. She tried her best to stay with her morning routine, but found herself wandering from room to room. She put toothpaste on her brush before realizing she already brushed her teeth. All she

301

could think about was Josh.

Her mind wouldn't let her rest. She looked at the phone and desperately wanted to talk to him, to hear his voice. Her shoulders sagged when she realized she didn't have a number for him. She took her everyday purse off the hook and set it on the table. Opening the little blue purse, the first thing out was the name and address of the boy at the gas station. She addressed an envelope, wrote a large thank you on a piece of paper, folded in a five-dollar bill and put it in the envelope. Her fingers trembled as she unfolded the thousand-dollar check. She smiled at it being for her college fund but knew there was no way she could keep it. She used a magnet to hold it to the refrigerator.

D owntown was deserted. Gone were all the people that had descended on the town for the holiday weekend. Julia walked into the post office and put the boy's envelope and a nickel on the counter. Dolly licked a stamp, put it on the envelope and tossed it into a mailbag.

"That must have been an exciting race on Saturday," Dolly said. Everyone's been talking about it. I think the whole town will be out there on Saturday to see if Doug and your friend can win again."

Julia smiled and made a quick exit. There's going to be a lot of disappointed people, come Saturday, but she didn't want to be the one to tell them.

Phyllis at the hospital was understanding with her excuse of feeling under the weather, but made sure to have Julia pass along her congratulations to Josh for a great race. Julia forced another smile. It angered her that it was probably going to be left to her to explain his absence. Her lower lip quivered. This was going to be real tough. She barely knew how to explain it to herself.

She still had more than an hour to kill before meeting Doug. Not sure where to go or what to do, she kept driving.

It wasn't long before she found herself on the highway where Josh and Mary had crashed. She slowed to a stop as she approached the spot. Putting her head against the steering wheel, she spoke her thoughts. "If that deer hadn't jumped out in front of them there wouldn't have been a crash. Mary would be alive and this whole saga of Josh being at The Glen would have never happened." She had a life before, now she had nothing. What would she do if he didn't come back? She continued to drive aimlessly through the countryside.

Josh Returns to Pine Lake

Josh wheeled the Corvette past the Pine Lake city limit sign. He drove directly to Julia's place and was surprised to see her car gone. Maybe he should have called to let her know he was coming. He'd try The Glen.

Nora shrieked with delight when Josh walked through the door. She ran and gave him a hug. "I knew you would come back. I just knew it."

"I drove by Julia's place, she's not there."

"I saw her this morning. She told me quite a bit about you."

'"Some of it good, I hope. Any idea where she might be?"

"All good. She's probably running around town someplace. Are you staying?"

"I have to be back in Waukegan on Monday. In the meantime, I'd like to rent your upstairs for an extended period of time. I plan on spending a lot of time up here and I need a place to hang my hat."

"It's yours for as long as you want it, Mr. Forrester." Nora giggled. "Maybe we can get rid of some of the flowery stuff."

Josh took out his checkbook. "The place is just fine. What do you think, will you take $200 a month?"

"Oh heavens, that's way too much," Nora said.

"Don't be silly. It's worth every penny," Josh said handing her a check. "Right now, I've got to find Julia."

"Wait a minute." Nora rummaged in her purse. "Here are the envelopes you gave me."

"Great, I'll take care of them."

The whistles and cheers went up as Julia walked into Teddy's. Her hand barely moved as she waved to acknowledge their applause. She lowered her head and walked to the back dining room. "Coke please," she told the waitress. "I'm waiting for Doug, we'll order when he gets here."

Josh pulled in front of the courthouse. The treasurer was talking to a woman when Josh walked into the office. Opening the envelope, he laid out the two hundred and fifty dollars on the counter. "I'd like to settle up on my loan."

The treasurer looked at the money. "That didn't take long."

"I'd also like to give you my medical insurance information. You can forward all my medical bills to them. They should take care of everything."

"This will make the taxpayers very happy," the treasurer said.

Josh thought about saying something, but just smiled. "Thank you again for all your help."

Josh made another pass by Julia's place, still no car. Parking in front of the liquor store, Josh saw the front door fly open and Fred come running out. "Holy Crap! Where did you steal the car?"

"I didn't steal it, it's my car." Josh said sheepishly. "Is Doug around?"

"He's in the office." Fred continued looking over the car.

305

Big Plans For the Icehouse

When Josh walked into the office, Doug threw the handful of papers on the desk. "Julia said you were still in Waukegan. I never got to thank you proper for working your magic during the race. People are still pumped that we won the thing."

"It wasn't magic. We caught a couple of breaks and that wind change sort of sealed the deal."

"The store has been doing great. We've had a real jump in business because of it," Doug said proudly. "And not just from town people but Lakeshore, too."

"That's good to hear. Pine Lake needs more things that bring people together."

"Are we gonna sail this weekend? The Lakeshore guys want another shot at us." Doug laughed. "They liked the competition."

"I'll be here until Monday. I guess we could go out and mix it up with them."

"Fantastic! I'll let them know. So what's the deal? What's in Waukegan? Are you coming back here for good?"

"Not full time." Josh saw the questioning look on Doug's face. "I found who I am. My name is Josh Forrester, I'm a CPA."

"CP what?"

"I'm an accountant. My sister and I have a number of business holdings in Waukegan but are looking to invest in Pine Lake. I plan to split my time between here and there."

"Holy Cow, you've got your memory back. How did this all happen?"

"I'll tell you all about it, but for now, the main thing is I've fallen in love with Pine Lake and would like to do some things up here."

"Things, what kind of things?"

"Do you remember our conversation about moving the liquor store and bait shop into the icehouse? You said if I found someone with the money you would consider it. Well, I'd like to go into partnership with you to do just that. There is so much room in the icehouse. We could add a gift shop, maybe a snack bar, and perhaps an ice cream shop to compliment your present businesses."

Doug sat up in his chair. "Have you got that kind of money?"

"Money won't be a problem. I'm also intrigued with your grandfather's photo collection. I think if we build a second story loft around the outer walls, we could make it like a museum with his photos and movies. People could walk around up there and see the history of Pine Lake through his camera lens. We could set up some sort of historic backdrop and let people dress up in costumes and offer old time souvenir photos of people."

"Gramps would love for people to be able to see his work," Doug said. "Like I said, there's eight to ten large boxes of old photographs and 8 mm movies upstairs. He also kept a journal with dates and descriptions of things that happened in town since the twenties."

"We can clean up the area by the lake and build a deck where people can sit, eat their ice cream, and watch the activities on the lake. We'll put out a pier so people can

307

come by boat to shop in the store."

Doug came out of his chair. We could use the deck to display some of the larger items used in the ice harvesting business. I think people would enjoy seeing some of that old stuff."

"You bet, and here's the kicker," Josh said. "I've talked to Joe Nelson and he's willing to sell us the White Wings. We can build a special pier for her and offer boat rides, moonlight cruises, and maybe even cater parties serving food and cocktails."

"How about an evening cruise ending with a world famous fish chowder cook-out like I do for my fishermen."

"That would be a natural. I also convinced Joe he should be the captain. With his family history and knowledge of the lake can you imagine how interesting these excursions would be? He knows the people and can tell a story about each one of those big homes on the lake. It would not only be a huge draw for the tourists but for people living within a hundred miles of Pine Lake."

"I could run my guide business from the pier," Doug said. "We'd pick up extra business in beer, liquor, and snacks from those people."

"I'd be willing to bet, with your guide customers, and Joe's boat rides every morning, afternoon, and evening, we'd have two hundred people a day coming through our shops. We'd sell a ton of ice cream and souvenirs and all the other stuff."

"I like it," Doug said, his voice cracking with excitement. "Do you really think we can do it?"

"No doubt in my mind. Another thing we can do is remodel the present store and convert it into a small office building. We'll need office space for our businesses and I would like to open an accounting and bookkeeping office. I'll need to be able to write off my travel expenses."

"Holy Cow!" Doug said. "How long have you been

thinking about this?"

"Since the first time I saw the icehouse. It's a magnificent structure and has such a wonderful history and connection to the town."

"When can we get started?"

"We'll need to get some engineers and an architect up here to give us some ideas, but I'd like to be open Memorial Day next year."

"Hallelujah!" Doug yelled. "We're going to set this town on fire."

"I've got a few more ideas for Pine Lake, like forming a chamber of commerce to promote the downtown, and maybe find new businesses to fill some of the vacant buildings. But, we can get into that at another time. Right now I want to find Julia."

Doug looked at his watch. "She's probably at Teddy's. We were going to have lunch. Do you want to take my place?"

"If you don't mind," Josh said. "She and I have a lot to talk about."

"You're not going to hurt her are you?"

"Good Golly no, I love her," Josh said without hesitation.

"I know she's crazy about you. You'd better get over there."

"I'll stop tomorrow. We can work on more of the details of the new Icehouse Mall & Museum."

"Sounds good, partner," Doug said.

"Oh, one more thing," Josh said, taking a slip of paper from his pocket. "You might want to give this girl a call. She's a school teacher, not married, and living in Saginaw, Michigan."

Doug read the note. "Peggy?" He flopped in his chair. "Are you kidding...how did you?"

"A friend, the DA in Waukegan, with a little help

from the Chicago Police Department. "I spoke to her. She remembers Pine Lake, the fair, and a funny kid with the flattop haircut. I wouldn't wait too long, you never know where this could lead." Josh watched Doug reach for the phone as he backed out of the room, bumping into Fred.

"Who's he calling?" Fred asked.

"A school teacher in Saginaw."

"A what," Fred asked.

"I'm sure he will tell you all about it," Josh said. "Right now I'm late for a luncheon date."

When am I going to get some time off?" Fred yelled as Josh ran through the store.

"Soon," Josh yelled back. "Doug will tell you about that too."

"Dammit," Fred said, "I'm always the last one to know what the hell is going on."

Will You Be My Girl?

The cheers and whistles erupted the minute Josh walked through the door of Teddy's Bar. He quickly waved his arms for the crowd to quiet down. Josh looked at Teddy and pointed to the back. "Is she back there?"

Teddy nodded.

Julia was sitting at the table looking out the window. Josh walked up quietly. "Mind if I join you?"

Julia spun around and jumped up. "When did you ..."

He put his finger to her lips, then took her into his arms and kissed her tenderly. She felt his heart beating in rhythm with hers.

The bar cleared, everyone came to the back and watched the lovers smooch. Slowly their lips parted.

"Will you be my girl?" he asked.

Julia giggled. "What, like go steady?"

"I know that sounds corny, but I love you. I know what you experienced in Waukegan was hard to deal with, but that's part of who I am. I'm hoping with time that you will see that being wealthy is not a bad ..."

She put her finger to his lips. "I just want to be where you are," she whispered. "I'm lost if you are not here with me." She laid her head on his shoulder.

He stroked through her hair. "I feel the same way. I woke this morning and all I wanted to do was come to you."

311

"What do we do now?" Julia backed away. "How is this going to work?"

"For starters, I've rented Nora's upstairs. Doug and I have a few things in the works so I'll be spending three to four days a week here. We will have lots of time to be together."

Julia pulled him to her. "If we're going to go steady, aren't you supposed to give me your class ring or something?"

Josh laughed. "Maybe we should just start looking for a ring with a diamond in it?"

Julia felt her heart skip a beat. *Oh, please, just ask, the answer is yes.*

Joe Van Rhyn
Author of "Born Yesterday"

Joe grew up in Green Lake, Wisconsin. His family operated a popular Steak House restaurant. In school, Joe divided his time between sports and carrying the lead in a number of plays. He uses the theater experience in his writing to build memorable characters, great dialogue, and compelling story lines.

In 1969, he left the family business and opened a silk screening shop. Combining his art and writing talents, Joe produced a set of historical wall plaques depicting some of the people and places of early Green Lake. A complete set is on display at the Dartford Historical Society. He has written many short stories and is a contributing writer for Thomas Gnewuch's, 1997 book "Green Lake Memories."

Joe moved to Las Vegas in 1978. He and his wife Elaine ran a successful promotional products company. Retirement presented a new challenge, how to channel the energy that still churned inside him. Joe decided to write a book. "Born Yesterday" is the first in a series of novels set in the small resort town of Pine Lake.

"Battle Born," the follow-up book, is due out on the fall of 2017. It is the Nora Jensen story, beginning in 1945 when she's an Army nurse.

Visit Joe's website at www.joevanrhyn.com to get the latest information on upcoming projects.

25915165R00178

Made in the USA
Columbia, SC
12 September 2018